PHENOMENAL PRAISE FOR
MOTH TO THE FLAME
By Kathleen Dougherty . . .

"Terrifying and riveting, Kathleen Dougherty has created that rarest of entities: a finely written, *original* thriller. The most intriguing blend of crime fiction, sci-fi and horror since *Falling Angel*."
—bestselling author
JONATHAN KELLERMAN

"Four-and-a-half stars . . . Kathleen Dougherty has made an original and stunning debut with this tight, fast-paced psychological thriller. For those looking for a suspenseful, edge-of-your-seat read, *Moth to the Flame* is for you, and Kathleen Dougherty is a writer to watch!"
—*Rave Reviews*

"I opened the first page and was hooked . . . truly scary . . . satisfying . . . If you like true teeth-grinding suspense, you will love this book."
—*Mystery News*

"The writing and story move at breakneck speed . . . full of suspense!"
—*Deseret Sunday News* (UT)

AND NOW, KATHLEEN DOUGHERTY PRESENTS HER MOST CAPTIVATING AND UNUSUAL THRILLER . . .

DOUBLE VISION

Diamond Books by Kathleen Dougherty

MOTH TO THE FLAME
DOUBLE VISION

DOUBLE VISION

KATHLEEN DOUGHERTY

DIAMOND BOOKS, NEW YORK

This book is a Diamond original edition,
and has never been previously published.

DOUBLE VISION

A Diamond Book/published by arrangement with
the author

PRINTING HISTORY
Diamond edition/December 1993

ISBN: 1-55773-963-3

Diamond Books are published by
The Berkley Publishing Group,
200 Madison Avenue, New York, New York 10016.
DIAMOND and the "D" design
are trademarks belonging to Charter Communications Inc.

PRINTED IN THE UNITED STATES OF AMERICA

10 9 8 7 6 5 4 3 2 1

To my mother
for her belief in all her children

ACKNOWLEDGMENTS

My thanks to:

Hillary Cige, Senior Editor, The Berkley Publishing Group, for always seeing what needs to be done;

Tim Katanik, my husband and biggest supporter;

Luci Zahray, pharmacist, and P. J. Coldren, pharmacy technician;

Charlene RaElle Raddon and the other fine writers of Wasatch Mountain Fiction Writers: Arlene Brimer Mailing, Barbara Dutson, Jackie Howa, Linda Aagard, Michelle Bell, Betsy Bennett, Dorothy Canada, Tina Foster, Edith Johnson, Janie Meier, Kathi Peterson, Wilma Rich, and Marilynn Rockelman;

Joan Bolling May for the use of the word "curdled";

Joel Bown for his knowledge of the university;

Murphy for his devoted presence.

I have felt the wind of the wing of madness.

—BAUDELAIRE

FIFTEEN YEARS AGO
THE CARRION EATERS

The dead, dry heat of the desert percolated up through his boot soles. His footfalls kicked up dirt clouds. Hot air tightened his skin.

He carried the shovel past sun-scorched sagebrush and prickly pear cactus. Birds orbited sluggishly in the hot sunlight, vultures with wingspans of six feet, smaller V-shaped silhouettes of ravens. Scavengers. An acid thickness rose at the back of his throat.

He hurried up the small rise. He had left her beneath the creosote bushes at the base of the slope. He stopped, his heart trip-hammered. The branches and the ground beneath swarmed with ravens and vultures. The carrion eaters. They shrieked and fought.

The stink.

The revulsion.

He wanted to turn back, let the desert and its minions have her. But he knew he couldn't risk leaving her out in the open. He rested the shovel upright against his leg, pulled a white handkerchief from his jeans pocket. The handkerchief was too small to tie around his nose and mouth like a bandanna. He held the white cloth to his face and

1

carried the shovel down the slope. He rounded the brush and halted, paralyzed by a grotesque fascination.

Ravens, their thick black beaks red with gore, clustered around her corpse. Pecking, tearing, swallowing. Two vultures, obscenely large, flapped at her head, stabbed with hooked yellow bills, croaked hoarsely. The bigger vulture yanked at the face, *her* face . . . and his paralysis broke. He stepped from the cover of the brush and swung the shovel. The creatures scattered, the vultures gaining the air with laborious flapping. When all the birds had taken flight, he forced himself to look. He reminded himself that she was dead, beyond suffering. He had taken care that her death was swift. Her arms sprawled out to her flanks, her fingers loosely curled. Skin of her chest pale, dark red at the buttocks where blood had pooled. Death gases had distended her stomach, but the real horror was her face.

The real horror was her face.

It had started then, the mad ricochet, the image that would rebound razor-sharp in his mind for years and years to come. He had not taken enough care, not nearly enough. Her death had been anything but swift.

BOOK ONE

PHANTASM

CHAPTER 1

Suzanne dreamed that the rabbits complained about the eyedrops. One, who sounded remarkably like a rap-style performer, explained that while the eyedrops lessened his glaucoma, they also stopped his heart. In demonstration of this, all the rabbits did theatrical kick-the-bucket routines in their cages.

Suzanne woke then, shifted position, the water bed making soft lapping sounds in the darkness. The ethyl group on that molecule, she thought. Oxygen bonded to hydrogen. O-H. She bet the ethyl group was the culprit. It enabled the drug, which did such swell work on intraocular pressure, to zing through the bloodstream to do some not-so-swell work on the heart's beta-receptors. The bunnies weren't dropping dead in their cages, but the slight decrease in heart rate was statistically significant. She frowned. Weis wouldn't like this side effect of his new wonder drug. He'd want to play Whack-the-Mole games with the analysis, smash the calculations with the statistical equivalent of a rubber mallet. Then the company would start clinical tests in a third world country.

5

Who'd complain if the poor dropped dead from a questionable drug?

She wouldn't let it come to that. But every encounter with Weis was going to be a battle.

She sighed and twisted, unable to find a comfortable position. The sheet tangled around her legs, trapped her, caged her the way the animals were caged. She'd never anticipated feeling so constrained. Years ago she'd felt only elation when she'd signed the contract with Bolton Pharmaceuticals. The company funded her pharmacology doctorate in exchange for four years of postdoctoral employment. Not great pay, but the experience more than compensated: She'd design and test psychotropic drugs, pharmaceuticals that lifted depression, compounds that quelled hallucinations of schizophrenics. For nearly a year and a half, that's what she'd done at Bolton.

Then the company's lawyers got cold feet, worried about side effects, wondered what would happen if a psychiatric patient became violent while taking a Bolton drug. Similar lawsuits had pulverized other moderately-sized firms. Her division was sold to the highest bigger. She was shifted, transferred to head the preclinical testing of medications for glaucoma. Honorable, worthwhile work. Necessary work.

Heartrending work.

The catch was the word "preclinical."

Animal testing.

Her eyes were squeezed shut. She opened them, stared into the darkness. If she quit, defaulted on the contract, she'd owe Bolton over sixty-thousand dollars plus penalties double that amount. She'd gone over the possibilities again and again. Even with the unlikely luck of landing another pharmacology position at the going rate, she'd never manage the contract-default payments. The housing market in southern California had taken nosedive after nosedive; selling was out of the question, not to mention that her parents had trustingly cosigned for the mortgage.

She'd hoped that Bolton Pharmaceuticals would be a stepping-stone in her career, the opposite shore being a teaching and research position in psychopharmacology. She'd expected to negotiate a part-time position at the university of California, Lake Forest—UCLF was within walking distance of her house—but her doctorate in pharmacology was a necessary yet insufficient condition. Teaching at the university required extortion or nepotism or murder. Even if it were possible, Weis wasn't likely to go along with altering her work schedule.

Two more years as an indentured servant under the thumb of a despot. Weis, the company's chief scientist, clearly wanted to bean her with the nearest *Physician's Desk Reference* and hire someone with the right genitals to manage the lab.

Boy oh boy, was he going to hate the latest analysis.

Her thoughts muddled around lies, damned lies, and statistics, and onion sandwiches on rye bread. She drifted into sleep.

Air currents moved her bangs, gusts as though a fan were being waved. Half-asleep, she turned her face to the side. A tickling over her nose, lips. "Paul." She smiled. Paul was tickling her, teasing her to consciousness, and in a moment she'd roll over to him . . . hey, she thought, Paul didn't come over tonight, he's not *here*. A sharp jab to her cheek made her open her eyes, bolt awake. A big blurry darkness hovered. Its smell hit her immediately, a disgusting stink like swamp gases. Fear catapulted her from the bed. One leg tangled in the sheets. She fell on her hands and knees to the carpet, squinted up and around and saw myopic nothingness. Where the hell was it? *What* the hell was it? That grotesque smell.

She fumbled for the switch to the lamp and knocked it over. No, she needed her glasses first, damn it, she couldn't see, she had to *see*. Keeping her nearsighted gaze on the still air around her, she patted the top of the defunct TV and scattered computer printouts. Her hands shook. She found her glasses on the headboard and jabbed an earpiece into her ear before slipping them on. The fuzzy dark resolved into a clearer dark. The thing wasn't flying, but it was in the room. She smelled that odor of decay.

She found and righted the lamp while her eyes strained to see movement in the darkness, fearful that the thing would attack again. In addition to the smell, she sensed something else, a wordless something. Malevolent intent, she thought. She wished she wore pajamas. She wished she wore a suit of armor. The thing wanted to hurt her.

She switched on the lamp. Light spilled over the room, the queen-sized water bed with Paul's blue satin sheets, the cluttered desk against the far wall, her barbell, weights, and crummy workout bench in the corner. No place for a beast that big to hide. The walk-in closet was closed, and its mirrored doors reflected the sink counter. The door to the commode and shower was open. The stinking thing, whatever it was, had to have gone in there. She pulled open the drawer set into the water-bed pedestal. The Colt and cartons of .32 caliber bullets rested in a black faux-leather case.

Wait a minute, wait a minute, Suzanne cautioned herself. This is the stuff accidental shootings are made of. She closed the drawer. Think, she told herself. Her rational mind scrabbled for a toehold. Allan, she thought, of course. Allan, her roommate, and his frigging Megachiroptera. Megabats, all of whom should be hanging from their respective perches in the zoology building on campus. She eased the sheet off the bed and wrapped it around her. She wasn't going to risk exciting the beast by rumbling open the closet door for her robe. Her muscles jittered as she avoided squeaky floorboards. The worn carpet cushioned her footsteps.

She stopped at the bedroom door. The mirror over the sink reflected the dark interior of the shower. The angle of incidence equals the angle of outcidence. Was the bat in there, gazing out at her reflection?

A flapping sound pulsated the air. She spun around, clutched the sheet, her mouth opened to scream, expecting this huge gargoyle to rush at her . . . nothing. She jerked open the door and closed it behind her. She flipped on the hall light. Suzanne, she told herself, calm down, it's all right. A big monster bat, whose neurons are scrambled, mistook your eyeballs for mangoes. It's perched in the shower, dropping guano, chewing on Ivory soap, and reading *Scientific American*. Allan is in his room, laughing himself silly.

She didn't quite buy it. Allan was shy, and while he might have a crush on her, this was hardly the way he'd pick to win her affection. But galvanized by the possibility, she passed by the phone on its shaky TV tray to the three bedrooms. Kelly, her eighteen-year-old kid sister, slept in the one on the right. The pink thread of the night-light shone along the bottom of her door. The bedroom on the far left was bare, empty since the last renter graduated from the university. She needed another renter in addition to Allan, and soon. She pushed aside money worries and tapped on the door of the middle bedroom.

"Allan," she whispered. Silence. She knocked louder. Fabric rustled.

"Just a minute," he said. More rustling. Footsteps.

The door opened and Allan peered out. As soon as she saw him, she knew he was innocent. His brown hair was rumpled, his eyes sleepy. Gray sweatpants drooped around his narrow waist. A slice of light illuminated his hairless chest and well-formed biceps. He was in his late twenties, a few years her junior, yet he seemed more youthful. Untouched. He hadn't, she thought, had much luck with women. The years would favor him, age his face to match his IQ. He was intelligent, but when relaxed his smooth features resolved into a buffoonish expression.

She began to feel foolish herself, wrapped in a satin sheet and nothing else. "I'm sorry to wake you," she said, "but there's something in my room."

His eyes registered her naked shoulders, the blue sheet. He stepped into the hall. "What's wrong?"

"I thought . . . I think it's a bat."

His face changed from concerned to interested. "A bat? I bet it's a *Tadarida*. I saw one in the woods last week. Let's take a look." He started for her room.

"Wait. Don't you need something?" Every wall of his bedroom was covered with cinder block and pine bookshelves. Except for his narrow mattress and Batman sheets in the center of the floor, everything was tidy and neat. Not that Allan owned much of anything. His was the spare den of a graduate student on fellowship.

"Like what?" he said.

"An Uzi."

He cocked his head.

"A net." She laughed uneasily. "A very large net."

"I have leather work gloves and a canvas bag in my truck. I don't have a net with me, but I can probably use the pool net. I'll take a look at the critter first."

The idea of the tiny pool net swiping at the thing she saw was comical. Actually, the idea of *seeing* what she saw was comical. "Hold on a second, Allan."

He waited while she collected her thoughts. She said, "You know, I must have been dreaming. Because now . . . thinking back on what happened, it's impossible. I felt something hit my face, I woke, I saw this huge—we're talking humongous, like a three-foot wingspan—this huge thing hanging over me. And I felt its anger, its intent to hurt me. I guess bats don't tend to be telepathic. Or maladjusted."

He cut his eyes toward her bedroom, still intrigued. "Bats native to southern California are pretty small. What you saw sounds like your basic nightmare."

"Deep with symbolism." She'd been thinking about Weis before she dozed off, a sure catalyst for night terrors. "I'm sorry about getting you up."

"Stop eating those onion sandwiches before bed." He grinned. His gaze dropped down to the blue satin. He flushed and studied his own bare feet. "Since I'm awake, why don't I check it out anyway?"

"I feel like an idiot." She glanced toward her closed bedroom door. "Did I tell you it stank? How many nightmares smell like sewers?"

"Come on." He walked toward her room. "It used to make me feel better when Dad checked under the bed."

She gathered up the sheet and followed him, feeling odd. Paul was the only man who'd been in her bedroom for the past two years. And definitely the only man who'd ever seen her wrapped in the blue satin sheet.

"A bat wouldn't actually attack a human. If it's hurt, it might fly aimlessly, knock into things, scrabble with its claws." His shoulder blade flexed as he opened the door. The action highlighted a narrow scratch, fresh and pink, stretched diagonally across his back. Not the sort of injury you could easily inflict on yourself. Hmmm. Well, well, Allan, you rascal, you. Maybe not so virginal.

Once inside, she sniffed the air, making snuffling sounds. Allan stared. "The smell is gone." She'd have to ask Paul about the olfactory component of hallucinations.

Allan scanned the furniture and walls. "Not many places to perch."

"The shower," she said.

He walked to the bathroom, turned on the light. He went in. She heard the shower partition slide open. He came out and closed the door. "Nope."

He checked the windows, open to let in the June breeze. "You must have dreamed it," Allan said when he was done. "There aren't any tears in your screens. And bats don't hide under things, but just in case . . ." He shook the comforter at the foot of the bed, lifted the pillows. "No, I didn't think so. You're officially bat-free."

"It seemed so real." She touched her cheek. A slight tenderness. "Come look at this." He followed her to the sink. She removed her glasses and squinted a few inches from her reflection on the medicine cabinet mirror. A pink round spot was just below her right eye. "This mark." She turned to him and pointed at her cheek. "What's that look like to you?"

"Like the beginning of a zit."

She pursed her mouth, considering. To her, it looked more like she'd been stabbed with something dull. Or pecked.

CHAPTER 2

Early the next morning, Suzanne sipped coffee and enjoyed the view. Beyond the sliding glass doors of the kitchen were the pool, spa, and gazebo that needed staining, then the rusted wrought-iron fence, then the broad bridle path with the occasional horse apples, then the woods of Serrano Park. Plumes of pampas grass glowed silver in the first light. Black phoebes, bluebirds, sparrows by the dozens tweeted like crazy. The staccato beat of a woodpecker floated high in the air from one of many hundred-foot-tall eucalyptus. The outline of the trees formed the edge of the world.

The coo of mourning doves felt like a reminder of something forgotten. What was she supposed to do before she left? She searched her memory, but nothing surfaced. Stop trying. Tip-of-the-tongue memories are better accessed without effort.

She knew, with the certainty of one who loves her home, that if she walked to the fence and unlatched the gate, she'd startle a tiny herd of cottontails furtively munching spring growth. If she crossed the bridle path and stepped into the woods, jumped over the stream, she'd still not be able to see the towering buildings of the University of California, Lake Forest, through the dense foliage. She might, however, see a coyote or two. The animals followed the stream from the nearby Saddleback Mountains, escaped the drought-dry valleys for the feral lushness—and bountiful rabbit population—of Serrano Park.

She'd dreamed last night about the woods, hadn't she? *The woods are lovely, dark and deep.* Was that the memory that tickled the back of her mind? Chasing a swift unknown through the darkness, undergrowth holding her back, slapping her legs, her bare legs . . . she shook her head. She'd been stark naked. Naked equals what? Relying on my intellect, she mused. The woods impeded her progress. So she was reaching for some difficult goal. Ha, not too hard to figure out what *that* was. Beyond the woods in her dream and in reality was the campus of UCLF, where she hoped to teach. Dreams. Paul's bearded face came to mind. She smiled. Spend enough time with a psychologist, you analyze everything.

Allan thumped down the stairs.

"Morning." He greeted her with a stare and a lopsided smile.

She smiled back. "You're up early today."

He still stared and smiled. It was as though he expected a wink or other evidence of camaraderie. Bemused, she finally said, "Help yourself to coffee. I'm on my way out."

"No, thanks." He stood there in her way, fidgeting in his sneakers and faded clean jeans and Batman T-shirt.

She was about to squeeze by him, when a vibration thrummed the soles of her feet. "Is that a little earthquake? No," she answered herself. Now she heard the accompanying low rumble of a massive engine from the El Toro Marine Base. The base was less than two miles away, a testosterone jungle of men and machines.

Like anyone who'd lived in southern California long enough, Allan didn't even comment on the vibration. "I posted more notices about the room for rent," Allan said. "The humanities building and the bookstore."

"Great. Thanks. Kelly thinks she can post some in the undergraduate library."

Allan cleared his throat. He watched Suzanne with a peculiar expression, one of growing puzzlement. He blushed furiously. "So how'd you sleep last night?"

Suzanne lifted and dropped her shoulders, tilted her head to one side. "Fine." In the two semesters that he'd lived here, he'd never asked that question before. He was working up to something. She smiled at him. "And how did *you* sleep?"

"And, ah . . ." He leaned toward her, giving her face the once-over. "That spot is gone. So no more bats?" he said.

"Spot? Bats?" Suzanne thought he was making some confusing reference to his biosonar research at the university, except that images niggled at the back of her mind. Last night. A black fluttering or spinning, the sheet wound around her leg, an odd sensation, a smell? And Allan. The memories strobed like flawed film. She laughed uneasily and said, "Well . . . I woke you, didn't I?"

CHAPTER 3

Elliot Trodd sat across from Suzanne and appeared about to vibrate into another energy state. His thin, nicotine-stained fingers drummed against the walnut conference table and his left eyelid twitched. His whole body shook, a seismic disturbance rising up from his jiggling foot. There was something insubstantial about Elliot, the wispy blond hair, translucent eyebrows, his angular greyhound build, his aura of barely contained anxiety. He was business manager of the biology, toxicology, and pharmacology labs at Bolton Pharmaceuticals, an administrator who monitored budget and resources. These last-Friday-of-the-month luncheons in the administrative building made him more nervous than usual.

Suzanne felt out of place herself, more comfortable with the antiseptic linoleum of her office and lab. She brushed at her white lab coat, and a few strands of rabbit hair swirled in the air. Here you sank ankle-deep into plush navy carpet, breathed the rarefied atmosphere of executive row, squinted from glare multiplied by polished furniture and mirrored walls.

Residues of Bolton's successful past, before its
narrowing down into the field of ophthalmics, lingered here: the solid cherry conference table, the
silver service, the antique rolltop desk. Sell that
puppy and the company could have afforded to
give someone a raise last year. Bob, Weis's secretary, hovered over the desk. He quietly arranged
bone china coffee cups, urns of steaming coffee,
and a crystal platter of deli sandwiches on the
desktop. His was a face designed to be forgotten, young, unlined, without the stamp of char-
acter that marked most past adolescence. Average
height, average build, a nondescript brown suit
that matched his hair. She looked down at her
notes for a moment, then up, and Bob was
gone. Poof. Presto chango. No doubt Weis considered him the perfect underling, useful and invisible.

At the head of the table loomed the man himself, Dr. Franklin Weis, Bolton Pharmaceutical's
chief scientist and great white hope. He was fifty-
something, a beefy man with remarkable thick
white hair that Suzanne suspected was a rug.
He wasn't tall, but his stocky build gave him
presence. He had pioneered the research of beta-
blockers early in his professional career and was
a tenured professor in ophthalmics in UCLF's
medical school. Thanks to him, Suzanne had two
medical school students doing gratis research in
her lab for university credit.

On Weis's right, in favored-son position, sat
Harold Ignasiak, head of toxicology. Harold was
a round, friendly Tweedledum, always grinning,
which seemed ghoulish—his lab determined the

dose that caused death. On Weis's left sat Ben Thibault, head of biochemistry, a thin business-like scientist with a permanent crease between his eyebrows from theoretical thinking.

Two empty seats formed the symbolic barrier between the trio and the untouchables, Elliot Trodd and Suzanne Reynolds. Though Elliot was immediate supervisor, on paper at least, of the three lab managers, he wasn't a researcher, which bumped him down an echelon or two. Suzanne, head of pharmacology, held the least favored position because of three things: At thirty-one she was the youngest lab manager, she was the only female, and Weis loathed her. She'd been an admirer of Weis from afar. Every pharmacologist studied his historical breakthrough with beta-blockers. Working with him this past year, though rarely seeing him, had eroded her awe.

"Dr. Reynolds, why don't you start." Weis leaned back. The leather upholstery creaked.

Suzanne walked to the wall panel and dimmed the lights. She slid the graph of Vitalol onto the overhead projector. Her presentation was precise and to the point, showing that the analog sig-nificantly reduced symptoms of glaucoma in test animals. Weis nodded and Thibault and Ignasiak bobbed their heads as if tethered by invisible wires. Weis said, "I'll incorporate that graph into my presentation. Good work, Dr. Reynolds." He turned to Ignasiak and said, "Let's see how toxicology did with the LD50."

"I have something else." Suzanne replaced the overhead slide with another. "This is a small study of nine animals over a two-week period, dosed twice a day with Vitalol. This solid line shows the significant decrease in intraocular pressure, as we saw in the previous slide. This dotted line shows a parallel decrease over time in heart rate."

There was a dead silence. She cleared her throat. "So heart rate is possibly lowered, a risk for the target population. It's likely that some elderly taking this drug for glaucoma may also have cardiovascular complications. I recommend exploring this possible side effect, including blood pressure—"

"To what end?" Weis was looking at her like she had cole slaw for brains. "You haven't shown standard error of the mean. The heart rate line could be flat, showing no significant change."

"The animals treated with Vitalol eyedrops appear unusually docile. I suspect this effect strengthens over time."

"Were these naive animals?"

"Naive? Yes, of course. These animals haven't been used for any other study."

"And don't you find that all naive animals, as they accustom to the lab, become more tractable? Naive animals present elevated heart rates as a matter of course, and we would expect to see a drop to normal baselines as acclimatization occurs."

Her temper flared. The greenest lab technician knew that test animals were excitable at first. She kept her voice even, reasonable. "That's certainly true, Dr. Weis, but in this case—"

"This is a business we're running, Dr. Reynolds. It's not in your purview to unilaterally waste test animals in—"

"Dr. Weis, I used a single bank, only nine rabbits—"

"We don't pull these animals out of a hat. I presume you had one of your technicians perform the study."

She knew what was coming. "Yes."

"Then we have not only the use of nine animals, but wasted man-hours to contend with."

In exasperation Suzanne said, "I'm simply recommending an additional study—"

"No." Weis turned to Harold Ignasiak. "Let's see the toxicology results."

Before Harold opened his mouth, Suzanne couldn't help herself, she snapped, "Why *not*, Dr. Weis?"

The other two lab managers stared at her as though she had spontaneously combusted.

"I said no, miss." The "miss" was intended to insult. It did. "You've stated your *opinion*"—he exaggerated the word to emphasize its contrast with solid scientific inquiry—"and it's been duly noted. Since you took it upon yourself to waste company money on unapproved research, I suggest you return to your lab *now* and determine how to function more efficiently."

She glanced at Elliot, who was absolutely gray, and decided to leave while she still had control over the steam pressure of her temper. She gathered up her presentation materials and walked to the door. "And one more thing," Weis called to her.

She didn't turn to look at him.

"Don't ever annoy me again with sloppy interpretations of data."

The critical mass was building. Just leave, Suzanne, she told herself. As she closed the conference-room door behind her, she heard Weis say, "Mr. Trodd, I assume you knew about this."

Poor Elliot.

Suzanne's anger evaporated during the walk from the administrative building, past the two tennis courts that needed resurfacing, to the gray-brick single-story research building. She went from being furious with Weis to being frustrated with how she handled the situation to being tired. Maybe sleepwalking with bats had sapped her energy, her ability to be diplomatic. She dismissed this, though. She never seemed to say the right thing to Weis. Weis had his sights set on bringing Vitalol to market; he simply wasn't receptive to advice to the contrary. What was the point of preclinical trials if data analyses were ignored?

She pulled open the glass-plated door. A nearly invisible filament of rabbit hair caught in her eyelashes and she had a dickens of a time plucking it out. The dander could slip under contact lenses if you wore them, which is why Suzanne didn't bother. She also thought that her wide-spaced eyes made her look too young, too puzzled, and that the dark frames lent her an air of professionalism.

Not that the meeting with Weis had given any indication of that.

"Hey, boss," Suzanne teased Mariette, the thin Hispanic woman typing furiously at the word processor, a wad of chewing tobacco swelling one cheek.

"Messages," Mariette said without slowing her fingers over the keys.

Suzanne plucked slips from the rack on the corner of the desk.

"An' I didn't get all those copies done. The repair man, he's working on the machine." Her fingers flew. She kept the nails short and lacquered a bright pink with a dab of stark white covering the crescent. Her feet were hidden below the desk but Suzanne knew a similar unique paint job decorated toenails peeping through open-toed high heels. The receptionist cum secretary cum administrator, in Suzanne's opinion, kept the machinery of the preclinical research division running smoothly. She had a Masters in Fine Arts, a much beloved son, and a husband who drank too much.

"Did you get your son to the doctor's?" Suzanne asked.

Now Mariette's fingers paused. She turned. Her blue-black hair caught a hard shine from the overhead fluorescents. "Manuel, he won't go. He's too macho, you know, too much the big man now, at fifteen, to see the doctor." Her tone was sharp, but pride glowed in her brown eyes.

"How's his vision?"

"He says it's fine now, but all the time he's rubbing that eye. Manuel's vain, like his daddy." She picked up a plastic foam cup and spit out the tobacco. "If he needs glasses, he won't be caught dead wearing them."

"It could be an infection, like we've discussed. You know, a conjunctivitis."

Mariette shook her head. Small medallions of
the Blessed Virgin Mary swung from her earlobes.
"I look, like you say, but there's no discharge,
no red."

Suzanne frowned. It was unusual for eyes to
unilaterally become myopic or hyperopic, but it
happens. "Put him in your car and take him to
that ophthalmologist in Santa Ana."

"I tell you, Dr. Reynolds, he won't go. But he
likes you, respects you"—Suzanne had helped
him a few months ago with some elementary
statistics—"then he might—"

"I can't examine him, Mariette. I'm not a physician."

"No, no, I understand, you told me. I understand. But if you, say, look into his eye, just pre-
tend, even, and tell him he must go to the doctor's,
he'd listen. You put the words right."

"I'll talk to him. But that's all."

"That's all I want."

Suzanne kicked through the swinging doors into
the corridor. In her office she settled into the admi-
ral's swivel chair, a gift from her parents when
Bolton hired her. The oak wasn't a magnet for
dander like the laboratory office chairs with their
nubby black upholstery. She thumbed through the
latest computer printout, an analysis of variance,
and tried not to think of that wretched meeting, an
effort that insured she would think of little else.
Fact: Weis was upset with her . . . again. Fact:
Elliot was upset with her . . . again. Elliot, by
the Law of Conservation of Agony, would have to
chastise her. So she wasn't surprised an hour later
when Elliot appeared, pointed at her, and jerked

his thumb toward his office. Not good, she thought, when he's speechless. She followed him, watched him collapse onto the chair behind his desk.

"Shut the door," he said.

She did, and sat on the straight-backed chair. Elliot fumbled in the desk drawer. His shaking fingers shoved things aside until he located his Benson and Hedges cigarettes. She felt guilty at how rattled he seemed. It would take only the slightest of catalysts to push Elliot over the edge, an activation complex, to state change him into gossamer. One day she'd enter his office and find his chair all aflurry with white gossamer strands and no Elliot.

"What is wrong with you?" Elliot hissed. "In the past year since Weis has been chief scientist, you've learned nothing about how to approach him. *Nothing.*"

He lit a cigarette, violently shook the match and dropped it, no, threw it into the wastebasket.

"This is research. This is science, not—"

"For Christ's sake, Suzanne, there are people involved here. Why do you have to butt heads with Weis at every damn meeting?"

"Because he's *wrong.*"

"You not only managed to infuriate Weis—"

"From whom all blessings flow—"

"—but you're screwing *me* in the process."

That stopped her. The throbbing vein in his forehead looked fragile, vulnerable. "You?"

"Why didn't you tell me you wanted to do an additional study?"

"Look, Weis may have been brilliant years ago when he developed the first beta-blockers, but today, now, his judgment is flawed. He's prejudicial and circumspect. And since he's been here, every recommendation I make is scrutinized, questioned—"

"Why didn't you tell me about the heart-rate study?"

Suzanne frowned. "It was only a two-week study using nine animals. You know we have a surplus of animals. The technician devoted less than twenty minutes a day to data collection."

"You expected that if you told me, I'd check with Weis, and he'd not approve the study. But maybe he would have. Instead, you spring that graph at the meeting and expect Weis to be thunderstruck with your genius? He sure was impressed with how well I oversee the labs."

"The study was my decision. Weis can't blame you. You had absolutely nothing to do with it."

"Exactly," he said bitterly, "I didn't. And I should have. Maybe you see loads of job opportunities out there, but I don't. You know how many management positions are open at pharmaceutical companies? Zilch. I've got three kids and another on the way."

Another on the way. Ah. More fiscal burden for Elliot. This didn't seem to be the time to offer congratulations.

"I'm not going to jeopardize my position here," he was saying, "by helping you lock horns with Weis in some sort of personal vendetta."

"Personal vendetta? I'm not taking opposing positions for the thrill of conflict." She stared at him a moment then said, half in jest, "So. Are you firing me?" If she was fired, she'd still have to reimburse Bolton for her education. With interest. Fortunately for her, she was cheap labor. Bolton, with its current lagging sales, couldn't afford a full-salaried pharmacologist.

Elliot looked at the long ash of his cigarette, tapped it into the wastebasket. "Not yet. You have to *think,* Suzanne. You insult Weis—"

"I didn't mean it personally."

"You *insult* Weis and this month I'm doing your performance evaluation. What am I supposed to do? Tell Weis I recommend a raise?"

"Yes. Absolutely. I went along with the belt-tightening last year, and my contract has me at a minimum salary as it is. I'm a good researcher, Elliot. You know I deserve an increase."

"Yeah, well"—he drew on the cigarette and exhaled a cloud of smoke—"you should have thought of that."

"I had no problems with Quiston when he was chief scientist."

"Well, Quiston retired. You've been transferred. Now you have Weis. *You* have to adapt, because I'm telling you right now, he is not going to change for you. The other lab managers get along with him."

"Thibault and Ignasiak aren't women."

Elliot rubbed his hand over his face, pulling his features so he resembled a high-gravity experiment. "Come on, come on, Suzanne. It's not that."

She leaned forward. "Elliot, these animals *are* showing signs of sedation. Slight but noticeable— How about a small clinical trial? Try Vitalol on a few humans. Me, you, Thibault, Ignasiak, the technicians. Remember a couple of years ago a group of employees signed release agreements and took drops of that pupil-dilating agent?"

"I remember. We can't do that." He swiveled his chair to face the window.

"At least then we'd be able to see the effect in humans. I guarantee there'd be a slight effect on heart rate and blood pressure—"

He spun around and jabbed his index finger at her. "I said no," he said through a clenched jaw, "and I mean no. Weis will never go for it. You *know* Weis won't go for it."

"All right." She held her hands out, palms up. "Why are we fighting?"

Elliot puffed furiously, lost in thought. She let the silence live. After a while his hunched shoulders relaxed.

"Are we friends again?" she said.

Elliot shook his head. "Not until you make nice with our chief scientist."

"How?"

"Talk to him."

"And say what?"

"Oh, no you don't." His tone hardened. "You're not that socially inept. You've been intentionally perpetuating a maverick attitude, which you know pisses him off. You understand perfectly well how to deal with Weis, you've just chosen not to."

She sighed. No point in defending herself. She didn't want to go toe-to-toe with Elliot again. "Okay. I'll talk to him."

"This is not an option. You have to straighten things out with Weis."

Maybe Weis didn't consider her economical at any price. "I mean it. I'll apologize. Or something." She meant it.

In her office she called Weis's secretary, who told her that he had left for the day. She made an appointment for Monday, and felt a sense of accomplishment. She'd have tonight with Paul, maybe the whole weekend, then mea-culpa herself before Weis, and all would be well.

CHAPTER 4

That night Suzanne stood at the range in her kitchen. Her latest concoction simmered in a deep stockpot. Behind her Paul Gershuny wrapped his arms around her waist, drew her to him, enveloped her. She liked being inside his embrace, yet a slight anxiety tainted the pleasure. Surely he must feel how well they fit together, physically and emotionally. She knew he enjoyed her and her house more than being alone in his cramped apartment. Yet his love was like a peal of thunder, large and meaningful, a tension promising rain that never fell.

"So what's this called again?" he said. His beard tickled her neck.

"Bayou black beans and rice. The wild rice"—she nodded toward a lidded pan—"is done."

"Beans, huh?" She felt him smile against her skin. "Maybe I shouldn't spend the night."

She knew he was joking about leaving. A tiny panic flared anyway. "You won't have gastric problems with these. All those nasty undigestible, soluble sugars have been soaked away."

"Did you see that I did my usual masterful job with the salad?"

"I did. And if you sauté that"—she pointed to a covered skillet on the tile counter—"we'll be ready to eat."

He released her and put the skillet on a burner. He was dark and bearish, a big man who could stand to lose a few pounds, easy with silences and delays. Had she ever seen him in a rush? For her, time skittered away, elusive and fleet. Paul slowed her down, uncoiled the tension in her chest.

Until she tried to deal with his aloofness.

He removed the lid from the skillet. "Is your sister eating with us?"

"Kelly met another freshman at the library orientation today. A nice girl . . . young woman," she corrected herself. "Cynthia. They went to Balboa Peninsula to see a film." She tapped the wooden spoon on the edge of the pot. "I don't know. Maybe I should have suggested they eat here, go to a movie in Lake Forest."

"Kelly's eighteen. She'll be fine."

"She's a very young eighteen."

"She's young, but she's not stupid. Give her some credit. She'll be fine." He squinted at the skillet. "What's in here? Chopped onions and some sort of imitation meat-tasting, meat-smelling tofu substance?"

"Nope. It's the real thing."

He placed his hand over his chest in mock surprise. "You mean you're compromising your values?"

"That sausage is only for you."

He turned on the burner. "Still, I'm touched. This beats the heck out of bean burgers. Where's

Allan?" He selected a wooden spatula from the wall rack.

"Out. He was in a hurry. Maybe he had a date."

He lifted his eyebrows. "So we're alone?"

"Yes."

"How alone?"

"*Very* alone."

He pushed the sausage and onions around with the spatula. Hot sizzles and pops entwined with the fragrance of spicy sausage and onions. "When was the last time we skinny-dipped in the pool?"

She turned off the two burners. "This is *always* better when it's reheated."

After they'd swum and made love, they carried dinner upstairs and felt decadent as they ate in bed. She told him about her encounter with Weis, her promise to Elliot.

"Elliot gave you good advice," Paul said.

"I don't feel like apologizing to Weis. He's wrong."

Paul shrugged. "Change your attitude toward him. You want to keep your job and eventually teach at the U. He's in a position to help. You have to consider, if he really is reacting negatively to you, that you might pose a threat to him in some way."

"I don't see it."

He smiled. "Think about it. You and he are in the same field, pharmacology. You're bright and young. He's older with all his discoveries behind him." He put his plate on the floor and pulled her to him. "Sometimes you have to make compromises to get what you want."

"You haven't made compromises. And now you

have the National Science Foundation funding your research."

"I'd study people who pick their noses, if that's what NSF was willing to fund. I'm hoping to publish a paper from this. I'd better, or I'll be lucky to stay an associate professor the rest of my academic life."

Suzanne nodded. A stable university career required tenure. Without tenure, you could never be sure of a position the next semester. No funded research, no publishing. No publishing, no tenure. This NSF grant was Paul's ticket to tenure and full professorship.

"When are you going to start?" she said.

"Monday. Psych 101 students. They earn extra credit by participating." He looked thoughtful. "I should get input on the setup."

"What sort of input?"

"The structure of the study is good. The subject free associates about a future event. The future event, *where* the outbound experimenter will be at a specific time, isn't randomly selected by the computer until after the subject free associates."

"Let me see if I've got it right: The subject attempts to predict where the outbound person will be. The experimenter doesn't know where the outbound person will be sent, since the computer selects the location after the subject free associates. This removes the possibility of telepathy. This research will show, if it shows anything, only clairvoyance."

He winced. "We scientists try not to use that word."

"Presensing."

"Thank you. Correct. Presensing. Like I said, the structure itself is clear, but the intangibles—like the best orientation for the chairs, the exact wording of instructions to the subject, whether something in the lab is distracting—those factors aren't quantified in the SRI research. I want to standardize them as well."

"The more variables you control, the better the study," Suzanne agreed. "Why don't you use me as a guinea pig? Tomorrow I'll be the subject. Run through the experiment just as you plan to do on Monday and I'll critique those intangibles."

He gave her a Cheshire-cat grin. "I was hoping you'd volunteer."

"You wuss." She chucked him under his beard. "Why didn't you just ask?"

"I've seen your expression when I talk about the presensory experiment."

She hoped she wore an earnest expression now. "I'm never scornful of good research." When NSF promised the funding, she'd taken special care congratulating him, knowing he'd get ribbed by his colleagues, other psych professors who put parapsychology in the same category as voodoo and faithhealers. As for herself . . . her mind balked. Well, admit it, she told herself. You think all psychic stuff is as credible as people being taken hostage by aliens who look like Gumbie. "I don't hold with testimonials, people claiming they predicted a plane crash, but only announcing it after the event. However, well-conceived experiments, that's what science is all about."

He angled his jaw to one side and lifted his eyebrows.

"What?"

"Oh, nothing. In any case, Kelly wanted a trial run. This will give her a taste before the actual trials on Monday."

"Thanks for hiring her. This is her first real job."

"I didn't take your sister on as a favor. If Kelly hadn't seemed capable, I wouldn't have hired her."

"I know, I know. I just wonder if I did the right thing, letting her stay here. She could have gone to a community college in Utah, stayed with Mom and Dad."

"You said you left home at the same age."

"I was different. Not so naive."

"Sure."

"I understood people better."

"Of course."

Suzanne smiled. Maybe she did worry too much. As a baby Kelly had a huge heart-tugging smile and curious eyes. Now her face seemed one of failed ambition, even before having ambition. Did Kelly wander through experiences without being aware of options, as though life were an unmappable landscape? Suzanne didn't know. Her little sister's mind was alien territory.

She stretched her arm around his chest. "Fib-and-fact." She said the three words like one: Fibnfact. "Tell me something."

"Oh, no. I went last time. Your turn." He eased one leg companionably over hers.

"Okay." She had to think of one truth about herself and one lie. Both must be equally plausible. This game became more challenging each time. "All right," she said. "In sixth grade during history class Crystal Dawson bit me on the ankle because she thought I was flirting with her boyfriend. That bite on my ankle hardly broke the skin, but it nearly killed me. Almost dying sparked my interest in pharmacology."

"I have a question," he said.

"How did I nearly die? The physician gave me a shot of penicillin and I had an allergic reaction."

"No. *Were* you flirting with her boyfriend?"

"Yes."

He laughed. "What's the second one?"

"The second one happened when I was about eight or nine: throwing stones at pigs completely and utterly changed my perspective on reality. I became another person. George started it, throwing the stones I mean, but I readily joined in. It began such an ordinary episode, children being thoughtless, even cruel, then . . . illumination."

He shifted his head to see her face. "That's it?"

"I can't give you *every* detail. Choose the fact."

She rested her ear against his sternum, listening to the thump of his heart, slightly faster than her own. She knew his pulse should be slower, but he'd rather eat lima beans, which he loathed, than exercise.

"You're becoming more tricky." His voice was resonant in the deep well of his chest. "Both sound real."

"Pick one," she said.

"I don't know. In one you're a victim, in the other the victimizer. I can't quite place you in either roll. I give up."

"Not fair. You have to guess."

"All right. The pigs."

"Jeesh. Even when you guess, you're right."

"What can I say? I'm good. Tell me the pig story." His right hand traced circles over the wings of her shoulders.

"We used to do our own slaughtering when my parents had the farm in Heber. We'd round up the cattle and pigs. I remember the men being more quiet than usual, subdued, almost reverential. George and I were hanging over the fence, tossing pebbles at the swine in the holding pen, bouncing pebbles off their big heads. We imitated their surprised snorts. It seemed terrifically funny at the time. Suddenly I was yanked off the fence, Dad's fingers digging into my arm as he spun me around. I cried, not that he hurt me, but at the fury on Dad's face. I'd never seen him so angry, never imagined that such anger would be directed at me. He lowered his face close to mine, so close that the smudges of dirt and blood on his cheek blurred. He whispered, but with exaggerated pronunciation, that these animals were giving their lives so that we could have food, and if I couldn't act with decency and respect, I should get the hell out."

Paul stopped stroking her back. He was very still. "How you must have hated him."

His remark puzzled her. No, not the remark, but the emphasis on the word "hated," as though he wasn't making a comment but imbuing the word with personal meaning. *Hated him. Him.* His own father. She hesitated, wanting to say that her father hadn't been abusive like his, but Paul must have realized how he sounded. He said quickly, lightly: "Was that when you dropped out of the food chain?"

She nudged him with her foot. "I haven't dropped out of the food chain. I eat meat."

"Seafood and chicken aren't real meat. Prime rib, filet mignon, that's meat."

"Let me finish. The point is, my father gave me a lesson in empathy that I needed. I don't know if I'd been aware, or aware enough, how other creatures, or people, felt. I was resentful of my brothers. Mark and Matt were born by then. I was always having to watch them, make sure that they didn't get into the barn around the tools, or that they didn't crawl under the porch because of black widows. I went to the other extreme, watched over my brothers like a hawk, couldn't stand to see anything suffer. My mother would kill a hen for supper, and I'd pester her about whether the chicken felt pain. I couldn't eat anything that ever had a face."

"Do you worry about being haunted by the ghost of Thumper?"

Suzanne frowned and rolled to her side.

"I'm sorry." His hand stroked her shoulder. "An insensitive thing to say. A stupid way to say what I meant."

"No. It wasn't what you said. Preclinical research bothers me even though I know how necessary it is." She turned to look at Paul. "Do you remember a few weeks ago when one of the network news stations reported on puppy mills?"

"I think so. A midwest state, dogs crowded into pens?"

"Right. Then a few days later the same anchor covered child abuse, showing photos of babies who'd been horribly burned, a toddler who'd been beaten to death."

"I remember."

"The station received hundreds of outraged phone calls and letters, viewers who deplored showing such cruelty on television." She sighed. "The outrage was for the animals, not for the children. Much more empathy for puppies than babies. Why is that?"

"Animals are seen as quintessentially innocent. Blameless."

"There was this animal-rights activist who claimed if her dog and her child were drowning, she wouldn't be able to choose who to save first. Probably that woman enjoys filet mignon and has had her health maintained by drugs developed through animal testing. I want to deplore her inconsistencies, yet I can't ignore my own. I should know better, shouldn't I? Three years of doctoral study, two years as a practicing pharmacologist. I know the value of preclinical tests. My great uncle Brian went blind from glaucoma. That was before drugs like these beta blockers were available. How many rabbits was his eyesight worth?"

"You're too hard on yourself." He pulled her to his chest.

She nestled her head on his shoulder. "I wish I wasn't the one supervising the research." Under her ear, his breathing reminded her of the surge and fall of ocean waves in a cave, a lulling sound.

She'd thought he'd fallen asleep, but then he

asked, "How much longer on your contract?"

"One year, ten months, three weeks."

"It won't seem so hard after more time has passed. You'll adapt."

Bolton's animal rooms were clean, the air fresher than she'd expected, the cages full of albino rabbits with twitching noses. "I don't think I want to adapt."

"You're not a strict vegetarian. How'd you resolve eating meat?"

"I didn't. Not really. Time passed, concern faded, Big Macs attacked."

Then it happened, a subtle shifting as though Paul had moved away, though her arm still encircled his chest. She'd sensed his withdrawal before, often following a particularly good weekend together. He'd make excuses for not coming over, grading papers or catching up on the journals. Sometimes he'd visit Rusty, a friend since childhood, a fascinating man who earned a living writing B-movie screenplays. Most evenings Paul telephoned from his apartment and they'd chat for an hour while Jarvis, his bad-tempered Amazon parrot, squawked in the background. At the end of the conversation, he'd say he missed her, which left her speechless.

What makes us resist things that give pleasure?

Would he retreat further if she pursued him? She took a deep breath, then another, and another. When she didn't feel much more comfortable and was in danger of hyperventilating, she simply said, "Have you ever thought about living together?"

He moved so he could see her face. He wasn't smiling. "Not exactly."

"I'd like to talk about it."

He let his head drop back to the pillow. He stared at the ceiling. "Sure."

"I hate it when you spend the night in your apartment. I know you like being here. I'm not asking for marriage. If living together doesn't work out, we can always go back to—"

"No. You can't. You can't go back."

"Where's it written down that we can't try?"

"It's very difficult to go from a position of greater intimacy, like living together, to less. Most relationships don't survive that transition."

"Living together will work out for us."

"You don't know that."

"I know it. I know *us*."

Suddenly he smiled at her.

"What?" she said.

"You're such an innocent."

"What's that supposed to mean?"

He pulled her to him and kissed her neck. "Nothing bad has ever happened to you, has it? You've never been *tested*."

His tone infuriated her. She stiffened in his arms. "I'm thirty-one. I've had my share of disappointments, like everyone else."

"I don't mean disappointments. I mean tragedies. The great reversals. Failed love affairs. Illness. Death."

"Are you saying your life has been harder than anyone else's?"

"No. I'm saying that, compared to you, I've been through more."

She knew he was referring to his father's alcoholism, his parents' nasty divorce, and, though he never discussed other women, a "failed love affair" or two. He was forty, nine years her senior, so she didn't have any illusions that she'd been his first love. But she intended to be his last.

"Maybe so," she said, "but being the oldest of six kids has to count for something."

"Suzanne, we're just *talking* about living together and already we're arguing."

"An ideal relationship is one in which there are no disagreements?"

He was silent a moment. "You're right. Give me some time to think about it. Get used to the idea." He hugged her and planted a nice brotherly kiss on her brow.

She relented, but didn't think getting used to the idea was the problem.

CHAPTER 5

Suzanne sat in a psych lab on campus, eyes closed, eyeglasses in her lap. Paul had finished the progressive relaxation sequence, suggestions for loosening the tension in her feet, then legs, and so on, ending with her jaw muscles. The technique worked better than she expected, though she'd recommended removing the headrest from the comfortable reclining office chair or an unusually tired subject might drift into sleep.

Paul faced away from her, another one of her inputs. Sitting with closed eyes and trying to free-associate while someone stared was disconcerting.

"Now," his voice said, "focus on where Kelly will be at two P.M."

His words were smooth stones dropped onto the calm transparent surface of her mind. Images burst like fireworks: Bolton's animal room with its banks of cages, the hummingbird feeder in her backyard, an electrochemical charge crackling along the axon of a nerve, her sister Kelly grinning and wrinkling her nose, Paul shrugging out of his underwear last night, already erect. She described these, declined to mention the last. The cassette tape would lack a description of Paul's crotch.

"Make a note that your subject shouldn't know you," she told Paul. "Shouldn't *personally* know the interviewer. I'm getting some great interference about you."

"Noted," Paul said. "Focus on where Kelly will be at two P.M."

His voice was professional, serious. This was Paul the researcher, Paul the psychologist, not Paul the lover.

"All right." She felt a tiny unease, as though pretending Santa Claus existed. Relax, she told herself. This is not a moral issue. "I'm getting a lot of mental noise, interference, related to Kelly. Snapshots. Kelly when Mom brought her home from the hospital, tiny and wrapped in pink like a baby doll. I suggest using an outbound experimenter, or whatever you call them, use an outbound person who isn't known to the subject."

Her eyelids twitched. Keeping them closed was an effort. "Okay. Kelly at two P.M."

A three-dimensional hydrocarbon structure flickered in her mind. "Just got a flash of the beta-blocker I'm testing. An exact structure."

Paul's instructions suggested that the clearest images tended to be nonsense, that fleeting images were more likely related to the study. She suspected any image, perfect or fleeting, was nonsense. "Okay, I sense an object, something being held . . . light in weight, small, an edge with strings . . . like a fringe."

"A fringe?"

"This fringe thing, I have a related impression of fluffiness, softness, something you could crush in your fingers. It's multicolored, warm colors like yellows, reds. No fragrance or smell."

Background noise, she thought, the logical mind trying to make sense of random synaptic firings in the cerebral cortex. "This is odd. I see this fringed thing tossed up into the air and it becomes a bird, like a magician's act. Poof. That's gone. A quick perfect image of a penny. Okay, here's a vague one. I see a long white ribbon, curved slightly like an arch."

"Good."

"This white ribbon bulges at each end. There's a vibration underneath it, a vibration of color, the way watercolor diffuses. A horizontal vibration. This vibration is not part of the ribbon. It's separate." Images came easily, a relief. She'd feared she'd be sitting here silently, useful as a blank Etch-A-Sketch.

"Kelly at two P.M. Fragrances? Odors?" Paul asked.

She shrugged. "Haven't a clue."

"Okay. Kelly at two P.M. The sense of touch. Textures."

"Nothing."

"Taste."

"I don't . . ." She stopped. A taste did occur to her. "There's a dark taste. A dark strong taste. Tar? I see tar or something black like sludge. Rubber, perhaps. Black rubber." She remembered a phenomena common to psych experiments where the subject unconsciously tries to please the experimenter. Well, these sensory experiences are unwelcome proof that I'm not immune to the power of suggestion.

"What will Kelly see at two P.M.?"

Paul's face appeared in her mind, the full neatly trimmed, grizzled beard and mustache, thick almost confluent eyebrows, menacing if you didn't look at his warm brown eyes or broad transforming smile.

"A clear image of you." She paused. "Okay, a sudden impression of a silver surface riddled with holes . . . this is rather odd but it's fleeting so I'll describe it." I'm bubbling over with images, she thought. "Visual impression of this perforated thing running the length of the long white ribbon, perpendicular to it. This perforated rectangle is like a mesh window screen viewed under a microscope. This mesh is above the white ribbon."

"The mesh is floating?"

"It's touching, forming a ninety-degree angle relative to the ribbon." The space between her eyebrows tingled, almost ached.

"I think I'm getting a headache, like eyestrain. Probably from trying to keep my eyes closed in this light. It'd help if you could dim the fluorescents."

A similar sensation, an uncomfortable resonance, started in her solar plexus. She pressed her palm to the area below her sternum. A deep breath didn't help. "How much longer?"

"A few more minutes. What will Kelly see at two P.M.?"

CHAPTER 6

Ten miles from campus a car poked along Pacific
Coast Highway. Toni clutched the steering wheel
of her mother's cobalt-blue BMW. Her mother's
new cobalt-blue BMW. She smiled at the chatter
of her passengers and hoped they wouldn't notice
how often the tires rumbled over the round metal
dots dividing the lanes. She kept her hands at ten
and two, like the driving instructor had told her,
but still the car drifted. Maybe because she was
tense.

Was it larceny to take your mother's car without
permission and drive around with only a learner's
permit? Could a fifteen-year-old be arrested for
that? Her uneasiness was mixed with pride at
having the two older girls, juniors at Laguna
High, in the car with her. Stephanie and Danielle
were popular, funny. Both tall, both blond, and
both poured into tiny Guess jeans. Toni was night
to their day. She was shorter, darker, unpopular,
had trouble understanding jokes.

"Get this beemer moving, Toni," Danielle said.
"You're driving like my old lady."

"You're not *listening*," Stephanie complained,
and poked Danielle's shoulder. Stephanie sat in

48

the middle, sucking on a straw protruding from a long pink thermos. "So then like, I go, what's it to you? And then he goes, get this, he goes, I been watching you. Like that old song, you know?"

Danielle put her Reebok-clad feet on the dash. "This is the guy with the diamond earring?"

"Yes yes *yes*. He knew everything, like where I live, my tanning salon, the stables where I go riding."

"What about Derek?" Toni asked, wanting to be part of the conversation.

Stephanie said, "You live in a cave or something? Derek's history."

Toni flushed. She didn't mean for it to happen, but the BMW swerved near a flame-red New Yorker convertible and its driver sounded his horn. He looked pissed. She stomped on the accelerator to get away from whatever he was mouthing.

"Way to go, Antoinette," Danielle said. "What a dweeb if he can't take a joke."

Stephanie craned around. "Nice car, though. So, as I was saying . . ." She paused to sip from the straw.

"Girl, give me that." Danielle pulled the thermos toward her. "I swear, you could suck the chrome from a trailer hitch."

Stephanie shrieked, spitting a mouthful onto the custom leather seat. Droplets trickled down the dash. Danielle thumped her feet against the dash, close to the CD player, and convulsed with laughter.

"Hey," Toni said. What was so funny? And she didn't want the car messed up.

In a nyah-nyah voice, Stephanie said, "She doesn't know what that means."

"We must educate this poor young woman." Danielle pressed the button to lower the window. She unbuckled her seat belt, leaned out the window, and yelled, "Antoinette doesn't know men have PECKERS!"

"Knock it off," Toni said.

"Oh, you can't knock them off." Stephanie shook her head. "Not only is that impossible, it's a very bad idea to even try."

Danielle slid back into the seat. "No, no, no. The expression is suck. You suck them off. But you don't actually suck them *off,* that's a, what-cha-ma-call-it?" She sipped from the straw.

"Exaggeration," Danielle said.

"A figurative expression," Toni said, unhappy with humor at her expense.

"Figurative! See, what did I tell you, Stephie? She's smarter than us. She doesn't use words like dick or pecker or twat."

"Ah, but perhaps she doesn't have a twat," Stephanie said.

Danielle giggled. "Is that the problem, Toni? Are you built like those dolls with just this tiny pee hole?"

"Twatless Toni. Kind of has a ring to it, don't you think?" Stephanie said.

Toni pulled over onto the shoulder of the road, floored the brake pedal. The tires skidded on loose gravel, then ground to a stop, throwing everyone forward. She was too upset and hurt to speak. She wanted to tell them to get out, but all she did was sit there and blink through tears, feeling miserable. She'd taken the car and everything, just to become friends with these two.

"Uh-oh," Stephanie said.

"Uh-oh," Danielle echoed.

"I think we've gone too far," Stephanie said.

"Again," Danielle agreed.

"We've been in bad taste," Stephanie said.

"Again," Danielle said.

"You know what we gotta do," Stephanie said.

"Grovel for forgiveness," Danielle said.

"I'm sorry," Stephanie said.

"I'm sorry," Danielle said. "Seriously. We apologize. We're often in the wrong. Here—" Danielle passed her the thermos,—"have a taste of this. Iced tea. Long Island style."

She shook her head.

"Come on. You'll feel better." Danielle shook the thermos. "We'll be good. Please."

"Puh-leez," Stephanie said.

"*Puh-leeeeez,* Toni," Stephanie and Danielle said in unison.

She looked at them. They pouted simultaneously.

"*Puh-leeeeez,* Toni."

She tried not to smile and failed. She put the straw into her mouth.

CHAPTER 7

In the psych lab Suzanne struggled to keep her eyes closed. She wanted to stand up, walk around, drive to El Paso, anything other than sit here, a punching bag for free-floating anxiety. A pneumatic drill drummed between her eyebrows. "My eyes are really bothering me, Paul. A twenty-minute session might be too long. Maybe you can get the same input in fifteen minutes."

"Almost over. What will Kelly see at two P.M.?"

The tingling in her solar plexus spread, trickled like an electric charge to her legs. Weird, she thought. Unpleasant. Maybe my conscience is beating me up, she reflected, because I'm violating some deep-seated Suzanne rule forbidding participation in superstitious mumbo jumbo. The thought didn't make her happy. She'd hoped that, at her core, she was both rational and nonjudgmental. However, if her lack of faith in the experiment caused the physical sensations, that didn't stop images from coming. "I see the *Physician's Desk Reference* opened to Oculol. That's the antiglaucoma drug of my company's competitor."

She inhaled deeply. Exhaled. "Okay, here's something obscure. A reddish-brown fabric, like a rug, and it's warm. You can run your hands through it. Maybe hair rather than carpet. Now it's changed, shrunk, become a reflective black, and there's a cone attached to it. Like a dunce cap, tiny, yellow—"

Without warning her mindscape spun crazily with sickening vertigo. Colors, sounds, and shapes kaleidoscoped.

A black lacy thrumming,
sulphurous blaze,
Kelly turns, pirouettes, hair fans out, light blond
whirling from green to white to flashing blue,
shrieks,
a metallic blue blur,
silver glinting,
and the metallic blue flashes toward her, over her, the angle is odd, slams into her right hip, a powerful blow that shatters bone. She falls, an endless terrifying fall as though she were falling off the planet, the fall of nightmares where hitting bottom means your death. She screams as the radiant blue crushes her legs, the surprising heavy treachery of blue. A hot rough surface grinds against her cheek and arms, wet red spatters black, black, the stench of burning rubber, the sun ignites her veins, searing, the pain . . .

His eyebrows raised. "You don't remember?"

"I do. Sort of." More came back to her, fuzzy and out of focus, the mental equivalent of myopia. Yes, she'd been up and about in the middle of the night. Something had scared the bejesus out of her. How could she have forgotten? A thin spike of uneasiness pinned her thoughts. There is a dark beneath the smooth terrain of the conscious mind. Her unconscious had made a subtle but major subterranean shift, similar to an earthquake, the sliding of strata that transmits only as tremor. She felt different in a wordless way.

Which was nonsense.

"I guess I wasn't fully awake."

"You looked awake to me."

"That's what my parents used to say. I was a sleepwalker when I was a kid."

A reaction, she suspected, to her position as only child usurped by all those brothers. She hadn't thought much about those youthful episodes, but recalled now the common element: that terrifying displacement in time and space. Like the night she woke with a start, completely disoriented, eyes focused on a ceiling that was all wrong, *wrong,* groping about and feeling the odd hard surface beneath her, her heart thudding with fright. She'd finally recognized that she was lying on the dining-room table.

Those times were years and years ago. She'd been just a kid, and like most childish things, she'd outgrown it.

Or had she?

CHAPTER 8

Paul's face, pale against his dark beard and moustache, floated above her. Anxious eyes. His mouth moved. A bright diffuse glow silhouetted his hair. Bright glow . . . what? The sun? That other reality had bolted, its brilliant burning flash suddenly absent, and now only the ghost of after-images, of terror, remained. Wherever Suzanne was now was thin and insubstantial, as though seen through a gauzy veil.

Paul was talking to her. "What happened?" he said. "Did you faint? Are you hurt?"

She recognized the inverted ice-tray cubes of the fluorescent light on the ceiling. She was lying on the floor of the lab, the linoleum cool and hard. Kelly. "My sister." She struggled to get up, her legs rubbery with fear. "She's hurt."

"Don't try to get up."

"Kelly's *hurt*." She clutched his arms, pulled herself up against him. Standing was difficult. Her muscles quivered as though she'd worked out too hard.

"Suzanne, she's in my office."

"She's—" Where? "She's outside. With that blue, that blue . . . " Images flickered, her thoughts tossed in a messy word salad, hot, blue, pain. She heard herself panting. "Her legs—"

"Listen." Paul helped her into the chair. "Kelly's still here. In my office." He pulled around the other chair, sat, and took her hands. His own were trembling. He wished he sounded more reassuring but panic had dried his throat. The reflection of another love, another time. He hardly dared focus on Suzanne in case he saw an expression he had seen once before: a look of pale, remote acceptance that meant that she was slipping away, from physical visible light, from his passion, into a shadow land.

"Your hands are like ice," he said, warming them with his own. "Listen. You and I've been doing the remote sensing part of the experiment. Right?"

She nodded. The veil began to lift. This was real. She was here.

"You had described something black with a yellow cone, then you stopped talking. I heard you fall. You must have fainted. That was just a minute ago. Not even a minute. You know the computer won't select a destination for Kelly until we're done. She's still here."

"Maybe she left. You don't know." She started to get up, but the urgency lessened. What had she seen? A blue what?

"I'll bring her to you." The two vertical creases between his eyebrows deepened. He touched her cheek. "You still look . . . Babe, I'm sorry. I didn't realize you were feeling sick."

His touch on her arms was firm, more sure.

"Kelly."

"I'll get her." After a lingering, uneasy glance, he left. The door's pneumatic hinge wheezed closed. She heard his quick footfalls. She blinked. Her eyes refused to focus. "My glasses," she said aloud. She stood and squinted at the tan linoleum, seeing the shiny blur of her frames near the table leg. She picked them up and slipped them on. The room seemed to tilt. She sat down again, leaned back, closed her eyes.

The memory of whatever had hurt Kelly shredded into filaments, evaporated the more she tried to grasp them, a dream-fade, leaving a slight emotional aftertaste of alarm. The ache of her hip reminded her of hitting the hard floor, though what had frightened her, the images, spiraled away. Gone. Kaput. Like a few nights ago. She'd had a nightmare about something—a bat?—in her room and had dragged poor Allan out of bed to investigate.

From the corridor came Kelly's muffled voice, rising high over Paul's deeper tones. The door swung open and Kelly rushed to her side. Nylon whispered from her disproportionately large thighs, her legs clearly intact under the pink shirtdress. The last of the Reynolds clan was barely over five feet tall and blond, as though the genes for height and color had been exhausted by five older siblings. Her sister's heart-shaped face, framed with hair the sheen of freshly pulled taffy, was pinched and concerned. She's fine, Suzanne thought, then felt surprised. Why wouldn't she be?

"What happened?" Kelly asked, touching Suzanne's shoulder. "Paul said you fainted."

Kelly's intent gaze seemed to peer into her thoughts, a mature worried appraisal.

"I had this ... impression ... that you were hurt."

Kelly shook her head. "An impression?" She glanced at Paul. "What sort of impression?"

"I don't remember exactly. Something about you being hurt." *She had been talking one moment, prone on the floor the next. If I were better prepared, this wouldn't have been such a shock. Prepared for what?* She had the eerie sensation that she knew something, but her emotional reaction had driven it underground. She felt different in a fundamental way. *What does it mean when your own thoughts mystify you?* She glanced at the downward draw of Kelly's face and joked, "I think Paul pushed me. I wasn't cooperating enough."

"What?" Kelly looked at Paul.

"Just kidding. I guess I fainted."

Paul said, "Might be a good idea to see a doctor." His voice was hesitant. He knew her opinion of the medical profession.

"Oddly enough, I feel great right now." *That was true.*

Paul opened his mouth to argue.

"But you're right," she said. "I'll make an appointment for Monday." A slight mechanical whir distracted her. She looked at the table. "Is that noise coming from the tape recorder?" It seemed so loud. Terrifically loud.

He walked over to the table. Suzanne heard the distinct rustle of pants legs, that fabric he was wearing making a singularly unique sound.

He pushed the stop button.

Kelly said, "I'll walk you home." They had trekked from the house through the Serrano woods to campus, a pleasant twenty-minute stroll.

"No, it's all right." She stood, her legs solid under her. "Allan's expecting me at Animal Sciences. We might have another housemate. And you have to buy your books today, don't you?"

Kelly nodded.

"Go ahead and do that."

Their combined concern, their reluctance to let her go, felt like a web she'd stumbled into. "I'm going downstairs. I'll ask Allan to drive me home. I'll be perfectly fine." She tried to look reassuring. "Don't forget, tonight Rusty and his latest starlet are coming over."

"I'll be over about six with hamburgers and hot dogs," Paul said.

"What about the experiment?" Kelly looked at Paul.

"Well," he said, "there's still time, if you want . . ."

"I'd like to finish," Kelly said.

"I'd better go have the computer select your destination." He pointed to the wall clock. "Twenty before two. You might need fifteen minutes to walk to your destination."

A shot of adrenaline spiraled up from Suzanne's stomach, an emotional echo. "No. I don't want her to go."

"But if I don't, that will mess up the experiment. We won't be able to see if your images match where the computer sends me." Kelly's eyes ricocheted between the two.

"This was dress rehearsal, not the real thing," Suzanne said. Paul looked at her with a sort of telepathic understanding and she felt a twinge of tenderness.

"I could go with her," Paul said.

"No. Not today. Besides," she hoped to soften her response, "there's too much interference when the subject—me in this case—knows the outbound person."

"What do you mean?" Kelly said.

"I kept getting images of you from the past, like when Mom brought you home from the hospital. A subject who didn't know you wouldn't have that interference."

"But this is just a dress rehearsal, like you said," Kelly persisted. "It doesn't have to be perfect. When the real experiment starts on Monday, the subjects won't know me. I want to go through the motions once before then."

"Tomorrow," Paul said. "We'll do this again. I'll find a subject who doesn't know you, Kelly."

"Okay." Kelly looked relieved.

"Oh." Suzanne touched Paul's arm. "The faculty tea is tomorrow."

"Not till two. We'll have plenty of time."

Suzanne left them in Paul's office, while he tried to locate another subject for the trial run tomorrow. She didn't have much time to reflect on evaporating memories, cerebral receptor sites, and the probable and fascinating electro-biochemical mechanisms. When the elevator opened and she strolled out into the fresh California air, a wave of nausea swept over her. She, of the cast-iron stomach, world-renowned onion-sandwich consumer, lover of three-alarm chili, creator of curried broccoli guaranteed to singe hair from nostrils, lost her lunch in the Japanese boxwood barely five feet from the women's room door.

CHAPTER 9

Suzanne trotted down the stairs of the zoology building. Barfing in the bushes had given her energy. Her spirits were high and strong, ready to combat all evils, solve all problems, rule the world. The dials of her senses were exquisitely tuned. Her high-top sneakers clutched around her ankles, her jogging bra slipped against her nipples, the crotch seam of her jeans pressed between her legs. Before today, had she been only half-awake?

Even before she reached the B2 level, where Allan had said his lab was, she heard the low distinct timbre and counterpoint of masculine voices in disagreement. The underground hall funneled the sound to her ears, wave forms pushing molecule against molecule and thudding against the thin membrane of her eardrums. She focused on the voices, followed them to a closed gray metal door marked LS-B22, but didn't need to see the room number to know this was the place. She recognized Allan's bass pitch. She knocked, but the argument continued. She knocked again and called out hello. No response.

The second man's voice was higher and nasal.

"Cripes, Allan, don't get so bent out of shape—"

"You don't touch the equipment unless I'm here, period. Don't. Touch. You got it?"

"Yeah, I got it. I got that you got a problem, man, a real problem. You think you're the only grad student on this project . . ."

Suzanne twisted the knob and pushed open the door. A trace of ammonia fumes stung her nostrils. At the end of three rows of black laboratory benches, stainless-steel sinks, and metal stools stood Allan and a small redheaded, bearded man, probably in his early twenties. Allan towered over the younger guy, anybody would, but the other man stood his ground, glaring up into Allan's face. The short man was bowlegged as though he'd spent too many hours in the saddle. The hem of his snug jeans, a thick roll at the cuff, hung low over his loafers. The sleeves of his blue plaid shirt hung to the knuckles of his fists. His ears were an impossibly bright red.

Allan stabbed him in the chest with his index finger. "You'll have a problem if you don't keep your mitts off the equipment." Another jab.

The short man backed away until he was against the bench. Allan followed. His six-foot height made the other man seem lilliputian. Allan ground out words through clenched teeth. "Next time you want to screw something up, how about trying to stop a buzz saw with your bare hands. Got it?" Another poke.

"Stop." The short man's voice quavered.

The aggressive behavior was so unlike Allan, so unexpected, that she gawked, stupefied. Her brain stripped gears trying to convince her this was someone else. But there was that faded Bat-man T-shirt, narrow waist, and skinny little butt in the Levi's with the hole below the left knee. It was Allan, all right. Her meek, mild roommate was about to jump down this man's throat. What had the little guy done to arouse such wrath?

Allan's eyes narrowed and he jabbed the short man again. He knocked Allan's hand aside.

This would go to blows in a few seconds. Suzanne hurried toward the two. "Ah, excuse me."

Allan shoved the other guy. He stumbled side-ways.

She said, "Allan!"

He swung at Allan, but was off-balance and only managed to clip his shoulder. His momen-tum carried him against a bench, his arm nicking and rocking a stoppered Erlenmeyer flask filled with a colorless fluid. Other flasks, glass beak-ers, racks of culture tubes, were aligned on the black benches. This was a dangerous place for a free-for-all. Too many chemicals eager to melt flesh. She noted a shower head mounted on the wall and the floor drain in a tiled depression, for emergency wash-downs. She hoped she wouldn't need to drag either man over there.

Allan lunged toward the short man and she yelled, "That's enough!"

The short man twisted toward her, startled. Allan grabbed his shirtfront and hauled him com-pletely off the linoleum. His loafer hooked a metal stool on the way up, which lifted along with him, then his loafer slipped off and the stool clattered to the floor.

The little guy grasped Allan's wrists, clawed to

pull them apart. His struggles failed to loosen Allan's grip. Allan looked ready to use him as a bowling ball.

Suzanne reached Allan, grabbed his arm, which felt like touching metal. He didn't register her presence. Icy needles prickled the nape of her neck. "Allan. *Allan.*"

His lips were a thin bloodless line. There was an alarming coldness to his eyes, his skin fixed into a mask that concealed an expression you wouldn't want to see in a nightmare. This fury was alien and inhuman, like a possession. His features drew tight into harsh angles, his lips curled back, and he lost all resemblance to the man she knew. This was a lethal and dangerous stranger who could sprout fangs and rip open the throats of prey.

She shook his rock-hard biceps. *"Allan".* Her heartbeat thudded in her ears.

His chin lifted, he blinked and looked at her. Recognition melted the frost. "Suzanne."

His arms relaxed and he let down the little guy, who flushed even redder. Here was an audience to his humiliation. He straightened his shirt with stiff jerks, panting. His beard trembled, his smoky blue eyes watered. He said to Suzanne, "He's fucking crazy, you know that? Goddamn fruitcake."

He pointed at Allan, who stood rooted to the spot, speechless. "Fucking crazy." The short man stumbled against the fallen stool. "Shit." He picked up his loafer, but didn't bother to put it on. He directed the shoe, like a gun, at Allan. "You're your own worst enemy, you stupid fuck." The little guy blinked rapidly, anguished. Suzanne looked at the gray and white linoleum, knowing her presence increased his embarrassment a hundredfold. His fist thumped against the door as he left.

Allan leaned against the bench, head down, arms folded. His chest rose and fell rapidly. Suzanne walked away, to give him time to recover. To give herself time to recover. This end of the lab narrowed into a short hall with two doors. Their small square windows were taped over and covered with a sign reading Chiroptera. The bat aviaries. Faint undefinable noises fluttered from within. A sheet of the calendar month hung beneath the sign, each day showing times and cryptic notations. She stared at these acronyms, a place to put her gaze while she wondered if everyone had a tripwire that caused craziness, if you could recognize when you yourself had become alien.

"Danny messed with the infrared timer."

Suzanne turned. Allan's face was pale, but it was his own again, smooth, unlined, high forehead, somehow older. Or maybe just weary. His shoulders slumped.

"The infrared timer?"

"The bats are on a diurnal schedule."

She paused. "I thought bats were nocturnal."

"It's . . ." He raised both hands, palm up, and let them drop. He shook his head with self-disgust. "Damn. This isn't important. What's important is . . ." He rubbed his face. "I'm sorry about . . . before. I don't usually have a bad temper. My dad was always pissed. I always swore I'd never lose control, be like him. He was a maniac."

"You don't need to apologize to me. Danny—"

"I know, I know. Being that short is enough of a burden without idiots like me bullying him." He winced. "God, I can't believe I did that."

"No kidding." She joined him at the bench, leaning back and facing the same direction. The fallen stool lay at their feet. "Allan, you didn't even see or hear me until—"

"This hasn't happened to me in years. I thought I'd outgrown that. But Danny is a guy who has gone way beyond his level of incompetence. He's been shown endlessly how to set the infrared timer and he still screws it up. Enough disruption of the schedule, and bats would die."

She began to say something, but Allan continued, "I know. That's no excuse for wanting to beat the living daylights out of him."

"Is that what would have happened if I wasn't here?"

"No." His eyes sought hers and locked in. "No. I couldn't hurt anyone. I'm not programmed that way. I am, however, amazingly capable of making a complete ass of myself."

"Uh-huh." She couldn't imagine him as the sort of man who ended up naked in a tower with a high-powered rifle. She playfully punched his arm. "Well, give me advance notice if I ever irritate you in any way."

He took in a deep breath, exhaled, and smiled wryly. "I guess your friend would find me an interesting case."

"What?"

"Paul. He's a therapist, right?"

"He doesn't shrink people, Allan. He does research, a mix of parapsychology and physics. All tied up with synchronicity and unrelated events having connections. It's almost . . . mystical, I guess. But he's basically a researcher. Like you."

Allan arced his shoulders as though trying to shake something off. He reached down and righted the stool.

"So . . . where's our potential roommate?"

He darted a glance at her, coughed, and studied his sneakers.

"Oh, no. Tell me it isn't so."

He grimaced. "Maybe Danny will accept my apology."

"He definitely deserves an apology. But I don't know if he'd be able to forgive. You mortified him. In front of me."

"Maybe if I gave him a cattle prod and let him zap the crap out of me."

"Sounds like a good idea."

"How bad are your finances?"

She shrugged. "Beware adjustable interest rate mortgages. It looked pretty good until the first eighteen months ended. Also I was due a raise last year, but Bolton put all salary adjustments on hold."

"I'll talk with Danny. He'll come around."

She doubted that.

Allan laughed. He put an arm around her shoulder and squeezed. "You wear your heart on your sleeve. Don't worry. Listen, I promise. I'll fix things with Danny."

He released her and smiled. "Now that you're

here, how about a tour of the lab?"

She wanted to get home and devour the contents of the fridge, yet she couldn't hurt his feelings by leaving. "Sure."

He grinned and looked boyish again. "Maybe it's just as well that Danny screwed up the timer. Wait here."

He loped in a long-legged gait to the farthest aviary doors and entered. A pool of red light spilled out, diluting to pink on the floor. The door wheezed closed behind him. A few seconds later he peered out. His dark brown hair gleamed with red highlights. "Come on."

She hesitated. "You're not going to scare the dickens out of me, are you?"

"You'll find this fascinating. Trust me."

"I hate when people say that." She walked to Allan and entered the aviary. Infrared bulbs cast a hellish glow on cages lining both sides of the broad room. Her pupils widened to their rims. She pushed her eyeglasses more firmly against the bridge of her nose. An astringent fetid odor, reminding her of a chicken coop, filled her nasal passages. Much worse than the rabbit rooms at Bolton. The air was warm, soupy. Small specific sounds echoed, the crepey rustle of leathery wings, the pings of tiny claws against thin metal bars, the whir of the ventilation fan. Ahead was a large enclosed area, chicken wire stretching to the ten-foot ceiling and across to either wall.

"Your vision will adjust in a minute," Allan said. "Want the minilecture? It's free with the tour."

"Absolutely."

"Like most mammals, bats have a sensitive circadian rhythm. The pattern of sunlight and darkness guides their feeding and sleeping cycles. These infrared bulbs create night for the bats, which is their normal waking time."

"Like zoos. The public watches nocturnal animals in action when infrared is used."

"Right." He took her elbow and guided her toward the large enclosure.

"Wait a minute." She pulled away. "What's that?" Now she could make out a huge jar he had pinched under his arm.

"You'll see in a minute." He released a latch on the enclosure and swung out a low gate. "This is the flight cage. Mind your head." He ducked and hunkered down through the opening.

"I'd rather jump in a vat of boiling oil than go in there. Don't bats get stuck in your hair?"

"Hogwash. Come on."

"And what about—"

"No. No rabies. Bats aren't any more susceptible than dogs, and these little fellas are all healthy. Heck, there are more rabid *cows*."

"Frothing Holsteins, huh?" She stooped under and pulled the gate closed behind her. Dark triangular shapes clotted the upper perimeter of the cage. She stepped back. The paper on the floor stuck to her feet.

Allan glanced down. "One of the better uses for the university newspaper, don't you think? All right. Stand right there. Don't make any sudden movements."

"Not to worry."

He walked to the middle of the cage. His lean

form glowed eerily in the dim red light. She smiled. He was completely in control, center stage, a magician about to perform a feat of prestidigitation. He unscrewed the lid to the jar and tossed its contents upward. Live insects—moths, she thought—fluttered and spiraled. There was an explosion of activity as dozens of bats descended. She reflexively hunched, but the bats were only interested in the moths. The size of sparrows, they swooped in graceful arcs. You wouldn't, however, confuse them with birds. Their wing flappage rate was much slower, and few birds flew in the dark.

"If you watch carefully," Allan said, "you can see how they catch moths with the underside of their tails."

She squinted, noticed the quick flip of a bat's tail toward its breast. It was an efficient, surprisingly quiet aerial display. Allan stood motionless, calm, at the heart of the darting shapes, the ruler of this little kingdom, until nearly all the bats had returned to roost.

"They're beneficial critters." He recapped the empty jar. "In one night a single little brown bat might consume a hundred cutworm moths or thousands of mosquitoes."

She believed that. Not one moth remained. It had been, as Allan promised, a fascinating sight. A slight pressure drew her attention to her pants leg and she yelped. An inky black-winged shape clambered up the fabric.

"It's okay." Allan tucked the jar under his arm, leaned over, and peered at her slacks. "This is an adolescent looking for a launching pad. Cute, eh?"

"Oh, sure." It's harmless, she assured herself. Beneficial. She gritted her teeth anyway while the bat scrabbled for a toehold on her leg. She noticed—scientific detachment at its finest—that it clutched more efficiently with its back legs than with the tiny wing-tip claws. The bat reached her hip and pushed off. The wings flapped past her face. Suzanne jerked, her shoulders banged the cage, and the wire structure jingled. Or maybe her nerves made an audible sound.

He touched her arm, steadying her. "All right?"

"Just dandy. Golly, that was fun." She still felt like something was crawling on her leg, but there wasn't anything there. "I think I'm ready for the vat of oil, now."

Allan pushed open the gate and waited while she left the flight cage. He exited and refastened the latch.

"The flight cage is for studying biosonar." He set the empty jar on a tall cage, its top level with her chin. "Bats use sound—"

"Echolocation?"

"Hey, no flies on you. Right. Echolocation." He reached over to the wall and turned on another infrared. Intense red spotlighted the tall cage. "Each bat emits sound, biosonar pulses, that tell not only the location and relative velocity of a moth, but also its wingbeat. Nothing in military aerospace matches their accuracy." He tapped the bars of the cage before them. "Here's something really interesting."

She peered inside. A furry curtain of Chiroptera hung upside down at the top, a few at lower elevations. One dropped with a small thud to the cage floor and crept to a large flat dish. It lapped the liquid. "They're a little bigger than the ones in the flight cage." She hunkered down and watched the bat drink. It had a squashed pug nose like a Pekinese. "A flat face and really pointed ears."

He crouched so his face was near hers. "These fellas are a different species. *Desmodus rotundus*. Our newest arrivals."

The fluid in the dish seemed darker than water. A lot darker. And viscous. She didn't think this was a trick of the infrared light. "What's it drinking?"

"Equine serum."

Horse blood. She scuttled back. "Where the heck do you buy that?"

Allan grinned. "There's biological supply warehouses for *everything*. Feeder insects, like the moths, bovine serum, equine—"

"Ah, that's all right. You don't have to explain. I grew up on a farm. When you slaughter animals, nothing goes to waste." The bat crawled to the cage bars and climbed. "So these are the infamous vampire bats. Are you studying echolocation with them?"

"No." He straightened. "The common vampire bat does use echolocation to search for prey, but other species, like the little brown bats, are less fragile, easier to maintain. Most research on the vampires has been done on the anticoagulating factor in their saliva."

"I've read about that in pharmacology journals." She stood. "The anticoagulating factor acts like heparin, prevents clotting. Might be useful for people with heart disease."

"We're not going to study that, either. Something more arcane and behavioral. Altruism."

"Altruism?" She pointed, but not too close, to the shifting wad of bats at the ceiling of the cage. "These fellas look chummy, but I wouldn't say they're in a gift-giving mood. And what about these loners down here?" Two bats, about a foot apart, clung near the floor.

"The ones near the bottom are subordinate males. This one"—he reached a finger between the bars and stroked the belly of a single bat a few inches below the ceiling cluster—"is the dominant male. The group is the harem, females with pups. The females engage in the altruistic behavior."

"Which is?"

"Food sharing. A vampire bat dies if it doesn't feed for two nights in a row."

She studied the dish of blood and the harem. "How does one female share food with another?"

"A hungry bat grooms the donor, licks under the donor's wings, then the donor regurgitates blood."

"Yum."

"The fascinating thing is that the altruistic feeding is antisurvival. It's maladaptive. Or, at this point, it seems so. The donor, just like the begging bat, *has* to get her nightly quota of calories or she'll die. So in and of itself, it's a curious evolutionary adaptation."

"Like sleep."

"What?"

"Like sleep. Mammals are defenseless when they sleep. Like altruism, sleep is a curious adaptation."

"I hadn't considered that, but you're right. In the wild, for a creature to be unconscious for any length of time is an invitation to predators."

A tiny bell of recognition chimed in her head. Recognition of what? "But sleep, like this altruistic sharing of food by the bats, must be adaptive, right? Otherwise the behavior wouldn't continue."

"We're starting there, assuming the altruism has a useful function. Perhaps, for instance, a donor bat on another night doesn't obtain a blood meal. Does she then approach the beggar and request food sharing? Or—"

He rambled on while ideas resonated, swirled in a vague, protoplasmic way. Adaptation. Mutation. Allan's talk triggered the impression that she'd been altered, genes recombined, that she'd been given the equivalent of a strange, complicated, powerful tool. The instructions for its use were indecipherable unless . . . unless what? Then a door in her mind unlocked and the memory of that night when she woke Allan—*before* she woke him, before she was awake herself—that dreamscape flickered. The heat, the dry desert, she couldn't move, and the revolting shadow that blotted out the sun, descending, stabbing—

—and it wasn't a bat, not even close.

It was a carrion eater. A vulture.

Seeking her eyes.

CHAPTER 10

"What's your dog's name?" Kelly asked.

"Trouble," the girl said. She hauled an energetic Irish setter, its leash over her shoulder. She disentangled the leather cord from her fine blond hair. "He wants to pee on everything he sees. Are you a college student?" The dog bounced on spring-loaded legs, jumping against the girl and Kelly.

"Yes," Kelly said, proud at the question. She felt like an adult for the first time in her eighteen years. She loved California and the university, its sun-washed man-made lake in the heart of campus, the tropical palm trees, the immortal youth. The endless possibilities.

Kelly ruffled Trouble's silky ears and he slobbered on her hand. She teased the girl the way an adult might. "How about you?"

The child drew together her white-blond eyebrows. "What?"

"Are you a college student?"

The girl laughed, pleased. "No way. I'll only be in the fifth grade."

They passed the pedestrian archway spanning Lake Forest Boulevard. Trouble lunged in every direction at once but the girl kept a two-fisted hold on his lead. At the light Kelly punched the button for the walk signal. On the opposite side was the university bookstore, where Kelly planned to buy used English lit and algebra textbooks. Thinking about algebra nearly gave her hives. Math had been her biggest nightmare in high school. She wanted to do well, to see a different expression on Suzanne's face other than that doubting, concerned frown. Her sister didn't think she was very smart. Actually, in Utah, she herself thought this was true. But here, with an interesting job doing research, just like Suzanne, with a new life starting under eternal sunshine, she felt she could do anything.

"Do you like licorice?"

The girl nodded vigorously. Kelly dug into her purse, found the cellophane package, and handed her a twist.

"Aren't you going to have some?" the child asked.

"Trying to give it up," Kelly said. I will, she thought. I'll lose weight. Maybe start jogging. Everyone ran, everyone was blond, tan, healthy, everyone wore running shoes with air pumps. She would become thin and precise as a knife.

Her thoughts stubbed against the memory of Suzanne in the lab, without her glasses, looking pale and fragile. A fainting spell. Maybe she wasn't eating right. You can't depend on vegetables. Not enough protein in brussels sprouts and lima beans and tofu patties and all those weird vegetarian concoctions. Tonight she'd make a hearty chicken soup from scratch and insist Suzanne eat it.

Kelly saw herself years from now, accepting an award for a medical discovery, something related to nutrition, and Suzanne would tell how Kelly had cured her anemia and returned her to glowing health, that Suzanne owed her *life* to . . .

The light across the street flashed the image of a person walking. The girl dragged her dog onto the black macadam, but lost her grip on the leash when she raised the licorice to her mouth. The dog bounded loose, toward Kelly and beyond.

"Trouble!" the girl cried, hands on her hips, the exaggerated outrage of a child with an audience.

Kelly turned to watch the setter tear onto the grass. A huge black bird with a yellow beak hunted for worms. Trouble lunged after the bird, sending it into flight. The dog sprang into the air, russet fur rippling, leash sailing, and yelped with delight. With its open mouth, lolling tongue, Trouble appeared to be grinning. Kelly laughed.

The rest happened in eerie slow motion. Kelly turned to look at the girl, who stood in the street under the smooth white bridge of the pedestrian walkway. Her blond hair shimmered. The girl squinted, shaded her eyes from the sun, and shouted, "Trouble! Bad, bad dog!"

Kelly said, "Come to the sidewalk," when the corner of her eye caught movement, a blue car rolling fast, way too fast, speeding and swerving, rocking violently side to side. Kelly had stepped onto the street and now she lifted her foot to step back up onto the curb, because the car was out of control, fishtailing, heading for her, the blue finish glinting, at that speed it would hurtle the sidewalk no problem. Then her heel hit the curb, she lost her footing, and she began to fall back like falling off the planet, a slow tumble in a void without gravity, the sun a white-hot sphere in the cloudless sky, a blue sky equaling the blue finish of that car, there's some algebra for you, she thought she heard laughing, or maybe crying, a girl crying, the little girl? Still mid-fall she looked to the road, the car spun around, tires screaming, like the driver had jammed on the brakes, only it was too late, too late, the blue car was totally at the mercy of a cruel impersonal force . . .

CHAPTER 11

Suzanne hunted around in the refrigerator until she spied the purple-lidded container. "Aha." She pried off the cover. The intense scent of olive oil and garlic wafted up. The puree was a darker yellow, but wasn't that innocent oxidation? She scooped a bit onto her finger and licked. It tasted fresh. However, with all the garlic, who knows what could be setting up house?

"What do you think it is?" Allan said.

"I told you what it is. Humus. Pureed chickpeas and sesame seeds, lemon juice, extra virgin olive oil, garlic, lots of garlic—"

"No, no, what do you think these dreams or visions mean?"

She looked at him. He hunched over the kitchen table, a brown leather work glove on his left hand, an eyedropper in his right. A decrepit bird cage with tortured bars rested before him. A tiny brown bat hung inside, snug under its wings.

"Now I know how Paul feels," Suzanne said. "Maybe this whole experience is a brand of instant karma to teach me tolerance."

He reached in his gloved hand and gently plucked the bat from its perch. Wings, like little hands holding the hem of a cape, grappled with the glove, then surrendered. Allan set the dropper aside and stroked the bat's head with his thumb. "Huh?"

"Your absent, patronizing tone—"

He pulled his attention from the bat. "Hey, I didn't mean—"

"It's all right. I think it's hard to prevent disbelief from creeping into your voice."

She approached the table quietly. "He's pretty tame."

"It's female. She's not tame, she's weak." The bat blinked at the daylight. Its velvet ears twitched.

"It doesn't look like a mouse," she said.

"Actually, bats are more related to dogs." He dipped the eyedropper into a small pink can, then wiggled the tip of the eyedropper into its mouth and squeezed the bulb. A slender pink tongue licked the glass tube. "Good. She's swallowing."

Suzanne turned around the pink can to see the label. "Infant formula?"

"Bat milk is one thing those biological supply companies don't have. The mother"—he dipped the dropper into the formula—"won't allow this pup to nurse. A few other nursing females have abandoned their young. Usually that means starvation for the pup."

"What causes that?"

He nudged the bat's chin with the eyedropper and it opened its mouth. "Sometimes the parent is inexperienced. Sometimes the pup is defective. But that hasn't been true lately." He glanced at her, then back to the pup. He flushed. "It might be the disruption of the diurnal cycle."

"Ah. Danny and the timers."

"Might be," he said. "I'm going to see if I can keep this one from starving." He suctioned more milk from the can. "I'll call Danny after I'm done and see if I can set things right." The little bat had to be nudged again with the dropper before it began to eat. "My mom's going to be pissed."

"Your mom?"

"I'm driving to Santa Barbara tonight, staying with my parents till Monday. Mom doesn't know it yet, but she's having another houseguest. This pup needs to feed every couple of hours. Now what about this dream of the vulture?"

That tone again. She sighed and held the humus toward him. "Does this smell all right to you?"

"That stuff never smells right. It doesn't look right, either."

"Come on."

He sniffed. "Smells like it usually does. It looks like—"

"I don't want to hear." She went to the sink and dumped the contents into the disposal. "This is the only thing I've eaten that no one else has, so it must be what made me sick. I can't see how it could have gone bad. I only made it a couple days ago." She ran water from the tap.

"What about that dream?"

"Dream isn't the right word. It was an experience, like stepping into another reality."

"You didn't remember anything until I asked." He held another dropper of formula. The bat had the idea now and opened its mouth. "How can you forget something like that?"

"It was so intense. Maybe it takes a certain Zen dispassion."

"What about that . . . experience . . . in Paul's lab?"

He used the word like it was synonymous with hallucination. She put the rinsed container and lid into the dishwasher. "I still don't recall much about that, just that I thought something had hurt Kelly. The idea of anything happening to her . . ."

She turned to him. "You see, Allan, that supports what I'm saying. I was very upset. Like when you were angry with Danny. You didn't hear or see me until I shook you. Strong emotions blot out everything."

"You'll get no argument from me on that." He maneuvered the bat into the cage and latched the portal. He swiveled in the chair toward her. "You don't really think something's going to happen to Kelly, do you?"

"No. I mean, I don't *want* anything to happen to her. Of course not. I don't sense impending disaster . . ." The sound of her own protest gave her pause. Inside her head was a tangled skein of yarn, near subliminal impressions of Kelly, mixed with desert images and yes, damn it all, a sense of doom.

"Maybe it's stress. The financial problems and whatever—"

She snapped, "Give me a break. It's not stress." The urge to convince him was powerful. Paul's voice sounded in her head, urging her to examine why she felt so hostile. I'm hostile, she admitted, because I need to convince myself most of all.

Maybe I should just shut up. "I'm going to clean the pool."

She let herself out, stepped over a scuttling garden lizard, and gazed down at the turquoise water and its mesmerizing sun diamonds. What was it about water that was so soothing, so restful? She felt the solid shift of a heavy piece of mental lumber settling into place. That's it. A state of peacefulness, like sleep, or like the relaxation sequence that Paul used in his study, that must be the key to eliciting the presensing experience. Yes. So now I should . . . should do what? Take what action? And why? What am I anticipating? Something. Dominoes were already falling. Gad, she shuddered, I do sound like a mystic. Predestination. Kismet.

The phone trilled. After a moment she heard the screen door grate open. She turned. Allan held the cordless phone. "It's . . ." He looked at the receiver like he'd never seen one before. "It's a police officer. He says your sister's been taken to Saddleback Valley Hospital."

CHAPTER 12

Suzanne barely registered Allan's mad drive to the hospital. She sat on the passenger side, motionless yet coiled, ready to act. Dread had eaten a hole in her chest, a beast with fangs and scales and poisonous drool, and in a heartbeat it would begin to howl, a shriek that would spin the Earth out of orbit—

"Did you hear me?" He thrust the truck through a yellow light. "I said I'd telephone Paul while you find your sister."

She nodded, an immense effort. Her essence had split in two and she whiplashed between them. One was very still with dread and awful recognition. The other part prattled that Kelly was in ER, not in intensive care, so it probably wasn't serious, right? After all, she'd be in ICU if it were serious, right? Or she would have been taken to triage at Fountain Valley Hospital, right? Every synapse fired with questions, none left over to understand his words.

"I'll get Paul. Okay?"

She had to be ready, she had to control the beast, yet there was this fly buzzing around her ears, the kind that bite—

"Suzanne, look at me."

—and she couldn't figure out what she was supposed to do, there was something that needed doing, she needed a tiny space, a moment in time to think, a moment to take a deep breath, but this beast had taken all the space in her chest—

"Suzanne." He grabbed her hand. "Your fingers are freezing."

She tried to pull away, but he held firm.

"Suzanne, come on, talk to me."

She exploded with sudden fury. "*What?*"

Allan wanted to keep her talking, to help her stay afloat above the turmoil she must be feeling. "Tell me Paul's number." He steered around a white van with black calligraphy that stated: El Toro Fresh Florist, We Deliver Happiness. "His home and university number."

She clung to the name. "Paul." Numbers. She knew about numbers. Standard error of the mean, analysis of variance, standard deviation—

He spoke sharply, "Suzanne, snap out of it. Tell me Paul's phone numbers. At home and the university."

The digits popped to the surface of her mind, carrying her out of dark tide pools. Paul's phone numbers. She was back together, one piece, in this reality, and Allan was driving her to the hospital. The Toyota swerved around an open bed truck filled with Hispanic men and rakes.

"Okay," she said.

Allan squeezed her shoulder and put his hand back on the wheel.

She rubbed her cold and clammy hands together, inhaled deeply, exhaled slowly. Shock. She

had been going into shock. She couldn't afford
the indulgence. She had to take care of Kelly.
"Okay. Should I . . ." The glove compartment was
held closed by a white Velcro tab. A layer of dust
grayed the dash. "Do you have a pen and paper?"

"I'll remember. One of my many talents."

She recited both. He repeated them correctly
while he twisted the wheel left onto Paseo de
Valencia. The truck seesawed on worn shocks.
The ivory colonnades and dome of the Taj Mahal
office building glowed under the harsh white sun.
A silver Caddy decelerated to a near stop in front
of them. Allan slapped the horn. The car lumbered to the right lane and turned into the Lei-
sure World entrance. Allan gunned the motor and
the truck surged forward. Saddleback Valley Hospital was a half mile ahead.

"Listen, Suzanne. This is a coincidence."

His words echoed down a long dark corridor and
at the end was a small-screen version of what had
happened in Paul's lab. The scenario flashbacked,
the light, Kelly, the slow pitch backward, the terrible crushing pain. Her heart clenched. Kelly's legs.
Terrible injury to the pelvis. She pressed her cold
fingers against her eyelids, which felt like they
were burning up. Why had the memory blossomed
now? The answer rotated to the surface from liquid
darkness—the sudden drop in millimeters of mercury, systole, diastole. You can't get much calmer
than shock, than when your blood pressure takes
a nose dive.

"A bizarre coincidence, sure, but nothing more,"
he was saying. "You're not responsible for—"

"It was a blue car."

"Come again?"

The Toyota turned onto the hospital approach. There was the emergency-room entrance. Suzanne pulled on the door handle. Allan said, "Wait till I stop, damn it—"

She had been warned, and she had done *nothing*. She pushed open the car door.

"Damn it, Suzanne, wait till I stop. *Shit . . .*"

She leapt out, and stumbled, like hitting the moving walkway at an airport. She reached the pressure sensitive entry of the emergency room before the Toyota had rolled to a stop. Inside were smells of pine disinfectant—fat lot of good that did for destroying the vehicles of viruses—and two women in flowered muumuus, the only patients. Too early on a Saturday evening for the walking wounded. A brunette in white, eyeglasses tethered to a rhinestone-strung white cord, pushed papers around behind the counter. Suzanne gripped the ledge. "Where's Kelly Reynolds?"

The woman's long red-tipped fingers jerked, as though Suzanne had shouted. Perhaps she had. Her head swam, a contact buzz from the proximity of pharmaceuticals. She realized dimly, the way you know your hand is there even when it's numb, that she was running on the very edge of control.

The woman squinted up at Suzanne. "Who are you?"

"Her sister. Where is she?"

"If you'll take a seat in the waiting room—"

Suzanne slapped the counter. The woman recoiled. *"Where the hell is she?"* Now she was yelling.

The woman must have seen something on her face, authority or madness. She pointed down the left-most corridor and said, "But you'll have to wait here. The doctor—"

Suzanne went into the corridor. A large room was partitioned by blue-green drapes on ceiling runners into six examining areas. Only two partitions were in use and curtained from view. A babble of Hispanic voices emanated from the one on her right. A man yelled over the Spanish: "Tell your mother that she must be admitted. Tell your mother that she must be admitted. Tell your—" The other curtained partition was quiet. In the space between the curtain hem and linoleum she saw a pair of white tennis shoes protruding from blue jeans.

A cold stone lodged in her stomach. Quiet. Too quiet for the injuries Kelly must have sustained when the blue car hit her. Unless it had been too late. She shoved away the painful thought and, on automatic control, made her way to the partition with the tennis shoes. She pulled aside the curtain. A doctor stood with his back to her. Fiery red curly hair, caught into a small ponytail, topped a rumpled white lab coat. His right hand, mottled by moisture condensing under a skintight translucent glove, moved up and to one side. He held a curved surgical needle by tweezers. She couldn't see the patient sitting in front of him on a white-sheeted gurney. She stepped inside.

She instantly recognized the back of Kelly's head, the narrow shoulders, the pink shirtdress. Kelly was alive, not seriously hurt. Relief made

Suzanne's muscles weak. Allan was right. A coincidence. Maybe she, Suzanne, was going nuts, hallucinating, but she didn't care. Her little sister was alive.

The doctor worked on the parietal area, just below the crown. He deftly tied a fifth black suture on a skull gash. The two-inch cut was the center of a large shaved area, reddened by Betadine solution. The russet-gold hair at the nape of Kelly's neck was matted and darkened with dried blood. A roan-colored stain spattered the shoulders of the pink shirtdress.

The doctor, an intern by his name tag, paused before starting the next suture. He looked at Suzanne. Red capillaries threaded his hazel eyes. Freckles had merged on his ruddy Irish complexion, making his nose and cheeks look tanned. "You family?" he said.

Kelly's torso rotated stiffly, as though her shoulders ached. Her normally rosy cheeks were pale. "Suzanne!" she said, and began to cry.

CHAPTER 13

" . . . and I fell, I missed my footing, and this car, this blue BMW, was headed right for me, and the back of my head hit something metal on the walk signal post—"

Suzanne nodded, held on to Kelly's leg through the quilt as though to prevent her from slipping away. Telling was cathartic. She had hugged Kelly and listened in the emergency room, in Paul's car as he drove them home, and now in her sister's bedroom. Outside frogs croaked in the dark, moths beat against the window. In here words rolled, but slower now, the dog, the little girl, the licorice, the dog, the car, the little girl. The blood. How the BMW had spun, slammed into the little blond girl, who had been standing in the street, shouting for her pet. How the BMW's driver and passengers, teenaged girls, had escaped without a scratch.

Kelly stopped. Time slowed, and she turned inward for a moment. Her hands, smooth Mona Lisa hands, plucked at a wad of tissue. Lamplight threw spiky eyelash shadows down her cheeks. She didn't rest back against the pillows, but held her head a bit forward. A white gauze pad, twice the size of the shaved area on her skull, was taped over the twelve stitches.

Suzanne let the silence live. There were more moths fluttering against the screen, eager to possess the glow inside the bedroom. Little lives of puzzling motivations. Her own emotions scattered and eddied. Sorrow for the dead child, for the anguish of her parents. Compassion for the teen-aged driver. But strongest of all, a hurricane-force wind, was her fierce gratitude that Kelly was alive. Hurt, yes, and in more ways than the scalp wound, but *alive*. She was young. She would heal.

"Suzanne." Kelly stared miserably at the tissues in her hands. "If I hadn't given her the licorice, she wouldn't have lost hold of the leash."

The wretchedness in Kelly's face clenched Suzanne's heart. She scooted closer and covered her sister's hands with her own. She waited.

"If I hadn't given her the licorice"—Kelly raised her eyes to Suzanne—"she wouldn't have been standing in the middle of the street." Her voice caught. In her face was the death of the little girl.

Suzanne struggled to keep herself from interrupting. Kelly had been working up to this. It needed to come out.

"If it wasn't for me, she wouldn't . . ." Kelly took a shaky breath. "She wouldn't have been killed."

This was the real injury, the pain of feeling responsible, rightly or wrongly, for the death of another.

Suzanne released her hands. "Tell me about the kids in the BMW."

Kelly's brow puckered. "The three girls?"

She nodded.

"I got up, I didn't know I had cut my head. The blue car was stopped in the middle of the street. It was almost pointing in the opposite direction. From when I first saw it, I mean. From when I thought it was going to hit me. Now the passenger side was nearest to me. Two kids stayed in the car. But this dark-haired girl got out of the driver's side. I couldn't really see her until she went to the back of the BMW. She was, like, walking funny. Staggering. I thought she was hurt, but later the paramedics said she'd been drinking."

Her eyes fogged, fixed on something inward.

After a moment, Suzanne said, "Go on."

"She . . . she was sobbing and saying, 'Oh God, oh God,' over and over. She fell to her knees near the back tire, the left back tire, and covered her eyes with her hands. She was screaming and crying now, rocking back and forth. I went to her and . . . and under the tire . . ."

"Okay. What might this girl, the driver, have been thinking?"

"That . . . that she had killed . . . that she had killed a child."

"Why would she think that?"

Kelly cocked her head to one side, lifted and dropped her shoulders. "Because she *did*. Because she was driving. She didn't mean to, but she did."

"How do you feel about her?"

Her lips pressed together. "That she made a stupid, terrible mistake—"

"What do you *feel* about her?"

"Angry. And . . . pity."

"Pity?"

"I feel sorry for her. She'll never forget this. She'll go to her grave knowing that, because of her . . ." Kelly sighed. She put the tissues on the nightstand next to the lamp. "The paramedic said it had happened so fast, the little girl hadn't felt anything. Suzanne, do you think that's right? I can't bear thinking—"

"Honey, at that speed—"she stared directly into Kelly's eyes and lied—"she was killed instantly. She couldn't have felt anything."

Kelly nodded, her eyelids drooping.

It was a lie because Suzanne knew that, in Paul's lab, she'd been sensing the future experiences of the little girl, not Kelly. The experience had been from the point of view, the perspective, the height of a child, and that child had suffered excruciating crushing pain before death took her.

Suzanne tried telling herself that she couldn't really know, that the world of external reality existed outside her mind, that no one had actually suffered. That her visions of the accident were reducible to neurons firing in the brain, simply acts of will, unconnected to black asphalt and the color of blood.

She wished she could convince herself.

Her sister settled down on the bed. The right side of her face pressed into the pillow. The bulky white bandage jutted out from her scalp. A breeze, thick with forest scents, swirled through the window. Suzanne tucked the sheet around Kelly. In a few moments her sister slept from exhaustion, the telling over for now.

Suzanne leaned over and switched on the pink night-light plugged into the wall. When she flipped off the lamp, darkness revealed the moonlight. Its cold beam saturated the quilt and her sister, bleaching her complexion a corpselike white, showing what might have been. Fear pierced Suzanne's heart like a blade. She moved to close the drapes when Kelly's eyes opened. "Look at the moon," she said.

Suzanne looked. The velvet sky was spangled, a glittering backdrop for the rosy sliver of moon. The cup of the crescent was tipped.

"Mom would say that the moon is spilling its rain." Kelly closed her eyes. The syllables slurred. "That we're due for a drencher. A frog-strangler."

Utah farmers had their omens. The tilted crescent was a portent for downpour, a welcome sign when cornstalks were shoulder high, unwelcome when seedlings struggled to root in the soil. Suzanne had never, even as a child, trusted omens. Never. Yet tonight this rose-tinted sliver, over two hundred thousand miles away, gave her pause.

She listened to Kelly's breathing slow into a smooth regular rhythm. But she watched the sky, stared at the ruby halo around the crescent. That reddish color. A blood moon. And what it poured wasn't water.

She shivered.

CHAPTER 14

Every strand of Rusty Rydalch-Ames's thick dark blond hair was in place, as though arranged by scientific instruments. A narrow sculpted nose centered between high cheekbones. Smooth-shaven and tan, he was saved from being too beautiful by skin slightly pitted and scarred from adolescent acne. Suzanne supposed he was ruggedly handsome, though in a self-conscious way. Maybe Hollywood did that to you.

Probably his date thought, as most did, that his slightly clipped accent, his precise almost military bearing, and his hyphenated surname meant that Rusty was British. Rusty was, however, a native Californian right down to his feet, knobby from surfing. His family and Paul's had been neighbors in Newport Beach. Rusty had fabricated a new persona, one that needed to delight and entertain others. Suzanne thought, though, that she'd glimpsed the real Rusty in her pool with neighborhood kids. He adored children. He was respectful and charming with his girlfriends, usually not much more than kids themselves.

His date was another in a long line of young leggy blondes, her hair long and straight, razor cut at the ends. This woman had a lyrical amused tone, which made her sound far more intellectual than she looked. A spaghetti-strapped dress of some silvery, clingy material threatened to slip down over breasts more perky than nature designed. Rusty and the blonde—what was her name? Angelique or Angela?—sat on the family-room couch across from Paul.

Empty plates, wine goblets, and a half-filled wine bottle littered the coffee table. The scent of charcoal and hamburgers wafted from the outdoor grill. Outside the pool glimmered with the flat sharp light of the moon.

"The movie business," Rusty was saying to his date and to Paul, "is no place for humans."

Angelique or Angela noticed her on the stairs. "How's your sister doing?"

Suzanne stepped down to the family room. Kelly's pastel pink shirtdress was bunched in her hand. She held it up, to say offhandedly that the material was ruined, when her gaze froze on the stains, dried to the color of chocolate, a violent Rorschach. Kelly's blood. She tore her attention from the fabric, fixed her stare on the bright candle-shaped bulbs of the ceiling light in the kitchen, a technique for stopping tears. It wasn't going to work. She'd need bigger magic.

Paul and Rusty must have immediately understood her stricken expression. Both were by her side. Rusty pried the dress from her fingers. Paul enveloped her in a hug, maneuvered her to the couch, and sat down with her. She leaned against his chest, into his love, grateful for his silence, the way he stroked her arm. After a moment she pulled off her glasses and rubbed at her wet eyes. He produced a white handkerchief and dabbed at tears that had escaped down her cheeks.

"Better?" he said.

"Yes." Her mouth twitched when she smiled. "I hate when that happens."

Rusty hunched down and touched her knees with his hands. "Something to eat, right? You must be starving."

Suzanne slipped on her glasses, nodded. A dull empty ache had settled beneath her ribs.

"We barbecued chicken fillets for you. I'll fix a plate." Rusty started for the kitchen, paused, and said, "Angela." His date rose from the couch in a fluid boneless motion, a practiced grace, and trailed in his wake.

"Kelly's dress . . ." She let her voice fade.

"Even small head wounds bleed like crazy. Look much worse than they are."

She wasn't worried as much about Kelly's scalp wound as she was about Kelly's heart. "Maybe I should send her home. To Utah, to Mom and Dad."

Paul let her words hang in the air. They had a clear view of the kitchen. Angela slid a plate into the microwave. Rusty said to her, "Nuke it for a minute. The other button. Above that. Right. Then two zeros." He stooped down to peer into the microwave, but from the way he crooked his neck Suzanne suspected he was admiring his own reflection.

Paul laced his fingers through hers. "What did Kelly say about going home?"

A good, open-ended therapeutic question. "We

didn't discuss it. But I . . . she'd be safer there."

"Safe from what?"

"From . . ." What words could speak her fears? She was worried about another world that possessed her mind, sand hot enough to burn skin, dry herbal scents of wasteland brush, the everlasting descent of a winged beast that blotted out the sun, rough shrieks as if all the lost souls in hell were howling. The searing anguish of a world-to-be.

"What, then?" Paul said.

"I just think it would be better if Kelly weren't near me."

His eyes crinkled in puzzlement. "Weren't near you?"

Rusty and Angela were coming to the family room. Suzanne shook her head in a gesture that said, "Later."

Rusty set a plate of barbecued chicken, baked beans, and cinnamon applesauce on the coffee table. He poured wine into a goblet. Warm smoke and tomato scents made her mouth water. The pangs of hunger reassured her. At least her stomach was working normally. Angela added utensils and a blue paper napkin.

"Thanks," Suzanne said, and began to dig in. She welcomed the distraction of food and company.

Rusty sank into the overstuffed BarcaLounger. Angela perched on the arm. Though she appeared to be braless, her breasts stuck together with an impressive show of cleavage. How did they do that? Magnets?

Suzanne tasted the wine, a tart dryness. She

rotated the wine bottle. A Beaulieu Vista cabernet sauvignon. Rusty's contribution, no doubt. "This is wonderful." She lifted her goblet and nodded at him. "Thanks."

Angela smiled, flipped her hair back. "You're welcome. It's one of my favorites."

So much for assumptions.

"Here, listen to this," Rusty said to Suzanne. "I'm writing a new script, and I could hire you as consultant."

"I meant to warn you," Paul said.

She sliced the chicken fillet. "Me?"

"A vampire holds a pharmacologist captive, till she formulates a sunblock with a skin protection factor of one thousand."

Suzanne kept chewing. It sounded like a joke, but Rusty had had stranger scripts optioned.

"It's a romantic comedy," Angela offered. "This Universal Studio executive went indie-prod—"

"Universal canned his butt," Rusty said.

"Yes." Angela crossed her legs at the knees and ankles, a pose designed to attract attention. Paul's gaze flickered over her and away.

"So now," Angela said, "he's an independent producer, and he's interested."

"What would you need me for?" Suzanne asked.

"The science end of it," Rusty said. "You should come with me when I see the producer next week. Take a meeting in the grand Hollywood tradition. See what sort of demeaning garbage a screenwriter has to tolerate."

"I tolerate enough demeaning garbage at Bolton." Was the meeting with Weis just yesterday? After today, apologizing to him would be anticlimactic. "And I don't think you want the reality of research, anyway. Why don't you stop by my lab? Get a feel for . . . for . . . whatever."

"The atmosphere?" Rusty stroked his chin. "That's not a bad idea."

Suzanne finished the beans. "Don't wear anything dark."

"Why not?"

"Rabbit hair." Suzanne wiped her hands on the napkin. "You can't escape it."

"You don't say." Rusty's eyes fogged, turning over some script possibility.

Angela untangled her legs and leaned forward. "I think it was so eerie that you predicted the accident. So awful about that little girl."

Suzanne whipped her head to look at Paul. He and Rusty traded glances. A tiny sense of betrayal made her cheeks warm. "What?"

Paul said, "I typed the transcript from your presensory session."

More ocular Ping-Pong between the two men.

"What's the big secret?" Her tone was sharp. She chided herself for being irritated that Paul and Rusty—and Angela—had made her a topic of discussion. "Tell me."

"When Allan called from the hospital, I'd just finished typing the transcripts from your tape." Paul rotated to face her. "I don't know how much you remember, but after you fainted, you mentioned 'blue' several times and that Kelly was hurt."

The machinery of her id maneuvered to a position of mechanical advantage. "That can't be very significant."

"The correlation between 'blue,' saying Kelly was hurt, and the actual accident as Kelly described at around two P.M. isn't strongly significant. You're right. But—"

"It feels significant to me," Angela protested.

"Significant in the sense of statistics," Rusty said to her. "The scientific method relies on facts. You can't go by feeling, even gut-level feeling."

Paul said, "But what is more startling are the images you had *before* fainting."

His body language reminded her of herself, trying to sell the blood-pressure research to Elliot. What was Paul trying to sell to her?

"The large white ribbon with the silver mesh," he persisted. "Remember?"

"Yes." She nodded. Her neck felt stiff, rusty.

"Kelly and the little girl were waiting near the crosswalk, under the pedestrian skywalk over Lake Forest Boulevard. That walkway looks like a long arched ribbon." His hands described the shape in the air. His tone became faster, impassioned. "Steel chain-link fencing—it looks like silver mesh—forms the walls for the bridge. And you described fur. The dog."

"God, this would make a great movie," Angela said.

Suzanne tapped her fingers on the couch. Internal radar beamed warning signals. Paul was working up to something. "Those images were so abstract."

"That's the way accurate presensory data present." Paul rubbed his hands on his thighs. "Here's a theory: For a while you presensed Kelly's experiences. Then—I'm guessing here, since you didn't say much when you felt the accident occur—you oriented on the little girl, whose sensations of terror and pain essentially drowned out Kelly. The little girl's experiences were so intense, so nonverbal—"

"Okay. All right." She winced at the memory. "What are you saying?"

"You might have a particular skill at this type of prediction. Some subjects in the SRI experiment were better at it than others. Some—like you— had *never* been psychic before, but tested strongly during the research. The technique suited their particular mind-sets. The relaxation commands prepared them to free associate about what the outward-bound person would see at a specific point in the future. Those who were exceptional at this type of predicting were worked with more closely and . . ." He hesitated. "These subjects got better with practice, Suzanne. What you did today already surpasses the results of the SRI studies. And presensing is a learnable, improvable skill. With additional training, I bet we'd exceed the results of all the old research."

A learnable, improvable skill. Like, for instance, if she became his own personal guinea pig, his ticket to publication and tenure. His eyes on her were intense, focused. Apparently she interested him more as an experimental subject than as a girlfriend. "It was like having a nightmare fully awake. I don't want to get better at sensing death."

Paul leaned toward her. "You remember now? Do you remember more than . . . "

"I don't want to know the future," she snapped.

"But, Suzanne, today was a . . . a freak accident. The chances that you'd presense a death again are very remote—"

"For God's sake, do you ever think about anyone but yourself?" She picked up the plates, making more noise than necessary, and carried them to the kitchen. Paul followed with the glasses. She ignored him, rinsed the plates, and stacked them in the dishwasher.

He massaged the back of her neck. The heat of his body warmed her. Whiskers nettled her ear. "I'm sorry, babe. I wasn't thinking. It's been a rough day."

His fingers lessened the tension in her muscles. "I know how important this research is to you, Paul. But this presensing business is torture. A nightmare."

"I hear you."

He heard her, all right, but she sensed his determination. They needed to talk. She was wondering how gracefully she could ask Rusty and Angela to leave, when Paul said, "Want me to stay tonight?"

The question hit her like a punch to the stomach. She twisted around in disbelief. "What?"

"I'll stay, if you want."

This was the same tune they'd been dancing to for the past two years, with her leading. She was sick of it. Always her asking him to stay, never an initiation by Paul, never an indication that the depth of his feeling for her had evolved to where he'd simply leave a few items of clothing in her closet, a few toiletries in her bathroom.

"You didn't bring your overnight stuff?" Him and

his blessed toiletry kit. She hated it, a small oblong leather bag that he brought when he stayed the night, as though he were at a hotel.

"I came directly from the U—"

She didn't hear the rest of his response, so great was her hurt. After last night, after nearly proposing to him, after Kelly's accident today—

"No." Her teeth clenched. "I don't want you here tonight."

He cocked his head. Somewhere in there, she knew he was trying to categorize her anger. Projection? Displacement?

He touched her shoulders. "Are you sure—"

"I want you to leave. Now."

"Suzanne—"

"*Now.*"

She felt like she'd kicked a puppy. Great. All she needed on top of everything else was a dose of guilt.

"Well . . . uh." He let his hands drop. "I'll call you in the morning."

She had yelled within hearing of Rusty and his pneumatic date, but she didn't care. After Paul left, she slumped onto the couch. "He's never going to get any closer to me, is he?"

She supposed her words contradicted her actions, but Rusty sat next to her and slid his arm around her shoulders. With his free hand he tapped his shoulder. She rested her cheek against that spot. The frame of her glasses pressed against her temple. Rusty was composed of angles and edges, bones thinly padded, not substantial and solid like Paul.

"I think I'll have a cigarette outside." Angela

rose and exited through the sliding-glass door.

"A complicated man, our Paul," Rusty said.

Suzanne nodded. "After two years, I can't read him. He loves being here with me, I know it, yet he assigns himself evenings away. Like some sort of duty."

"Some take time to develop relationships. When we met as boys, I recall that he seemed distant. Cool."

"You're his best friend. Did that take years?"

"I can't say. I think I had made most of the moves. He's cautious. And more so after that business with Carolyn."

The unfamiliar name was jarring. "Who?"

Rusty's shoulder stiffened. He coughed. "He hasn't talked about Carolyn?"

She had the sudden sense that the floor was falling away, that she was becoming smaller and smaller. "He's never mentioned her."

Rusty pursed his lips, his gaze turned inward, contemplating what to say.

"Is that . . . is that who he spends his time with when he doesn't come here?"

His smile was wry. "Possibly." He stroked the skin above his mouth with his forefinger and frowned. "Look here, that was ill-advised. I didn't realize that Paul hadn't . . ." He was uncharacteristically flustered. His skin pinked unevenly over the old acne scars. "I'm . . . I feel I've overstepped my bounds."

"I understand." She sighed. It was the right thing to do. Friends. Rusty and Paul. Friends come with obligations and intimacies, secrets. She imagined Rusty's lips with a closed zipper, the brass one on Paul's toiletry kit. "No wonder he's kept his distance. I hadn't considered he was involved with someone else." Her vision blurred. She removed her eyeglasses and rubbed her eyes.

He touched her knee. "I haven't been clear. You haven't flesh-and-blood competition. Not any that I know of, at least."

She blinked. "I don't understand."

"It doesn't seem like it, but it's been a long time. Carolyn's been dead for years."

BOOK TWO

VORTEX

CHAPTER 1

Carolyn.

Dead.

A dead lover? One of life's great reversals. One of Paul's great reversals, anyway.

Suzanne punched the pillow. She lay on her stomach, then rolled onto her side. The water bed gurgled in protest. Her left arm felt trapped. From the bathroom came the complaining chirp of a cricket behind the dry wall. The rasp of its saw-toothed legs was intermittent, plaintive, a lost soul seeking its mate. Aren't we all, she thought. After Rusty and Angela had driven away, she had telephoned Paul. The mechanical whir of his answering machine had crackled on. She left a message asking him to call. She wanted to drive to his apartment, but she didn't want to leave Kelly. Not tonight. She'd been tossing and turning since then.

The unknown is the worst torture. Did Paul's isolation have this long-dead Carolyn at the core? Was he still grieving her death? They needed to talk. She needed to understand, he needed to explain. If he was suffering, she would help him

work this through. If Paul still loved Carolyn . . .
she stopped herself. These random speculations
collapsed in on themselves, as pointless as the
legendary dodo bird, chasing its own tail and flying in ever-decreasing circles till it disappears up
its own rear end.

Rays from the street lamp angled through the
miniblinds and painted a blurry glow on the satin
sheets. She squinted into the darkness. Anything
could lurk in the myopic soup of her uncorrected vision. Fanged serpents. Gargoyles, demons.
Gelatinous ghosts. Stop this nonsense, she told
herself. You're a scientist. A breeze stirred the
eucalyptus outside her window and the miniblinds
shuttered. Light slithered to and fro on the bed.
She retrieved her eyeglasses from the headboard
shelf. Through the lenses the lamplight on her
sheets sharpened into distinct bars. If only it
were so easy to bring the rest of her life into
focus.

Like the images from that night. The desert,
the helplessness, the sharp beak aiming for her
eyes.

If that premonition came true as the one for the
little girl had . . .

Ludicrous. And maddening. What's the message? she wondered. Avoid desert wastelands?
Don't take a snooze under carrion eaters? And
why were these weird things happening now?
She'd been as clairvoyant as yogurt before this
week.

She wished Allan were here instead of visiting
his parents. Maybe he was right. Maybe stress had
set her neurons marching to the wrong drummer,

maybe her synapses had been sieged by a chemical storm. The brain was a three-pound universe. A delicate electrochemical balance kept it healthy. Too much of the neurotransmitter dopamine and the bizarre voices of schizophrenia start whispering in your head.

No. There was objective evidence, the blue car, the death of the little girl, that belied the possibility of hallucination. She swept her arm out over the smooth satin. Paul would have been here if she hadn't . . .

She sat up, irritated with herself and Paul. He had visions of full professorship dancing in his head. And images of an old, long-gone love? She listened to the cricket for a while. Then she checked on Kelly, left another message on Paul's answering machine—was he gone or in his apartment listening?—came back to her bedroom, thumped the bathroom wall until the cricket quieted.

She removed her eyeglasses and stretched out on the sheets. Paul had said that presensing was a learnable, improvable skill. If she did indeed possess this ability, could she summon it by technique? She inhaled slowly, held the breath, exhaled to a count of ten. Again. And again. Then she willed her muscles to unclench, using the relaxation commands of the presensory experiment.

The resonating sensation under her sternum, the jitter of small cold stones, alerted her. Just like this afternoon. Adrenaline buoyed her into tense apprehension and she had to start over, breathing with slow control, melting the resistance in her calves, thighs, neck. Her conscious mind kept yanking her to the surface, aware that tranquillity was a mockery. If this worked, she'd be descending into a maelstrom.

It didn't work.

She gave up. The idea of purposefully becoming calm as the ticket to entering a possible state of terror was antithetical. Peaceful horror was an oxymoron and her nervous system rebelled. She yawned, grateful for the weariness. The water bed cradled her. Her thoughts tumbled, whirled, grew wings that carried her into—

—*the white-hot ball of the sun. The heat. From the sun, from the hard-packed earth. Trapped between the two burning orbs. Torrid still air sears lungs.*

Parched low bushes cluster at the base of the slope. Spindly branches beckon. Demand. Perspective is slightly off. Scorched atmosphere vibrates with something other than heat. Dark movement. Hellish mirages percolate up from sand, desiccated tearless ghosts. Sweat trickles between shoulder blades. Skin hot as fever. Panic is a searing dryness in the throat.

Been here before. Yet alien . . . and strange.

Legs pump, stutter on uneven ground. Stumbling down, down to the brush. Footfalls stir up a fine choking dust. A white cloth sails to the dirt. Both hands grip a hard rough cylinder, swing it like a baseball bat. Dusty flappings and harsh cries, rising up, an explosion of black wings and cruel eyes, uncovering a dread grotesque, putrid odors swirl, thickened by the fanning, the anguish of a heart shattering into a million pieces—

Suzanne came to with a start and scrambled off the water bed. She pressed her hands against her chest to stop its thundering. The nubby berber pressed up against her feet. Not sand, not sand. Carpet. My bedroom. She made her way to the bathroom, hung over the sink, and splashed cold water from the faucet onto her face. She leaned there a while, water dripping from her chin, her reflection fuzzy in the mirror. When the roar of blood through arteries quieted, she was able to think. The disgust and horror lingered, but those weren't her emotions. She experienced them just the same, like being helplessly caught in a riptide.

That's it, she thought, that's what was happening. I'm along for the ride. I'm a tiny homunculus riding the central nervous system of someone else, privy to the complete network of sensory data, the reptilian receptors of sensation and thick dark emotion. A coconsciousness. But she didn't share thought. Only her own captive mind, an unwilling dybbuk, stunned and shocked, absorbed the intense stimuli. She did not share his thoughts.

His thoughts.

A man. It was a man. The proprioceptive cues, the sensations that delineate one's body, give it form and place in space, those cues weren't her own. Weren't female. She had inhabited someone's body like an ill-fitting suit. That's why the perspective seemed off. She was wrapped in the sensory inputs of a person taller and bigger, with a visceral sense of maleness.

She reran the images. The man swatted away birds, horror and dread possessing him in full measure *before* he saw what was beneath. He already knew what—who—was beneath the hungry swarm of scavengers.

The body of a woman.

CHAPTER 2

Suzanne tightened the sash of her white terry bathrobe. The walking dead must feel like this, she thought. Head full of cotton, limbs slow to respond. Whirling thoughts had kept her up until near dawn, when she sank gratefully into a druglike slumber. This morning all the jagged contours had softened.

She left her bedroom and saw Kelly in the hall bathroom, studying her reflection in the mirror. Her fingers plucked at the white scarf draped around her hair and knotted at the base of her neck. She dug around in her leather patchwork purse, retrieved a lipstick, and applied a light mauve coating to her lips. She moved her head with ease. Her heart-shaped face was as smooth and undisturbed as a clean page in a laboratory notebook. The physical and emotional pain of yesterday had not marked her. Suzanne's love throbbed in her chest like a physical ache. Thank God for the resiliency of youth.

Kelly spied Suzanne in the mirror and pirouetted. "I probably look like a dweeb, don't I?"

Suzanne smiled. California talk. She was learning fast. "No, you don't." Kelly wore a thigh-length loose white shirt over a gray skirt and white high-top sneakers, clothes from their shopping spree at the Laguna Hills Mall. She looked like what she was, a young coed with all of life's bright lights ahead of her.

Suzanne made a palm-up circular gesture. "Let's take a look at the bandage."

Kelly turned to the mirror, her image a good five inches shorter. Suzanne lifted the point of the scarf. The white compress was squashed but still in place. No sign of bleeding. "How does it feel?"

"The tape pulls on my scalp. Itches. The cut doesn't hurt at all. I wish I could shampoo my hair."

"We can remove the bandage on Tuesday. I'll help you wash around the stitches." The intern had shaved a large area, a conservative if aggressive approach. "Stitches out when?"

"Next Monday. I'm going to look like I'm wearing a reverse mohawk."

"Your hair will grow back in no time." She settled the scarf over Kelly's head and pulled the length of her baby-fine hair over the knot. The strands were silk in her fingers.

And then Suzanne was absorbed by the echo of a long-ago spring, Mom coming home from the hospital, a pink bundle in her arms. The four boys gyrated and bounced around her, but she laid the bundle in Suzanne's lap. The soft blanket framed a tiny peaceful face. Kelly. Her little sister's scalp was thick with blond wisps sticking out in all directions like the down of a newborn chick. She smelled of milk and baby powder.

"What are you smiling about?" Kelly asked.

"You." Suzanne wrapped her arms around Kelly. "I'm so happy you're all right."

She tilted her head to look up at Suzanne. "I prayed for that little girl and her parents. And the teenager who was driving the car. I feel . . ." She blinked. "I feel like I've been given a second chance. You know, to become something. I won't disappoint you. I'm going to work hard."

"Hey, honey, you can't disappoint me."

"Even the algebra," Kelly insisted.

Math had always terrorized Kelly.

"Well, then, you'll do better than I did."

"I thought you aced everything."

"Not those 100-level introductory classes."

Kelly gave her a speculative look. "Suzanne . . ." She paused.

Suzanne released her. "What?"

"I was wondering. Just what . . ." She turned to her. "When you were in Paul's lab, is this what you thought would happen?"

Suzanne chose her words carefully. "I thought you were hurt. I didn't know it was going to be a scalp laceration." That much was true.

"Oh." Kelly's brow puckered.

"What is it?"

"Paul said that I should ask you. I guess I was expecting a different answer, from the way he sounded."

"Paul?" Suzanne's heart did a little jump. She glanced out the bathroom to the stairs. "Is Paul here?"

"No. He called earlier to see if I still felt like doing the trial run."

Suzanne hadn't heard the phone from the depths of her zombie state. "He called? This morning?" She couldn't keep the exasperation out of her voice.

"A couple hours ago. What is it? What's wrong?"

"He knew I wanted to speak with him."

"Oh. He said he'd see you at the faculty tea. He didn't want to disturb you."

Sure, Suzanne thought. More like he didn't want to be disturbed by me. She wished she hadn't thrown him out last night. Though then she wouldn't have learned about Carolyn. But if Paul was more forthright and open, he would have told her about Carolyn himself . . . Her thoughts began to tangle again.

"And Allan called from Santa Barbara to see how I was. Wasn't that sweet of him?" Kelly rotated her wrist to see her Timex. "It's eleven. I have to go. I'm supposed to meet Paul at the lab. I'm going to time how long it takes to walk there."

Kelly swung the strap of her purse over her shoulder and stood on tiptoe to kiss Suzanne's cheek. She stopped on the stairs. "I talked to Paul about how I felt. About the little girl and everything." She paused. "He's a good listener. I'm glad he's your boyfriend. He's really a nice man."

The sad irony was that Kelly was right. Paul was a nice man, a man Suzanne loved and, even after two years, didn't understand.

CHAPTER 3

Suzanne stood before the yawning front door of Kurt Poole's house. The low oceanic murmur of voices floated from inside. During the summer the humanities tea was more of an open house. Professors from other divisions were invited. Conversations ranged from the sighting of a new star to the discovery of another subatomic particle. A man's voice drifted out of the bay window: "How many therapists does it take to change a light bulb? Only one, but the light bulb has to *want* to change." A spatter of laughter. A clinical psychologist, she guessed.

She tugged on the bottom of her white linen jacket. She wasn't sure she should have come. After Kelly had left, she had called Paul's apartment, no answer except the machine, then Paul's lab, only to listen to continuous ringing. Later she tried the lab again and Kelly answered, saying Paul was busy with the subject. He had never phoned Suzanne at home. His avoidance hadn't left her in the best of moods. She felt frustrated and reckless. If she couldn't get answers from Paul . . . she considered Kurt Poole. He had been Paul's doctoral dissertation adviser at the Uni-

versity of Southern California years ago. She had
half a mind to ask Kurt about Carolyn. Her conscience piped up right away, warning her against
doing anything that might further alienate Paul.
While she stood on the porch debating, Kurt Poole
glanced out the door and did an exaggerated double take.

Kurt opened his arms and smiled. She stepped
into the two-story entryway and into his hug.
The dean of the humanities division and acting
chair for the psych department was an angular
greyhound of a man, black straight hair neatly trimmed, smooth-shaven, large liquid tell-me-
everything eyes. Everything about him exuded
the therapeutic touch.

The two-story entryway was a foyer like many
others in this moderately priced housing development in Silverado Canyon, yet Kurt and his
wife—with a tribe of children and on a tight budget—managed to create the exotic atmosphere of a
Mediterranean villa. Gild-framed mirrors graced
the walls, dozens of tropical ferns flourished, and
red Spanish pavers covered the floor. At least
downstairs had that decor. The upstairs bonus
room was the domain of Kurt's youngest children,
the six-year-old triplets and ten-year-old Sunny.

He kissed her cheek, then peered out the door
behind her. "Paul's not with you?"

"No." She tried to keep the sharp edges from
her tone. "He'll be coming from the U. He's doing
a dry run of the presensory experiment. You probably know my sister's working for him."

Kurt's X-ray vision settled on her a moment, his
emotional Geiger counter tuned in. He was unread-

able himself, except for supreme acceptance. He'd never blanch at anything. Perhaps fathering seven children had immunized him against the petty vacillations of everyday life. The years of listening to the limitless problems of patients had taught him to savor life, rather than to become cynical.

"Where's Beverly and the kids?" She looked up at the ceiling, expecting to hear the playful thumping of the triplets.

"She hauled them to the San Diego zoo. The boys have reached the age of critical mass. They're lethal to innocent adults. How's your sister doing?"

Had Paul talked with Kurt about the accident yesterday? Or did Kurt mean how was Kelly doing since moving from Utah? You never knew how much this man knew. Suzanne quelled the urge to tell him everything, the death of the child, the desert images of last night, her frustration with Paul, Paul's nimble avoidance of her today.

"Kelly likes California . . ." The reflection in the foyer mirror snagged her attention. The image was herself from the back, the hip-length white linen jacket and coordinating navy skirt with white piping.

"Döppelganger," she said. However, the titan-red hair coiled in a braid wasn't hers, neither was the deep throaty laugh when the woman tossed back her head.

Kurt followed the direction of her gaze. He took a step, rotated his face 180 degrees toward the reality in the living room. He looked at Suzanne's identical clothes, then said, "It seems introductions are in order." He took her arm and guided her to the small group near the white baby grand.

"Olivia."

The woman spun away from the gathering, energy and grace in the movement. She was Suzanne's height and build, but there the physical similarity ended. She was square-jawed, ruddy complexed, with deep radial lines at the outside corners of the eyes, as though her forty-some years had been filled with more than the usual laughter and tears. The coil of her long reddish hair was haphazard, hurriedly braided and pinned. She pointed at Suzanne's outfit. Her hazel eyes snapped with intelligence.

"Ha! I'll be damned. Professional Elegance catalogue. Am I right?" Her voice was gravelly as though she'd been shouting for a long time.

"I buy almost everything mail order." Suzanne smiled. "I loathe clothes shopping."

"What intelligent woman doesn't?" She thrust out her hand. "I'm Olivia Flandro."

"Suzanne Reynolds."

They shook hands. The older woman's grip was firm and bone-crushing, her fingernails short, her thumb splayed at the tip like a spoon. Her biceps defined themselves under the sleeves of the jacket. She was surprisingly flat-chested, like an Amazon who'd cut off her breasts to better aim the arrow from her bow. A clean antiseptic scent, like bleach, eddied about her.

Kurt said, "Olivia Flandro is currently our vice president of administration and our next university president."

Olivia snorted. "Don't I wish."

Kurt excused himself to greet new arrivals.

"Suzanne Reynolds. Your name's familiar." Olivia's alert eyes clouded for a moment, then cleared. "You're the research pharmacologist at Bolton. I remember Paul Gershuny telling me. You must know Franklin Weis."

Suzanne hesitated. "I know him."

"Frank was supposed to be here. I'd hoped to see him."

Great. Suzanne couldn't prevent her head from swiveling around the room. She was all geared up for a Weisian encounter *tomorrow*.

Olivia laughed. "Don't worry. Our professor emeritus isn't here. His kid had a soccer game this afternoon. So"—her expression was rueful, penetrating—"Frank has been his usual charming self."

Suzanne flushed. "We don't always agree."

Olivia rolled her eyes. "Does that ever sound like Frank."

It didn't seem smart to discuss Weis in the negative. She changed the subject. "What's this about university president?"

"You know how many women have been president of UCLF? Zip. If I want this position, I'll have to do a lot of palm-pressing. It's very much like running a political campaign. The search committee and the Board of Regents have narrowed candidates down to myself and three men. Hell, I've put my time in. I've been in university admin one place or another since God was corporeal. Women don't know how to play contacts." She scanned the room as if to demonstrate. A lot of men, very few women. "That revolting buzzword 'networking.' Men, it's in their genes."

Suzanne knew what she meant. Paul was a case in point. When Kurt landed the psych chair at UCLF a few years ago, Paul contacted him and Kurt brought him on as an associate professor. Last semester Kurt moved up to head the humanities division and the psych department sought a new chairperson.

"For instance, Frank Weis. Your good buddy. He mentored me into UCLF, recommended me for the administration VP slot. I had to ask him, we'd been friends forever, he bloody well knew my ambitions, but still I had to ask. Actually, plead and grovel was more like it. You know the man."

Jeesh. Weis helped Olivia? Maybe he wasn't a male chauvinist pig. Maybe he was just a butthead. A butthead, she reminded herself, who hated her guts. But then, as Elliot had pointed out, Suzanne had never exactly cultivated Weis's favor.

Olivia nodded to a young man with an ascetic build and blue eyeballs that threatened to pop out of his head any minute tethered on springs. "Hey, Binky. How's anthropology?" They chatted briefly, then Binky mentioned the pedestrian death, the little girl, yesterday on Lake Forest Boulevard. Olivia hadn't heard. Discussions about the car accident bounced around the room like a tennis ball. No one knew, apparently, that Kelly had been there. Or, thankfully, about Suzanne predicting the event. After he wandered away, Olivia said in an aside, "Binky Jurkowski, three Ph.D.s—count 'em—before he was twenty-two, heads anthro, youngest member of the Board of Regents. He's already committed to voting for me."

Suzanne began to feel rather flabby and spine-less before Olivia. The woman seemed to be a more evolved species. Formidable. No soft pad-ding of fat on her body. She had presence, charis-ma, that rare indefinable essence. Suzanne had the strong sense that she was, indeed, in the company of the next university president.

"The man talking with Kurt." Olivia indicated the direction with a lift of her chin. "Recognize him?"

The man wore a bright wide smile that could sell toothpaste. He was tall, over six feet, and his lean frame complemented the brown suit. Dark-framed eyeglasses gave him a studious look. The temples of his blue-black hair were brushed with gray. He would photograph well.

"He's a House of Representatives candidate. Blake Evans."

Was this one of Olivia's networking contacts? Suzanne wouldn't have recognized him even if his toothsome face graced a billboard on her lawn. She had a difficult time keeping politicians straight.

"Blake Evans. Sounds like a politician, doesn't it? People are affected by names like you wouldn't believe. Now, my parents named me Olive. Can you imagine calling a child that? They claimed that when I was born my eyes were that color, a sickly green like pool water contaminated with algae. Speaking of pool water, do you swim?"

Olivia's quick mind was the sort that leap-frogged all over the place. Before Suzanne could reply, a rich baritone said, "Don't let my wife hustle you." The voice belonged to Blake Evans.

He took Olivia's hand, raised it to his lips for a quick kiss. "She never mentions she had the same trainer as Mark Spitz until it's too late."

"I was an Olympic hopeful eons ago." Olivia wrapped her arm around his waist and regarded him with undeniable fondness. "Freestyle."

"She still whips my butt at the swimming pool."

That explained the slight scent of chlorine. Olivia introduced her husband to Suzanne.

Blake covered Suzanne's hand with both his own, making a sandwich, and he pumped just the right amount of time. Suzanne disliked the ersatz intimacy the handshake implied. As though reading her thoughts, he said, "We're taught this in Politics 101." He grinned. "Glad-handing and grinning."

The self-deprecation worked. His smile was infectious. Suzanne mirrored his and said, "You're doing very well."

"Good thing, since a handshake is often all the contact I have with any one person. It's supposed to make you want to vote for me, regardless of my politics. My campaign slogan is 'a confused man for confused times.'"

"That has a certain appeal."

"Ah." Olivia nudged her. "Look at Kurt."

Suzanne turned. Paul, the charcoal-gray plaid suit coat with the suede elbow patches swung over his shoulder, was in the foyer with Kurt. His shirtsleeves were rolled up, revealing powerful forearms pelted with fine dark hair. Her frustration melted into relief. In the back of her mind had been the fear that he wouldn't show. Paul spoke into Kurt's ear, who listened and nodded somberly.

"Kurt Poole, Father Confessor," Olivia said. She shook her head and smiled. "Everyman's therapist. When he emerged from his mother's womb, I bet the obstetrician told him his problems."

Kurt said something to Paul and then both men looked in Suzanne's direction. When their eyes met hers, Suzanne felt a zapped sensation like static electricity.

"Hey, you two," Olivia called out in her good-natured raspy voice. "Get your butts over here."

Something icy chilled Suzanne, like the phantom of an ancient premonition. Something beyond thought. Whatever the source of this wordless dread, it was close.

CHAPTER 4

"It's all right about last night." Paul stroked her arms. "I know you were upset about Kelly."

He was forgiving her. She could see he needed to feel magnanimous. That was all right with Suzanne, God knows she hadn't been on her best behavior last night, though she kept her arms crossed over her chest. He kissed her, but the usual comfort wasn't there.

They were in Kurt Poole's study. After an agonizing amount of chitchat with Olivia, Blake, Kurt, and others, she'd managed to maneuver Paul in here. The sandstone carpet was landmined with dozens of red, blue, and yellow blocks. Some were arranged in a shape that brought a castle to mind. She'd been in this room a month ago, when she and Paul had visited the Pooles for a cookout. She had sunk into the huge burgundy chair, its leather worn to a shiny patina on seat and arms, and helped Beverly sort through an extensive collection of coupons. Beverly had little pieces of paper for cents-off on deodorant, ibuprofen, bathroom cleaners, ground turkey, corn cereal in the shape of little clown faces, panty liners with embossed daisies. The scarred mahogany desk still supported an awesome pile of unsorted coupons. Beverly was the financial wizard of the family and this was part of her craft.

The oak veneer floor-to-ceiling bookcases were jammed with children's books on the bottom, grade school textbooks and a children's encyclopedia set in the middle, and adult mysteries peppered with classics and psychology tomes at the upper echelons. But the thing that first struck your eye upon entering the study was the photographs. Kurt's Ph.D. diploma hung on the wall, a tiny island in a sea of family photos, class photos of the children, sepia prints of infants in lace gowns, a much younger Kurt in cap and gown, their oldest daughter Arline in beaded veil and lace wedding dress, Beverly juggling three identical fat baby boys, snapshots of Kurt and Beverly squinting into the sun of various vacations. Lives lovingly and inexorably intertwined.

"I needed to talk with you," Suzanne said to Paul. "Why didn't you return my calls?"

He leaned back against the bookcase, his arms behind him. A blindfold and he'd be ready for the firing squad. "I didn't realize there were any messages on my answering machine."

"Sure. There's only one thing you're anal retentive about, and that's checking that blasted machine." She waited.

"Suzanne, I just didn't. I phoned this morning, you were asleep. I knew I'd be seeing you here."

Over the tide of conversation from the living room rasped Olivia's laughter. The thought of the other woman's self-possession spurred Suzanne on. "So you're saying you never heard the phone ringing, you never listened to my messages on the machine?"

He lifted his hands, palms up. "That's what I'm saying." He let them drop. "Let's rewind for a second. You're angry about me not returning your call—"

"I called three, four times—"

"All right, your calls, but I don't think that's really it. I mean, I don't think that's what you're really upset about."

He touched his beard, a contemplative gesture. Suzanne sensed that he was slipping into his Freud routine. She felt her own shields clanging down into place.

"Your not calling me is symptomatic. You give me mixed messages, Paul. You say you love me, then you avoid me for a couple days. Why don't we discuss that? About how conflicted you are? About what that does to me?"

His brow corrugated. His brown eyes quirked at the inner corners as if some interior vision had stung. She hoped it had.

"Well?" she said.

"Guilty," he conceded. "I'm sorry." He shook his head. "You are the most important person in my life. I don't mean to hurt you. Or confuse you."

He leaned forward and grasped her hand to pull her toward him, as though the apology had made everything all right. She resisted.

"Just a minute. I'm not interested in making you feel guilty. And I'm not much interested in your good intentions. I want to know what's going on."

"I don't know what to say." He lifted and dropped his shoulders.

"Give it a shot."

Now he crossed his arms over his chest. "It's nothing more complicated than what many men wrestle with. A fear of intimacy."

"Damn it, Paul. Don't talk to me in psycho-babble. Be specific. Clue me in."

"I don't know what more I can say."

A spark of anger made her start bluntly: "So who was Carolyn?"

"How did you . . ." He caught his lower lip with his teeth. "Carolyn has nothing to do with us."

Suzanne closed her eyes for a moment. After a beat, she said, "Don't do this, Paul. Who was she?"

A few seconds passed. She opened her eyes. Paul had his hands in his pockets, his back to her. He stood by the window seat and stared out the window into the backyard. Outside Kurt's two golden retrievers played with a large rawhide bone. "It was a long time ago. We were going together when I was in graduate school."

"Going together?"

"Engaged."

"How did she die?"

He rotated his head to look at her. "Carolyn had allergies. You name it, she was allergic. Dust, penicillin, licorice, ragweed, shellfish. She died from a severe reaction to wasp stings."

He stepped away from the window toward her. "That's it. That's all. An old loss, long before I met you."

Behind his words scurried an odd tension, strumming her emotional tripwires. "I don't understand why you've never mentioned Carolyn."

The muscles in his forehead contracted into a frown. He made a sound of exasperation. "Suzanne, it was finished years ago."

"It's part of you. And there's something you're not telling me."

"There are things about me—and about you— which have nothing to do with our relationship."

"Carolyn has nothing to do with how you react to me?"

"Nothing."

He was lying. He knew she knew it. He had the grace to blush. What little there was left of trust crumbled.

Suzanne walked to the study door. "You used to say that our relationship was special, like magic. Even magic has its monsters. Especially magic. I don't know who I am for you. When you figure out if I'm something other than a source of ambivalence, you know how to find me."

"C'mon. Don't leave like this."

She left.

CHAPTER 5

Suzanne made her way through the throng at the tea, reached the foyer, and realized that someone had been calling her name. She slowed but did not stop. Her body was on automatic pilot, set to escape. Olivia came abreast of her on the porch steps.

"Are you leaving already?" Olivia studied her from those startling hazel irises. She didn't comment on how unraveled Suzanne must look, but said softly, "I meant it about the swimming."

"Swimming?" It was hard to change gears after the torment with Paul. For him to recognize that he held her at arm's length, then to immediately do it again. For him to therapize out the yin-yang about fear of intimacy.

Damn his soul. How could he be so arbitrary? What was it about Carolyn that he was refusing to tell? That he still loved his allergic dead fiancée? That he had consecrated himself to her forever?

Was he using Suzanne as a sort of temporary fix until she, Suzanne, got sick and tired of him jerking her chain?

Was she sick and tired of him jerking her chain? The question cut too close to the psychic bone and she pulled outside herself.

She had stopped by her white Buick Skylark. Through the window she saw tan foam poking through the navy cloth of the driver's side where the seat belt rubbed. Superimposed above that, like ghosts, were the transparent reflections of two women in identical white jackets, one with dark hair, the other with light.

The air was heavy with expectation. Olivia must have said something that required a response.

She had a question of her own. She turned to Olivia. "How long have you known Paul?"

"Gershuny?" The non sequitur question didn't seem to surprise Olivia. She pursed her lips. "Maybe six, seven years. I think the first time I met him was soon after he was hired at the U. Kurt and Beverly brought him over to our place for dinner."

"He's never mentioned you or your husband to me." As though this proved something. Why was she seeking more evidence? How many times did she have to be hit over the head?

Olivia blinked into the sun and hesitated. In this light Suzanne noticed pinguecula, a slight yellowish raised area on the inner corners of her eyes. It was an innocuous phenomena, common to the elderly and those who were often exposed to irritants like sun, wind, chlorine.

"There's no reason Paul would have mentioned us," Olivia said finally. "Blake and I are no more than acquaintances to Paul."

These acquaintances were running for university president and the House of Representatives.

However, Olivia had a point. Paul was as much enamored of politics, campus or otherwise, as Suzanne was.

While she cogitated, Olivia said, "Let's go somewhere and talk. Peppino's. Noisy as hell. We can bitch all we like." Her eyes wandered to Kurt Poole's house.

"Oh, no. I don't want to take you away from the gathering. Besides, I'd like to check in on my kid sister."

Olivia didn't ask for an explanation. "How about I get a gym pass for you? The U has an Olympic-sized pool."

"I'm not very good. I float, do some sort of bastardized side stroke. I think. Anyway, I have a pool at home."

"You can't *swim* in a backyard pool. I usually go to the gym late afternoon, about five-thirty. Why don't you meet me there tomorrow? I'll show you the real honest-to-God side stroke. And"—she smiled—"it's cathartic as hell. You'll feel great afterward."

Not since college had Suzanne spent time with a woman she could call a good friend. How did that happen?

"I've always wanted to learn to dive. Never had the guts. Think you could teach me?"

"Guaranteed."

Suzanne smiled. "I'd like that."

After she gunned the motor, not pleased with the throaty sound of the muffler, Suzanne pulled the Buick away from the curb and waved to the older woman. The brilliant afternoon sun reflected a nimbus around the golden red of Olivia's hair.

Something about her seemed oddly familiar, like a faded memory. Then Suzanne realized what it was. With the identical clothing and similar build, seeing Olivia was like seeing a better designed version of Suzanne herself. Or what she should strive to be.

CHAPTER 6

Suzanne kept a firm grip on her own psyche. Row row row your boat, gently down the stream. This stream was the id-consciousness of the person feeling—

the piercing glint of reflected light, rippling, seen from a high place. The unruly brightness imprints on the retina, superimposing dark splotches over a large square with gold trim. A small voice crackles in the right ear.

The sensations were ill-defined, muddy. Sounds were like those from a distant station, crackly with static; images like trying to see a distant landscape using binocular lenses smudged with butter. She'd experience more if she let go, immerse in the visceral, but fear kept her clinging to the boat of her own mind. She was learning, wasn't she, a baby taking its first steps and falling, and getting up again. She clung to the identity of her own thoughts, though she paid a price in clarity.

The air is stuffy. Hot. Flesh is moist and sticky at the crotch, a man's genitalia. He adjusts himself, then tilts his head up and down with weariness. An ache throbs at the small of the back. Long nimble fingers twist a knob. A background voice sings muffled nonsense. The snugness of long narrow cloth around the neck is loosened, then in a heartbeat—

EVERYTHING STOPS, and for a few nano-seconds Suzanne was alone, more alone than a sensory deprivation tank of body-temperature water and complete darkness, an aloneness worse than all descriptions of hell, the mind unmoored in dreadful nothingness. No sight, no sound, no touch, no smell. The host had checked right out, all circuits dead, and had abandoned her in a void where sentience was torture—

A sharp sting to the inner arm, a tiny stabbing pain, sparks him to groggy wakefulness. A flat hard surface presses up against his shoulders, buttocks. Dull ache to the back of his head. Sharp angles swim, spin, and flatten into an ant's view of a large dark piece of furniture. The visual field orbits in a sickening whirlwind. Eyes closed, he grasps something, pulls to raise himself, and the thing crashes over onto him. His skull bangs into a sharp edge. He retches, gags, then stays prone. Exhausted. A winter cold suffuses his hands, his feet.

A cerebral accident, a stroke? But what was that dartlike pain at the crook of the elbow? Had to be an injection. He's certainly concussed, going into shock—

His diaphragm paralyzes, becomes static and unresponsive. He can't inhale. His lungs are empty of air. The reflex response to oxygen starvation commands him to breathe, but he can't. The muscles that control respiration have shut down. A hungry anguish. Terror and the animal will to

live jolt him to action. He shoves aside the fall-
en object, drags himself up against the sturdy
oblong furniture. Black spots strobe in time with
his laboring heart—

Good Lord, she was in the mind of a *dying*
man. Would his death condemn her body to a
permanent vegetative state while her spirit suffocated in an empty void? In his compromised condition, he would suffer brain damage in a couple
minutes, death close behind. Her sanity wouldn't
survive another split second of that vacuum. Got
to get out, got to get out NOW. She willed herself home, back to her body. There was a surge,
increasing momentum in infinite space, her mind
a fiery comet rushing away from a small dying
star, faster, faster, faster until the speed itself
seemed an agent of destruction—

CHAPTER 7

"What time is it now?" Suzanne asked Bob, Weis's secretary. His gamin face reddened and he tapped the knot of his sedate navy tie as though it were a Star Trek communicator. Beam me up, Scotty, the natives are unfriendly.

"I am sorry, he's taking an awful long time, isn't he?" He touched his tie again. "It's half past eleven. Maybe I'll . . . if you'll just give me a moment . . ." He eased up from behind the cherry wood desk, opened the office door, and went in. Weis's office was huge. Suzanne had been in it plenty of times before Quiston retired, but not once since Weis came on last year. The way things were going, she might never see the interior again.

This was the second time this morning she'd been sitting here, shedding rabbit hair onto the plush maroon armchair. Earlier Weis had kept her waiting and waiting and waiting, so she'd told Bob that she'd go back to the labs, and to please call when Weis had a free moment. The walk from the research building took less than five minutes. The secretary had called and said eleven would be fine and here she was once more, like an idiot, hanging around until Weis deigned to talk with her.

She was determined to apologize, but more importantly, to see if Weis was the man of last night's presensory ride. She welcomed the break from her personal concerns about Paul. The thing about self-absorption, the more you scratch, the more it's going to itch.

Bob returned. He came over to Suzanne and bent down, his hands pressed prayerlike between his knees. "I'm awfully sorry, but he's not going to be able to talk with you." A good secretary, making excuses for his poor excuse of a boss. "He's a bit irritable. Maybe he's sick."

Yeah, Suzanne thought. Sick of me. She kicked her conscience. If he's really ill, if he's the man of the remote sensing experience, then he's a candidate for a terrible death. "When can I see him, then?"

"Oh . . ." The secretary's cheeks reddened again. "I'd have to check with him . . . I mean . . . I don't know."

Hmmm. Weis must be royally ticked. Maybe she had gone too far over the line at last Friday's meeting.

"Is he in?"

"Why, yes."

"In there?" Suzanne pointed to the closed office door.

"Yes." His look said, who did you think I was talking to, myself?

Suzanne rose and walked toward the closed office door before the secretary registered what she was doing. "This will really only take a minute."

The secretary's protests were polite and feeble. Suzanne turned to Bob as he made to follow. She pointed at him. "Stay," she said, and closed the door behind her.

Weis sat at his desk, twin oblongs of gold-threaded black marble supporting a broad slab of highly polished mahogany. His thick white hair was reflected in its hard smoothness like a cloud in the calm surface of a lake. A red bow tie with black spots was tied jauntily around his neck. His charcoal-gray jacket bunched at the shoulders as though too large. He didn't look up, but turned another page of a stapled report. "I told Bob I wasn't available."

"I know. I wanted a chance to—"

"Is there anyone, yourself included, who can control your behavior?"

She approached his desk. Behind him two walls of tinted glass joined. From here, the eighth floor, you had a bird's-eye view of Irvine. A twin-engine plane glided down toward the John Wayne Airport runway. The silver wings tilted, sending a dart of sunlight to her eyes, then straightened, then tilted, as though the horizon were unstable. Was this the light, seen from a high place, that had flickered in the host's eyes?

"I want to apologize about last Friday. The study I did on Vitalol heart rate. You should have been informed. Asked," she amended. Weis held the sheaf of papers in one hand, his eyes locked on the type.

"I just thought—"

"I don't want you to think about what studies to do." He directed his speech to the desk, enunciating as though it were a slow-witted child. "I want you to do as you're directed. It was only some fast talk by your supervisor that prevented me from firing you last week."

That jolted her. She'd thought she was too inexpensive an employee to warrant termination. "I apologize. Dr. Quiston had a different . . . management style. I've had . . . difficulty getting calibrated to your methods." Diplomacy wasn't her strong suit. Neither was detective work, apparently, since she hadn't come up with a subtle way of getting the answers she wanted. Screw subtlety. "Look, I came here to apologize, which I did, and to find out some things. They may sound like crazy questions. Actually, they are crazy questions." She was talking too fast. She crossed the room to the matching mahogany bookcase with tambour doors shielding two shelves from view. "Do you have a CD player in here, something with on-off dials or volume knobs? Or a radio, the station selector. It has to be round, the kind you twist."

"I don't know what kind of game you're playing, Dr. Reynolds, but I want you out. Now."

"Okay. But just one more question. Please. It's important." She turned to him. He looked at her, his eyebrows lowered in suspicion. Not a happy face. She stepped up to his desk. "Are you, or is someone, injecting you intravenously"—she touched the bend of her right arm over the median veins—"with a substance that could cause cardiorespiratory collapse?"

His face suffused. "I don't want to see you again. Do you understand?"

"I'm talking about a pharmaceutical you might use here. In your office." Very diplomatic. It sounded like she was accusing him of using illicit narcotics. "Maybe I should explain."

"Get out."

His hands shook. The papers he held were her last report, which included the results of the heart-rate study. He had been reading her analysis. When she didn't move, he stood suddenly, and a small piece of paper dislodged from the rest, floating like a miniature magic carpet to her feet. Suzanne picked up the rectangle, noted that it was a Kodak moment of a much younger Weis and a dark-haired teenaged girl. She set the photograph on his desk.

He spoke through clenched teeth. "Get out!"

Her report crumpled in his grip. He didn't look so much ill as furious. The sort of fury that could burst blood vessels.

"Well, golly, yes. I'd say Dr. Weis is a tad irritable," Suzanne said.

Bob swiveled away from the word processor. "He'll want my ass for letting you in."

"No doubt. Sorry about that, but it was critical that I speak to him."

"It's all right. I'm used to it. He fires me about once a month, anyway."

"No kidding."

"It makes him feel better. Then he apologizes and gives me a raise. Once he drove out to my house, way out in Diamond Bar, to ask me back."

"What about the freeze on wages?"

"In extraordinary situations, they can bend the

rules. Weis uses me as a whipping boy. He always wants me back."

"Hmmm. I don't think I'd be so lucky."

"I don't know. I've heard him say that you were one of the brightest researchers he'd ever worked with."

"Not possible."

"It's the truth. I hear everything in this place."

"Huh." Bob had heard wrong that time. "Well, listen, I am worried about him. He doesn't seem well. I'm concerned about him being alone in there, in case he . . . uh . . . faints or something."

He rolled back the chair and stood. "You think he's seriously ill? Should I—"

"No. No. Nothing like that. Just a . . . concern. A hunch. You know, woman's intuition." She smiled, but grimaced inside. A lightning bolt should strike me dead for perpetuating that stereotype.

"He's not in there alone too often. I'll keep an eye out for him." He studied the floor so intently that she looked down. Nothing there but the plush navy carpet and their feet, hers in sensible black pumps—she'd been influenced by an advertisement of women skipping through marathons in them—and his in shiny leather loafers.

"Have you had a buffalo burger?" he said.

"Buffalo?"

"There's a restaurant at the airport at the top of Catalina Island."

"Oh." Uh-oh. He's revving up to ask for a date. "Aren't the buffalo a protected species?"

"Catalina's grazing lands are pretty small. The law allows them to control the herd size, so . . . anyway, I have this little single-engine plane, a

Cessna. I have a spot, a tie-down at the John Wayne Airport."

"Wait a minute. You own a plane?"

He grinned. He had the sort of cheeks her grandmother would pinch. "Kind of a Tijuana taxi. She's old, but she's in perfect running condition."

"And a house? Your house? Or do you live with your parents? Tell me you live with your parents."

"My house."

He must be mortgaged out the wazoo. She stuck her hands into the pockets of her lab coat and leaned in. His ear looked like the profile of a tiny face with protruding jaw. "Listen, this is a personal question, I know. Unforgivable. But . . . just how much is your salary?"

He told her. This young man—he looked just barely legal—topped her salary. She blew a gust of air that lifted her bangs. "I've got to go. There's some radiators I need to beat my head against."

Outside she paused in the parking lot between her building and administration. A dozen cyclists zoomed by, taking a shortcut from the noon traffic on Von Karman. They were the serious sort, tight lycra pants with padded fannies, helmets that looked too little, gloves with the fingers cut off. Bulging calf muscles pedaled furiously. They passed her, rumps aloft. A sweaty breeze gusted in their wake. Like creatures controlled by one mind, their bikes angled, hugged the curve, and they disappeared around the corner of the building. She gazed at the air where they used to be. A bunch who knew where they were going, and went. Had her life ever been that linear? How did one unravel complexities, return to simplicities? She'd be satisfied if she could make some sense of last night's presensory excursion. She'd kept herself so distant, so closed, that the sensations were blurred, remote. Was Weis the host? If he wasn't, then who? Maybe it wasn't even anyone she knew. Maybe she'd blown her chances of identifying the man by not immersing herself fully. One thing she did know, especially since last night. She didn't have the courage to risk sanity by a psychic bungi jump into a dying host.

CHAPTER 8

Suzanne watched Linda Yoshi through the window of the tomograph room. The young woman was outfitted in black, as usual, from her black ankle-high boots and stretch pants to her shiny blue-black cap of hair—black, that is, except where a rooster tuft of maroon sprouted from one side. Top the outfit with the spotless white lab coat and you've got a weird-looking kid, bloodred fingernails, exotic epicanthic folds to the eyes, high cheekbones, delicately sculpted chin and lips. She was twenty, the youngest and newest research technician, and by far the most natively intelligent. She had a BS in Biology and was slumming at the lab. Inexperienced, but never stupid.

Three albino rabbits were on the cart, their bodies zippered into protective canvas sacks, heads with twitching noses protruding. Docile. Calm, even given that lab rabbits were calm animals. The Vitalol bunnies.

Sadness pricked at the edge of Suzanne's mind. What she wouldn't give to have the term of her contract up.

Linda lifted one animal and placed it on the counter, her movements gentle and firm. A few strands of white fur spiraled in the air. She checked the number tattooed on the pink under-side of the animal's right ear, verified the number in her lab book, then plunked a drop of lidocaine, a topical anesthetic, in the rabbit's right eye. The rabbit blinked lazily. She lifted the stylus from the tomograph, a tan metal instrument the size of a bread box. Its red LED readout showed zero millimeters of mercury. Linda gently touched the rubber-capped flat tip of the probe to the rabbit's cornea, the transparent cells above the iris. Red numbers flickered on the tomograph's readout. The instrument beeped when the pressure read-ing stabilized on twelve millimeters of mercury, a healthy reading for intraocular pressure.

Suzanne entered the room. "How's it going?"

"I'm glad you're here." She did the same read-ing on the animal's left eye. "This last bunny has lateral nystagmus. I think," Linda said noncha-lantly. Suzanne smiled. Linda had been doing some extra reading. Linda exchanged rabbits from the cart. This last one's head, cocked to the left, moved back and forth as though silently disagreeing about something. The left ear drooped slightly.

"Darn it," Suzanne said. You work with enough rabbits, you eventually see this symptom. "This is the Vitalol group?"

"Yep."

"I guess this small study sample's going to become smaller. Were the data on this bunny within range of the others?"

Linda wrinkled her brow, thinking. She lifted the rabbit's right ear to see the number tattoo, then traced a crimson-tipped finger down the chart in her lab notebook. "Uh-huh. Right in line with the rest."

Suzanne studied the rabbit, its constant side-to-side shake. "It was good you caught this symptom so quickly. Have you ever watched the eyes of a little kid when he's dizzy?"

"Yeah. My sister was dancing once with her little boy in her arms, he was about a year old, and after she spun around his eyes rocked back and forth. He looked drunk."

"Ah. Well, I wouldn't recommend doing that too often. Anyway, that jittery motion of the eyes is similar to lateral nystagmus. This animal presents with a different symptom."

"Its whole head is shaking, favoring the left side. Its eyes are steady."

"Right. This isn't lateral nystagmus. It's a classic case of otitis media." Suzanne scratched the rabbit between its ears. "An inner-ear infection has spread to the brain. This shaking indicates permanent damage."

"Can we treat it?"

Suzanne shook her head. "The damage is done, and progression is swift. She's probably off her food. Have you weighed her?"

"I'll do weighings before I leave."

"You'll find that she's lost weight. Soon she'll self-mutilate, chew on the left ear, left paw. She's suffering now. Worse suffering is in her future. It's better not to let the infection spread to that point."

"What if we treated it with antibiotics, keep watch on its symptoms?"

"The problem is, the early stages are asymptomatic. By the time an animal has the symptoms, the infection has progressed too far. This rabbit was infected at the breeder's, long before she reached us."

Suzanne's heart felt heavy, her usual reaction to seeing the test animals, innocent creatures like the pigs she'd tossed stones at when she was a kid. She reflected on statistics, good honest analyses of data, and how they translated into predictions. She thought about the animal data, measurements from rabbits like these, that justified testing a chemical on a human being. Most researchers would no doubt experience an ultimate satisfaction when their work could be reduced to a specific person placing one drop of the drug in each eye, a simple action that prevented blindness for the rest of that person's days.

She envisioned her grandfather, a long-time sufferer from angina, using Vitalol. Would the drug be poison to him? Slow his heart too much? Stop his heart? The target population, the elderly with glaucoma, often had cardiovascular complaints. What if Vitalol were tested on elderly with bradycardia, abnormally low heart rate?

If I could go back in time, she thought, before Thalidomide reached all those pregnant women, before those pregnant women gave birth to deformed infants, I would have thoroughly tested the drug on animals.

Weis pinned big hopes on Vitalol, that much was clear. Bolton Pharmaceuticals needed another good drug on the market. Tough patooties.

"Where's the new shipment of rabbits?" she asked Linda.

"The front half of room four."

"Let's go." Linda followed her down the hall to animal room four. When they pushed through the doors, cage-thumping sounds started and stopped. The new rabbits regarded them from the farthest reaches of their cages. A clean lemon scent rode in the air, punctuated by the fragrance of kibble and carrot greens. Banks of female albino rabbits towered from both sides. Each bank consisted of a wheeled metal frame holding nine large cages in a three- by-three-by-three tier. The card outside each cage showed the rabbit's ID number, the date the animal was delivered to the lab, and what study the animal participated in. The new arrivals didn't have a study noted on the cards.

"These two banks." Suzanne gestured to one side. "Tomorrow start taking their intraocular pressure, heart rate, and blood pressure twice a day."

"And eyedrops twice a day with Vitalol?"

"No flies on you."

Linda gave her a rare smile. "The test group."

"Right. And these two banks"—Suzanne pointed to the opposite side of the room—"same procedure exactly except that they'll be treated with saline."

"The control group."

"Right. Mark their cards with Vitalol/heart rate/BP. Set up your lab book for a thirty-day study, but leave room for sixty. Let me see the charts and how you worded the premise."

Linda left to retrieve the animals in the tomograph room. The rabbit at eye level to Suzanne munched on carrot greens, nosed them outside the cage. She caught the stuff as it fell, and poked the long pungent stalks back in. The rabbit skittered to the back of the cage, regarded her a moment, then hopped forward and continued feeding. "This study has to be done," she said aloud.

At least she didn't have to deal with Elliot right away. He had taken the day off. He rarely entered the labs, though he sometimes checked on shipments of new animals. How long would it take for him or Weis to discover her latest, possibly fatal transgression? Talk about career-limiting decisions. If she kept her head down and didn't mention this study to Elliot, she might be able to complete the data analysis before Weis fired her. If not, then she'd make sure her concerns were included with the FDA reports. Her work now, with Vitalol, was more important in preventing rather than enabling the drug's travel to the marketplace.

Which made Weis her adversary.

CHAPTER 9

Suzanne was all alone in her office, her and the eye. The poster was a large cross-section of the organ in heavily saturated colors. The white sclera, the perfectly transparent cornea, the blue-green iris. The iris is a radial muscle that widens or shrinks the diameter of the pupil, the black opening over the crystalline lens. And behind the lens the vitreous humor, the fluid protecting the retina. By a wondrous alchemy of the brain, light reaching the retina is translated into a rich visual field of coherent images: a colorful poster of the eye or black laboratory notebooks—pages awaiting her initials—or a phone with index finger poised over the numbers. Yes, indeedy, that's my phone, all right. And that's my finger.

She read the phone number in her address book. Yes, still the same. Hasn't changed since a second ago. She poked the buttons. Three ascending notes sounded, then the usual recording that tells you in a polite way that you screwed up the numbers. She dialed again. He probably isn't in. Ringing. Ringing. Then a connect.

"Poole."

"Kurt?" she said.

"Yes?"

"Is this a bad time?"

"Depends. Who is this?"

"Suzanne Reynolds."

"Suzanne! You didn't sound like yourself."
Then an aside: "Make ten, no, twelve copies."

"You're busy. I'll—"

"Not that busy."

Silence.

"Suzanne?"

"Kurt, I'd like to teach a 400-level class
in psychopharmacology. Antipsychotic drugs of
choice, side effects, the latest research on anti-
depressants, symptom modification, Halcyon and
other disasters in the annals of pharmacology.
A course geared to the non-medical profes-
sionals. How do I go about approaching the
psych department?" She rocked in her admi-
ral's swivel chair, its black spring twanging in
tune with her nerves.

"In the case of a faculty member," Kurt said,
"the professor submits a class description to the
undergraduate committee. If the committee votes
that the program looks worthwhile, then the
class plan is submitted to the academics in the
department. The other approvals up the echelon
are rubber-stamped, provided there aren't any
budgetary constraints."

"And since I'm not a faculty member—"

"Since you're not a faculty member, you'll also
have to submit a curriculum vitae, emphasizing
any supporting experiences, and letters of recommendation. Why don't you do this: Prepare

a curriculum vitae and a study plan with three suggested textbooks. Let me review those and if it looks good, I'll help push from there."

"Kurt, thanks . . . I thought somehow that this was going to be a horrible struggle."

"Oh, there's plenty of horror to come. It's built in to the unwieldy structure of the university. But you'll have a head start over most applicants."

"In what way?"

"You'll have a respected member of the faculty mentoring you."

"Who?" She hoped he wouldn't say Paul. Or Weis.

"Me, of course."

Jeesh, she sounded dense. "Thanks. I appreciate your help. How long will this process take?"

"The sooner you have those materials prepared, the better. If all goes well, you could be in the course schedule for the spring semester."

Spring. Far away, but a definite start. "I'll have everything by this weekend. Why don't you bring the family over for a swim on Saturday? You and I can review what I've written then."

"I don't know," he said, laughing, "those triplets, they're lethal weapons. Even my ten-year-old, a miniature version of Mother Teresa, loses patience."

After firming up plans for Saturday, Kurt Poole disconnected. She swiveled the chair, laced her fingers over her stomach, and smiled into the sunshine. She'd been beating her head against the brick wall of the medical school, applying for positions there, when all along she'd had a major contact in the undergraduate school.

She thought of Olivia and their scheduled swim after work today. If Olivia was hired as president, czar over the medical school and the university, she'd be a friend in a very high place indeed. The older woman would be sympathetic to Suzanne's goal of teaching at the medical school. She made a mental note to avoid shying away from asking for help. Particularly now, when Weis may fire her, contract or no contract. The financial problems . . . well, she couldn't do much about them except hope to negotiate a kinder payout. Still, her spirits floated. Damn the torpedoes, full steam ahead.

She toyed with the idea of confiding in Kurt about the presensory experiences. What had Olivia called him? Father Confessor. Sure, she could hear herself explaining things right now. Yes, I'd like your opinion about my being in this murderer's head, well not exactly his current mind, but his future mind, when he decides to kill a woman in the desert. Maybe me, but I'm not quite sure. It's kind of like a scene from Alfred Hitchcock's *The Birds*. And then there's another man, different from the killer—I think—who's going to die from respiratory paralysis, maybe as a result of an overdose of something given intravenously.

Not exactly the qualifications of a person wanting to shape young minds.

A knock on the door. "Come in," Suzanne said.

Mariette came in and handed her four slips of paper. "You forgot to pick up your messages."

Suzanne glanced at them. One from a computer sales rep, three from Paul. He had called while she was busy giving Weis a coronary. He had called twice last night, while she had been taking a post-dinner walk on the bridle path. Her anger had receded, but she wasn't ready to talk with him yet. Maybe later tonight.

Mariette still stood before her desk, wobbling as though her feet hurt. "You busy?"

"Not at the moment. What's up?"

Mariette turned, went into the hall, and pushed in a reluctant Manuel. "I go," she said to her son. She gave him a gentle shove. "You listen." The ticking of her high heels receded down the hall.

The fifteen-year-old shook his head, closed his eyes, wincing in exaggerated embarrassment. The sleeves of his white European-style shirt were rolled up, the buttons partially undone, a look of casual elegance that was enhanced by his dusky skin tones. His black hair was tied back in a short, tidy ponytail. He was well on his way to being six feet tall. With the baggy pleated-front trousers cinched tight at the waist, he was a candidate for the cover of *GQ*. Handsome but with a thin mouth that could go cruel. Was this kid really only fifteen?

"Hey, Manuel, good to see you. Take a load off." She pointed to the regulation black chair in front of her desk.

"My mother"—he rolled his eyes—"she's . . . she's . . . what can I say?"

"Persuasive."

"Yeah. Bummer." He dropped into the chair, legs wide apart.

"How'd you finally do in sadistics?" Suzanne angled forward on her elbows, but from this distance his irises were a solid dark brown, the black pupils indistinguishable. However, the sclera, the whites, looked clear. No sign, as Mariette had said, of rampant infection.

"Well, you know, that was a tough class. The teacher was a real bast . . ." He flushed. "A mean old guy. Most of the kids pulled F's. Getting a D in statistics is considered a real accomplishment."

"I don't care about most of the kids. I want to know about this kid. Did our slaving over those problems help?"

"You know, considering he flunked half the class, I was lucky to get"—he smiled, showing beautiful straight white teeth—"a solid B."

"That's great. After all that whining"—she stood, came around the front of her desk, and leaned back against it—"and complaining—"

"I didn't whine or complain."

"Not you. Me."

He laughed, his eyes crinkling. Anyone who heard this boy laugh would be charmed. He looked up at her, lifting his face into the glare of sunlight from the window, and what she saw under his long dark lashes gave her a chill. Anisocoria, pupils of different size. The pupil of the right eye was inadequately constricted. Her mind automatically cataloged causes, central nervous system diseases, syphilis, inflammation of the iris.

She twisted around and punched the extension for the lab. "Bring the ophthalmoscope and a penlight to my office right now." She turned back to Manuel. "I want a close look at your eyes."

He tossed his head. "Oh, man—"

"Listen, Manuel. Healthy pupils—you know what pupils are? The black dot, actually a hole, at the center of the colored part of your eye? Healthy pupils are the same size. You have such dark eyes, it's hard to see, but your right pupil is much larger than your left. Have you noticed that?"

"No. But anyway, that's my weak eye. I just need eyeglasses."

Linda came in and handed Suzanne the ophthalmoscope case and the penlight. "Thanks, Linda." She waved the young woman away and closed the door.

Manuel started to rise. She pressed her hand down on his shoulder. "Sit."

"No way I'm going to wear glasses. Only jerks wear glasses."

"Thanks," she said dryly. She walked around the desk and pulled down the window shade. The room dimmed.

"God, I didn't mean you. You're a scientist. I meant guys my age."

"Too late." She opened the black case and withdrew the instrument. "You've insulted me and now I have to torture you."

"What's that?" He blinked several times and his Adam's apple bobbed. His cocky sureness had melted into little boy fears.

"This won't hurt. I'm not even going to touch your eyes." She showed him the flashlight-sized device. "An ophthalmoscope. Here's the light source"—she tripped the small switch—"and this is a dial for selecting the lens strength. I'll set it for plus eight. Okay. A funduscopic examination is when I shine this little beam of light through the pupil and look through the ophthalmoscope lens at the retina."

"I don't know—"

"Let me take a look. Please. I'm worried as shit."

Her swearing convinced him. "All right."

"I want you to stare at the top of my filing cabinet." She gestured behind and to her right. "Good. And keep your face"—she touched his chin, skin soft as a girl's—"in this position, facing me. Keep your eyes and your face perfectly still. Look up. A little more to your left. A bit more. That's good."

She placed the instrument over her right eye and angled her head so her nose was parallel to his right eye and cheek. Starting twelve inches away, she aimed the beam of light through his right pupil. The normal golden-red reflex was dull and spotted with black. Not good.

She moved closer until about three inches away, rotating the ophthalmoscope lens, seeking the optimal magnification for a distinct view of the inner eye. The image sharpened and she exhaled in dismay. Damn damn damn. Morning Glory retina. The delicate membrane, rooted by the optic nerve, floated partially free of the nourishing capillaries beneath, resembling a red-hued flower. The slightest movement of his head tore the sheath more away from its blood source. When the retina died, vision died forever.

He still had some acuity in that eye. There was hope.

She yanked back. "Get up," she told him.

"What is it?"

"I'll explain in a moment. Do as I say. Get up."

He stood and she shoved the chair to the side of her desk. "Lie down."

He laughed uneasily. "You got to be kidding."

"You have a detached retina. If we act quickly, we might be able to save your sight."

"But . . . it's just dim. Like a fog—"

"Soon there will be nothing. *Nothing*. Lie *down*."

He shifted, stuffed his hands into his pockets. "Dr. Reynolds, I'll go to that doctor."

"There's no time. The longer you stand and move your head, the more you're ripping loose your retina. When you lose sight in one eye, Manuel, you lose depth perception. You can't tell exactly how close or how far away things are. You want to drive? Fat chance, when you can't tell where other cars are. You like to play sports? You can kiss them off, football, tennis, golf, racketball, basketball. Want to join the service, learn to fly jet aircraft? No way. You'll spend most of your time trying to avoid walking into walls. *So get down on the damn floor*."

She exaggerated to scare him, and it worked. He lay down on his back, his chest rising and falling rapidly, a frightened child.

She knelt next to him and adjusted the position of his head to allow the retina to sink back against the network of capillaries. "Good. Close your eyes. The less you move your head and eyes, the better. Okay?"

"Okay."

"*Don't nod*. Keep your head perfectly still."

The next few minutes Suzanne talked with Mariette, contacted a good ophthalmic surgeon, and arranged for an ambulance to transport Manuel to the surgeon's clinic. If operable, he'd be admitted to Hoag Hospital in Newport Beach. She explained the surgical technique, leaving out the word "staples," though that best described how the retina was reattached.

Mariette knelt next to her son and held his hand. "What causes this detached retina?"

Suzanne said, "Sometimes it's an inherited tendency. Often a knock or blow to the head—"

"My father." Manuel spat the words.

Mariette said, "Last week there was an argument—"

"He would have hit her." Manuel's voice cracked.

"My husband was angry. Manuel stood in front of me and my husband hit him here." She placed her fist against her right temple. "He hit Manuel here several times."

"Till I fell."

"He was angry." Mariette stroked his hand.

He pulled his hand away. "He was drunk."

"Yes." She looked at her son's face, his closed eyes. "He was drunk."

CHAPTER 10

"I can't do this."

"Jump."

"It's not natural. I've changed my mind. Why don't we just swim around awhile?"

"Jump."

"Flinging yourself headfirst at anything is insane—"

"Suzanne, for God's sake, move your butt."

She threw herself with misgivings, knowing she looked more like a statue toppling off its base than someone diving. The pool slapped her like a wet sheet. Chlorinated water filled her nose. Blurry underwater bubbles fizzed, then her face broke through to the air. Her nostrils stung. Thank the gods for buoyancy. She swam to Olivia and hauled herself up. Rough concrete scraped her knee.

Olivia shook her head. The white cap, hiding her red hair, emphasized the masculine features of her strong face. Well-developed pectorals over-whelmed her breasts, mainly visible as erect nipples under the slick black swimsuit. "Your visualization's all screwed up."

"I'll say. I can't see a darn thing without my glasses." Suzanne retrieved her glasses from atop the white towel and slipped them on.

"Get prescription goggles. But I'm not talking about your eyesight, I mean the image in your head of yourself diving is all wrong. Watch me. Pay attention. Curl your toes over the edge, like this." Olivia demonstrated at the pool's edge. Watching the play of muscles in her calves made Suzanne feel flabby. "Then bend your knees slightly, lean forward"—buttock muscles tensed under the high-cut swimsuit—"and push off." She dove into the water, her slim body merging with rather than penetrating its surface.

"What a wimp I am," Suzanne said aloud. Olivia snaked through the pool like it was her natural element, with powerful thrusts from muscled legs. She reached the opposite side, somersaulted underwater, and glided back. She joined Suzanne and wasn't even winded.

"Let's work on your visualization. Watch me a few more times, but imagine that you're diving." Water dripped from the tip of her nose. "When I hit the water, hold your breath, feel the pressure in your ears. Pull in as much sensory detail as you can."

Suzanne obliged, superimposing an image of herself over Olivia. Actually, she borrowed a bit of the older woman's body for herself—this is fantasy, right?—those delineated muscles of her legs and back, strong and beautiful in action, the flat stomach. While Olivia demonstrated with apparently inexhaustible energy, Suzanne's thoughts strayed to her phone conversation with the ophthalmic surgeon, who had admitted Manuel to the hospital and had scheduled surgery early tomorrow. The boy was a good candidate for retinal reattachment. Much longer, the surgeon had said, and the retina would have died. The small victory had boosted her spirits.

After a few more dives, Olivia said, "Can you see yourself diving like me?"

In a pig's eye. Though Suzanne did have a mental video of herself, an improved model, springing gracefully from the side of the pool. "Yes. I guess I'm ready." She dropped her glasses onto the towel. She moved to the edge.

Olivia crouched down. Her grip, positioning Suzanne's legs, was firm and painful. She was unaware of her own great strength. Olivia straightened. "Good. Arms up. A little higher. That's right. Head down in line with your upper arms. Okay. It's a go."

Suzanne leaned, realized she needed to flex her legs more, and tried to rewind. She windmilled her arms but it was too late. Gravity won and she crashed into the pool. She splashed and flailed before orienting her myopic vision to the pool's edge.

"You have to trust." Olivia reached down for her hand and helped her up. "Wrong-think. It's easy to do. Your thoughts are paralyzing you."

Suzanne arched herself at the pool's edge. "It's not my thoughts stopping me, it's the fear of dying." She did a few experimental knee bends.

"Trust that the water is there. Head just a bit lower. All right. Trust your instincts."

"My instincts tell me not to jump."

"Do it!"

Like committing suicide. Okay, I'm killing myself and it's okay it's okay—

"Jump!"

She pushed off from the edge, managed to do a painful belly flop. She treaded water. Her skin stung from chest to thighs. "Ouch."

The other woman hunkered down, ran a palm over her nose and mouth, ending with fingers over her lips. Hiding a grin.

"What?"

"You're much more motivationally impaired than I'd ever imagined."

"I agree. Let's swim. Show me the side stroke."

"Oh, no. You're a challenge. Get back up here."

Olivia had her try again and again until her leg muscles quivered and she was starving. And until Olivia admitted that there seemed to be no hope.

"Maybe you'll be better tomorrow," Olivia said.

"Tomorrow?"

"Same place, same time."

"I don't think letting my fear incubate is going to help."

"Trust me, you'll be better. Tonight visualize throwing yourself into the void."

"Sounds too much like flinging yourself at death."

"All challenges are like that." She clapped her hand on Suzanne's shoulder. "Welcome to the NFL."

In the locker room they undressed and stepped into a large white-tiled area with a half-dozen shower heads.

"From the Olympics to university president." Suzanne twisted on the shower and tested the temperature. "How did that happen?"

Olivia stood under an adjacent shower head, water cascading down her firm high breasts, her hair reaching the dimples at the small of her back. "I didn't have the speed for the Olympic team. I don't know, maybe I didn't want it bad enough. Anyway"—her deep voice carried clearly over the patter of water against tile—"I graduated from a college back east with a liberal arts degree, about as nebulous a degree as you can get, and joined the Peace Corps. Ended up in a swampy one-mule town in Belize, close to the Guatemala border, sweating and pretending to teach English. I assisted the doctor who came to town once a month, if the muddy roads were passable, and distributed medicine in between. It rained nine months out of the year. The Mayan Indians couldn't understand why a wealthy North American would want to be eaten alive by mosquitoes in their poor town. The poor see no virtue in poverty. After a short while, I didn't either."

Olivia soaped her underarms, stomach, and unself-consciously the faint auburn triangle between her legs. "Every native wanted to live in Belmopan, in central Belize. Belmopan had just been made the official capital, and rumor had it that there were jobs, running water, indoor plumbing, and television. Finally the whole bunch, about sixty adults, picked up and headed south for Belmopan. My assigned town left me. I got dysentery and the Peace Corps shipped me home. The kid I was then, I needed a little slapping around by reality. Got my doctorate in Business Administration, consulted while working up to dean at the University of Massachusetts."

"And soon UCLF university president."

"Damn straight. Every time the going gets tough, I tell myself, 'Olivia, this isn't so bad. After all, you could be in Belize.' "

Suzanne turned off the water and reached for her towel and eyeglasses. "I called Kurt Poole today." She relayed their conversation, Kurt's willingness to help her teach at the undergraduate level.

"He's a good guy, bless his little pointed head." Olivia bent over and wrapped the towel turban style around her hair. "You should try the med school. Get Weis to help."

"I don't think he's a fan of mine."

"The man's ninety percent hot air. Let him blow off steam, but use him. He'll help, but you have to persist."

Suzanne pulled the towel around her torso, knotting it between her breasts. "I don't think he'll help me under any circumstances."

"You're too sensitive. You won't know till you try." She walked before Suzanne to the lockers.

A memory percolated to the surface. "I saw a picture of Weis's daughter. How old is she?"

Olivia looked over her shoulder. "It's a he, not a she. A boy. I guess he's about eight. What's this I hear about you participating in a psych experiment?"

"What?"

"Yesterday. At the tea. Paul asked Kurt about requisitioning the EEG."

"EEG?"

"Electroencephalograph. You tape electrodes to the skull and get brain wave—"

"I know what it is. You say Paul has the equipment?"

"At the tea, Kurt Poole said he'd approved an interdepartmental requisition for an EEG. Paul wanted it."

Suzanne stopped by the varnished pine bench. This was news. "What's the EEG for? One of his classes?"

Olivia gave her a long side glance. "For you. They were talking after you left. I didn't catch everything. Paul's research, I thought."

"No kidding." She sat down and toweled her arms with harsh quick jolts. "I already told Paul I wasn't interested in being his darn guinea pig."

Olivia combed her wet hair. The ends reached the small of her back. "I might have misunderstood. Or Paul's making contingency plans. Those intradepartmental requests can take weeks."

"Do you know the subject of Paul's NSF grant?"

"No."

Suzanne patted the bench. "Have a seat. This will take a few minutes." She explained about last Saturday, the images, the little girl, the inexplicable desert experiences. When she had gotten that far, Olivia said, "You don't know who the man is in the desert?"

Suzanne shook her head.

"You don't know where this desert is?"

"No."

"Or when this might happen?"

"Ditto."

"Yet you're sure this murder hasn't happened?"

"I think that's right. But . . . I'm assuming it's in the future, since the incident with the little girl was predictive. If the victim is myself, then of course it hasn't happened yet. If it's some other woman, then . . . I guess it could be in the past . . ."

Olivia cocked her head.

"I know," Suzanne said. "It sounds nuts."

"Even if this is a true ability, there's so few identifiable facts, it's as useful as tits on a bull."

"Tell me about it." Suzanne sighed.

"It could be worse."

"It could?"

"Yes." She leaned sideways. Her naked shoulder touched Suzanne's. "You could be in Belize."

Suzanne laughed. "Well, I might as well tell you about the last presensory trip . . ." Abdominal rumblings made her pause. Her hunger began to transmute into a definite barf mode. She walked quickly to the sink and splashed cold water onto her face. Damn. Too late. Salivary glands went into overproduction. She ran to one of the toilet stalls and hung her head over the commode. Her pulse raced.

"Suzanne?"

Olivia squeezed into the stall, held her head while she fought the nausea. The overpowering floral air freshener pushed things over the edge. She retched, an alien force trying to turn her inside out and pitch her headfirst into the commode. Olivia's firm grip helped. Must be getting something, she decided. The symptoms dissipated and hunger, perversely, began to make its presence known again. She waved an okay sign,

Olivia released her, and they rested back on their knees.

"Better?" Olivia said.

"I think so." What a sight, the two of them, naked and kneeling on the tile before the white mouth of the toilet. Worshiping at the throne. "This is the second time—" Little lights lit up all over Suzanne's cortex. A memory flickered, her mother hunched over the kitchen sink, holding a wet washcloth to her face, her mother's huge stomach, the smell of vomit. She said, "Oh, no."

"What's the matter?"

"I need to get to a pharmacy."

"You need some of the pink gunk for upset stomachs?"

"No. A pregnancy test."

CHAPTER 11

Kurt Poole was in his former office, the psych department chairman's, located on the fifth floor, west end. Most of his belongings had been moved to the larger humanities suite on the opposite side of the building, top floor. For old times' sake, he decided on one last meeting here. When a new head for psychology was hired, he'd relinquish his old position with regret. There was a simplicity to this office, and to the position of psych department chairman. The evolution of his career, he guessed, would always be a moving away from simplicity toward chaos. And toward more money. With one child in college and four more to follow, he'd have to keep rising above his level of incompetence.

He liked this time of day the best. Below sparkled UCLF's man-made lake. The lowering sun painted ducks, swaying rowboats, and the twelve-story engineering building with amber hues. Occasionally light glinted with surprising strength off the water, like the sudden discovery of lost treasure. It had been hot today, in the nineties, and as usual maintenance had shut off the building's air-conditioning at six P.M. Now, barely thirty minutes later, heat rose through the lower floors to this corner office like a huge invisible cloud. Too bad about the windows, they were sealed shut. He'd already tossed his suit jacket on the couch. Even the old cojones stuck together. He shifted, pulled at the trouser fabric around his crotch.

The phone trilled. He lifted the receiver, punched the lit button, and his wife's voice slid into his ear. "I'm a woman in desperate need of counseling, Doctor."

"Therapy Are Us aims to please. How's the tribe?"

"You'll never believe what Ginger told the principal—"

Kurt leaned back in the swivel desk chair, phone to his ear. Beverly gave a rundown on each child. It would take a while. He stared, grinning, at a polished-brass framed photograph of his family, taken at Christmas. Seven children, two dogs, three cats, his wife, and himself. The tribe. The last child had turned out to be three, triplets, all boys, now six-year-old hellions. So a recounting of the day's events took some time.

"—so I had to leave my groceries in the cart and literally drag him by the scruff of his neck out of Ralph's, the clerks looking at me like I'm killing him. Actually, I felt like killing him." She laughed. "Oh, for September, when all three of them are in school."

"Did you give Alex his just deserts?" Alex, the middle triplet, was always the one in dutch with his mother.

"I *withheld* dessert. And no Nintendo tonight."

"I'll beat the tar out of him when I get home. A show of parental unity."

"Yeah, sure. You're such a pushover. He'd be eating brownies and playing Nintendo in a minute."

"Brownies?"

"We saved some just for you. When will you be home?"

Below on the lake, a magenta glow rippled in the wake of a mallard with places to go, ducks to see. Water stars sparkled. Gorgeous.

"Kurt?"

"By nine."

"That late?"

"Yes." He'd promised to keep this meeting in confidence. As a therapist, he was a keeper of secrets. Years of professional silence made it second nature. His wife knew not to ask.

"Before I forget," he said, "Suzanne invited us over Saturday afternoon for a pool party."

"What time, and what can we bring?"

"Uh . . . I don't recall. . . ." He lifted one haunch to withdraw his wallet from the back pocket. He found the Post-it with Suzanne's home number. "Here's her number. Would you check with her?" He recited the digits, tossed his wallet onto the desk, then relayed his conversation with Suzanne.

"I bet she'd be a great teacher," Beverly said. "She's got a lot going on behind those eyes."

After they disconnected, he rolled up the sleeves of his white shirt. Black splotches, a negative aftervision of the sunlight, peppered his vision. The Band-Aid and cotton wad at the crook of his left arm surprised him. He'd forgotten about having blood drawn at the medical school, done every month to keep track of his irascible cholesterol. He'd been trying to control his 300-plus count and wretched low-density lipoprotein levels with diet, but having little success. This was his last chance. If lab results showed no improvement, he'd have to take medication that would, his doctor assured him, make him fart incessantly. Poor Beverly.

He peeled off the bandage and cotton. On the pale skin of his inner arm were three red dots and the purple blossom of a respectable hematoma, like an oddly placed hickey. The student nurse had finally managed to insert the needle correctly, apologizing profusely all the while.

Kurt left the office and walked through the secretarial area, checked that the door to the hall was wide open. He returned to his office, his old office, and left that door open. He stretched. Joints in his neck popped. Getting old, Kurt. He slipped a tape of Mel Tormé into the portable cassette player, punched the play button. The Velvet Fog bubbled over with scat, a great soundtrack for the light reflected in russet and gold streaks on the lake. A twist of the volume knob and Tormé's liquid tones filled the air. He pressed his palms on the dusty windowsill. The beat of the sun weakened as it dropped below the horizon. He dusted off his hands, slipped his fingers under the knot of his tie, and pulled . . .

. . . and he was lying down, barely conscious. He'd blacked out. The back of his head throbbed. A merry-go-round of faces pulsed in his mind, his long-dead grandparents, his best friend in grade school, Beverly, the kids. All with enlarged fore-heads. The word "macropsia" occurred to him, a pathological condition where objects appear larger than they are in reality.

The floor creaked. Earthquake? His left arm was being held, thumped in a way that made him think he was back at the medical school with that pink-cheeked young nurse fumbling the needle into his vein. Was he in the hospital? Had his coronary arteries succumbed to his fondness for summer sausage and smoked cheddar? But there was Tormé's voice, fading in and out, singing in the distance, an acoustical ghost.

A sharp sting at the crook of his arm. The pain cleared his mind a little; Tormé's song returned to full throttle, yet his vision spun furiously like a dervish. His stomach lurched and he squeezed his eyes shut. Footfalls moved away.

"Hey"—his vocal cords felt rusty—"Help me." He was no competition for Mel Tormé.

The office door made its peculiar honking sound as it was pulled into its out-of-plumb frame. How many hundreds of times had he caused that sound, closing out the world so that he and a colleague, client, or friend could talk in private? His mind took a little holiday. Ducks ate brownies and talked on the phone, singing and squawking. Jazz notes, big black sixteenth notes, squeezed out the back of his head, a painful exodus. He should call 911, he was giving birth.

The phone. I'm in my office, I'm hurt. The phone. He opened his eyes, felt them rocking in their sockets, fighting to steady the whirling. He reached up, felt for the arm of his chair, and grabbed. It skidded on its casters and fell over onto him. His head knocked hard against the bottom edge of his desk. The world revved up to higher rpms and the inside of his skull was taken over by weasels, running round and round. His throat constricted with reverse peristalsis. Shit. He lay there a moment, hoping the carousel in his head might wind down, that he might not vomit. He needed to think straight. He shuddered. Cold perspiration beaded on his brow. His hands and feet turned to ice. Had the temperature plummeted to zero?

Then the horrible happened. He exhaled and his diaphragm froze. His chest was in a vise. No oxygen in his lungs. Terror released adrenaline. He shoved the chair away, dragged himself up against the desk, scattering the blotter, memos, the framed photograph, his wallet. The horror of being unable to inhale was a torture unlike any he'd known. He fell over onto the desk, panic robbing him of more of the precious oxygen reserves rapidly dwindling from his body. Weakness coiled around his chest like a snake, swirled up toward his head. Everything swam as though tossed on high seas. Black spots pulsed. His heart thonked against his ribs, attempting to compensate for the lack of oxygenated blood. Mel Tormé's singing faded, as though being moved away, until there existed a complete silence, as pure as that of the congenitally deaf. He couldn't cry out, speaking required the diaphragm to thrust air up past the larynx, and *he had no air*. He fumbled with the phone, got the receiver off its cradle, the hunger for oxygen was painful in a way he'd never

dreamed, felt buttons for outside lines but the
room had become a dark soupy screen and even
the sensation of touch abandoned him. His mind
was cocooned in a terrifying nothingness, physically dislocated.

The sun hung mid-sky and a fragrant breeze
drifted off the ocean. A puffy cumulus cloud
drifted. Feather-soft white sand cushioned his
body and he licked his lips and tasted sea salt.
He lay back, drowsy and content. His children
laughed over the ebb and flow of waves. They loved
the beach. Ginger, the ten-year-old, smiled at him.
Sunlight strobed through her tangled blond hair.
While he loved all his children, this one was
something special. She had gotten, he thought,
the best from him and Beverly. She peered down
with those clear inquisitive eyes, cornflower-blue,
and within her eyes you saw the possibility for
everything, shining bright and with promise, the
ecstatic recognition of the many roads to be trav-
eled, warmed by the sun . . .

CHAPTER 12

Suzanne's skin was finally cooling down. A fan hummed from its perch on the weight bench. The water-bed sheets bunched around her foot and she kicked them aside. She took a deep breath, inhaled a warm musky scent. She lay on her stomach, facing Paul. Candlelight, from stubby candles in brandy snifters, reflected in his eyes. There was a softness, a tenderness in his expression, something she hadn't seen before. She liked it. His right hand traced lines down her backbone, stopped to knead here and there.

She touched his lips, stroked his beard. "You're hired."

He kissed her fingers. "Not done yet. There's the postcoital refreshment." He stretched toward the headboard shelf, retrieved a white onion, and handed it to her.

She rolled onto her back. The water-bed glugged. "I've been wanting to try these for the longest time." She glanced around the smooth satin sheets. "What happened to the pillows?"

"Over here." He gathered them up from the floor, placed one behind her head.

"I tore out order forms from *Sunset* magazine,

but they were a jillion dollars per pound." She hefted the onion, peeled of its outer skin and the size of a tennis ball. On the ten-pound box had been the sentence, "The only time you'll cry is when they're all gone." She sank her teeth into the white flesh and tore off a hunk. Sweet as an apple, a faint onion tang, obscenely crunchy.

"I'm in heaven. I'm going to have Vidalias for breakfast, lunch, and dinner. Here"—she held the onion to his mouth—"taste."

He took a gargantuan bite and munched. "This can't be an onion. It's more like a fruit."

"I'll make sandwiches." She took another bite. "Slice the onion thin, several layers, a mild cheese like Havarti, on Russian rye with tofu mayonnaise."

"I was with you until that last ingredient." He hooked his arm under her neck and they finished the onion.

He said, "Do you have any idea where I had to go to find Vidalia onions?"

"Georgia, I hope. That's where they're grown."

"Even worse. The Farmers' Market in Newport Beach. Now I understand why people shoot each other on the freeways."

"Ah"—she nuzzled him below his beard—"but it was such a nice peace offering."

He stirred, grasped her buttocks, and pulled her hips against his.

"Again?"

He held her tight. His eyes sought hers. "I missed you. I must have called you a dozen times at work. You never called me back. It was so . . . I don't know . . . "

"Mean?" she helped. "Insensitive? Thoughtless? Smug?"

"All right, all right. Yeah. I never realized how you've always been there for me—"

"You'd say 'Jump' and I'd say 'How high?' You'd say 'Run' and I'd say 'How fast?' "

He pressed his lips together and frowned at himself. "Was I really like that?"

"Yes."

"I don't know why you put up with me." His eyes glistened. "What can you say when you've behaved so stupidly?"

" 'I'm sorry' would do."

"I'm sorry, Suzanne. I've behaved like a bastard." He traced a finger over her cheekbone, across her lips. "After yesterday, after you left the tea, I was pissed. You were always so needy, I thought. You always wanted me to read your mind. But I was angry, and I had to examine that anger. Why was I so defensive? It didn't take too much soul-searching before I realized you were right. I'd been acting at cross-purposes, telling you one thing and then doing another. It astounded me that I'd been working so damn hard to get you to end our relationship. And when you wouldn't return my calls, I figured I must have really blown it."

She thought about what he said. His insights were more than she expected, but insights were only valuable if acted upon. So she said honestly, "I feel like I hardly know you."

"I won't shut you out anymore. Our relationship is the most important thing in my life. It's a chance to redeem myself. I know we can't heal all at once, but I want to start. I'll need your help."

"You don't . . . emote. As soon as we get close to something that's affected you, you clam up. You pull away."

"I'm here, ready to emote. What do you want to know?"

She hadn't told him about the desert premonition, the presensory experience of the man's death, the PosiBlu pregnancy test waiting in its Savon paper bag on the bathroom counter. She wanted to tell him, but she wanted to take this slow. He was eager to prove himself to her. She wanted to give him that chance. "Tell me about Carolyn. How you met, your relationship with her, how you felt when she died."

He held her hand. "This was when Rusty and I were students at University of Southern California. Rusty was a psych graduate assistant—this was before he dropped out to become a rich screenwriter—and he ran numerous experiments on undergraduates. I was beginning my doctoral dissertation. Kurt Poole was my adviser. Rusty enlisted my help in pulling off a particular study. USC was set up like UCLF, the Psych 100 students had to participate in research if they wanted extra credit, mandatory if they wanted to ace the course. We herded all these freshmen into the room and had them sit at tables. Each table held an oscilloscope and nasty-looking electronic gear bristling with dials and indicators. Carolyn was noticeable in the crowd for two reasons: She had this unusual coloring, white-blond hair, eyebrows and eyelashes to match, very Nordic-looking, though

she was petite, small-boned. And she wore—
this was the beginning of the fall semester, so
it was hot—she wore a gauzy flowered dress
with a high lace collar, long sleeves, and the
hem reached her calves. Other students wore
shorts, the guys had on muscle shirts. I mean,
this is University of Southern California. Lots
of skin showing. Except for Carolyn."

He squeezed her hand. "Sure you're all right
with this?"

"It's okay." She watched Paul very closely. Had
his soul-searching delved deep enough to uncover
why he was so defensive, so secretive, about
Carolyn? Would he trust her, Suzanne, enough to
reveal what had been haunting him? She hoped
he would. It was the only way she could rebuild
faith in him.

"Anyway, this experiment was a variation on
the peer-pressure/authority-figure routine. Rusty,
wearing a lab coat and stethoscope, explained that
the equipment was for electroshock, that pain
tolerance was being tested, including parameters
like sex differences. Rusty was good at the BS
part, no surprise there, huh? Psychobabble was
his forté. The test would be very painful, he
assured them. Electrodes would be hooked up to
one arm and succeedingly greater shocks would
be administered. It was great, the looks on these
kids' faces. Rusty said that in unusual cases there
was a lingering numbness and redness, though
actual injury was rare. He distributed liability
waivers. The language was horrendous, stating
that there was no recourse if injury, like paralysis
or burns, occurred. Every participant would have

to sign this statement. He also told them that if they decided not to participate, they would not get credit. Anyone who wanted to leave should do so now. My job was to wait outside the lab door and nab the kids who left. Of course, that was the whole experiment. Tell them they were to be subjected to painful, possibly harmful electric shock, see how many stayed and how many left, then give questionnaires to the bunch. What do you think you would do?"

"Leave. No class credit is worth pain and injury."

"Hmm. That's what you'd think most of these kids would do. But they didn't. The only one who joined me in the hall was Carolyn. I found out that this independence was characteristic of her. She didn't give a damn what strangers thought. She was used to battling the odds to do what she wanted. Allergies and asthma plagued her all her life. It was as if the whole world were toxic to her. When she had a reaction like a rash, she'd simply cover up, like she had the day of Rusty's experiment, and go on with her life. She was stubborn."

His eyes disengaged, as if the past had materialized around them, a past that she couldn't see. After a moment, he said, "By the time she was a junior, we were engaged."

"What were you just thinking of?"

"That I had forgotten I loved her. This was, what? Seventeen, eighteen years ago. Intellectually I remembered, like seeing a movie without sound. But viscerally . . ." He shook his head. "I was in my early twenties, we were terrifically incompatible, and I couldn't see it. My love for her in part was misguided enthusiasm. Carolyn had a lot of problems. I believed, with my Ph.D. tucked securely under my belt, that I could be part of the solution."

"What sort of problems?"

"The theme was the same. She tried to ignore her symptoms, as though refusing to deal with them would make them go away. Like the time we had dinner at some friends' house. This was a couple she'd known since high school. During dinner, she excuses herself. When she doesn't return to the table, I go looking for her. The bathroom door is closed and I knock, call her name. No answer. I'm alarmed. I press my ear to the door and I hear wheezing. She's having an asthma attack. I jiggled the doorknob. It's locked. I ask her to unlock the door and I barely hear her, in between labored breathing, telling me to go away. The couple pop the lock, they had a toddler and had done it before. Carolyn's in there, sitting on the closed toilet, hunched over, gasping for breath, her lips blue, and *the aspirator is in her hand*. She was holding the damn thing, but hadn't used it. There were times when she simply refused to carry the aspirator in her purse."

"She must have known that untreated asthma could kill."

"Absolutely. Oh, I was full of theories for her obstinacy: convoluted aggression, death wish, you name it." He hesitated. "Then came the day Rusty drove us to Joshua Tree. He had just bought a used Jeep with his first advance for a screenplay. We loaded two coolers, one in the back with

Carolyn, the other with her knapsack in the storage area. With the four-wheel drive, we were able
to go a good distance on the unpaved roads. We
didn't stray far from the Jeep. It was too hot.
Rusty and I wore cutoffs, but she had these khaki slacks, she had to be careful because of sun
poisoning. We kept the hardtop on for shade. The
cacti were in bloom—"

"Cacti?" The desert? Her heart beat anxiously.
"Where is this place?"

"Joshua Tree National Monument. It's a national park, out in the middle of nowhere, past Palm
Springs. Joshua trees are a species of cactus with
branches. Carolyn had wanted to see them in
bloom." He gazed at her curiously. "What is it?"

"Nothing. Go on." No. Not Paul. The desert
vision of the woman hadn't happened yet. Right?
It had to be in the future.

"The Joshua trees were in bloom, large white
spectacular flowers. The nightmare started when
we decided to leave. Carolyn was in the back,
Rusty and me in the front. He had only been
driving a few minutes, lurching the Jeep over
this rutted trail, when she yelled for Rusty to
stop. I turn around, we're bumping along, and
see her crawling out the window. Rusty pulls to
a stop but she's already fallen out. I'm unlatching
the shoulder harness when red-hot needles stab
my legs. I don't know what the hell is going on,
all I can think of is getting to Carolyn. I'm out of
the Jeep, running, my legs on fire. She's sitting on
the ground and frantically rolling down her khaki
slacks. She can't kick them off over her sneakers.
She slaps at her thighs and calves, brushing away

black insects. Hornets. They keep stinging and stinging." He stopped, absorbed by the echoes of that long-ago day.

The telling made him pensive, but not distraught. Yet something twanged her sensory tripwires. Something.

If he had been responsible for Carolyn's death, had hidden her body in a desert grave, wouldn't he be more upset? But then, someone who'd do something like that would have to be psychopathic, devoid of normal guilt. "And she hadn't brought her antidote kit?"

"It's ironic. The bee-sting kit was in her knapsack. She had, for once, brought it and her aspirator. The irony is that the antidote was unusable. The syringe was cracked. I tried to inject what serum there was, but air and fluid bubbled out the crack."

"Did you leave her?"

"What? Leave her there? God, no. We injected what we could of the antidote. It took us close to an hour to drive out of the park, then another forty minutes to make it to the hospital in Palm Springs. By then it was too late."

A muffled ring sounded from the hall phone. It was half past ten. Bad tidings hasten in the candle hours. Suzanne rolled out of bed and hurried to the closet. While she shrugged on the robe, a tapping sounded at the door. "Phone for you, Suzanne." Allan's voice. He must have just gotten home. She tied the belt, opened the door, and stepped into the hall.

"It's Beverly," he said. He wore black Levi's and a black T-shirt, his skulking-in-the-woods-for-bats outfit. "I didn't catch the last name."

Kurt's wife. "Thanks, Allan. How did that little bat do at your parents'?"

His gaze dropped to her robe, then fell to the floor. A flush crept up his neck. He matched her gait. "Good. My folks are actually baby-sitting. They'll feed the pup until I pick it up this weekend." He stepped down the stairs.

Muffled noises came from the television in the family room. Kelly must be downstairs. "Allan?"

He stopped, blinked at the carpet.

"Thanks for . . . for the other day. Driving me to the hospital. Sticking around until Kelly was released, until Paul arrived. I . . . that was . . . well, thanks."

His lips quirked, he nodded, and continued down. "You're welcome."

She lifted the receiver. "Beverly?"

"Hi, Suzanne.. I'm sorry to call so late . . . but . . . I know this sounds silly. He was supposed to be home by nine. Kurt, I mean. It's so unlike him. I even let the boys stay up till nine . . . anyway, I can't reach Kurt at his office."

Tendrils of alarm coiled around Suzanne's throat. She had never been in Kurt's office. Could he be the man who suffers pulmonary arrest?

"I think he had a meeting with Paul tonight," Beverly was saying, "but I only get the answering machine at his number. Do you know where Paul is?"

"He's here. Hold on."

Paul stood at her bedroom door, wearing only his jeans. She beckoned to him. "Beverly wants to talk with you. Did you see Kurt this evening?"

He walked across the hall. "I left campus before six."

She handed him the receiver.

"Hi." He listened a moment. "No, I didn't have an appointment with him tonight." A pause. "I have a building key. The U's only a couple minutes from here. Why don't I drive over and have a look around?" Another pause. "It's no trouble. I'll call you from there."

When he hung up, Suzanne said, "I'm coming with you."

CHAPTER 13

Paul rapped his knuckles against the door, called out, "Kurt?" then placed his ear against the wood. The brass plaque read Humanities Division. Suzanne paced behind him. A reverberation, a resonance, strummed her neurons. She felt primed to explode. This was the reaction she had expected in Weis's office today, a vibratory recognition of the environment and man she had presensed. Did Kurt have an office with a view?

Paul knocked again. "I don't think he's in there."

She didn't sense that, either. But Kurt was here. Oh, yes, he was here. She had been in Kurt's mind, rather, in his body during the presensory experience, and the event in real time was near. "His car's in the lot. He's got to be somewhere in this building. Where else would he meet someone?"

"Let's try the psych department. His old office. It's two floors below this, but on the opposite corner of the building. The lake side."

A view of the lake. Reflections glinting off water. That's what she had seen. She pelted toward the red exit sign, yanked open the entrance to the stairwell. Her feet stuttered and she pitched forward, grasping the railing.

Paul caught up with her. "Slow down, Suzanne."

She threw herself down the steps two at a time. His keys in his jeans pocket jingled behind her.

He panted, "Kurt doesn't use the psych office anymore."

"Then we'll check every damn room in this building. He's here, Paul."

She burst through to the fifth level, leaving Paul behind, and ran to the west end of the corridor. Another brass plaque that simply said Psychology. She gripped the door handle, depressed the latch, not expecting it to be unlocked. She stumbled as the door swung easily, releasing a climate that was dry, stuffy, still. Dark.

Her fingers groped for a light switch, flicked. A secretarial area, two desks, typewriters, a word processor. No windows. A closed door to the far right. Even before she reached the interior office, a terrible sense of déjà vu, of worlds in collision, told her this was the place. She thrust the door open, bouncing it against the door stop. A dim liquid glow filtered in from the window. She fumbled for the light switch, inhaling an acrid scent. A round dial under her fingers. She twisted it on. Fluorescents flooded the room. Paul joined her, breathing heavily. Her gaze ricocheted off the dark brown blotter half off the desk to the framed photograph on the floor to Kurt's prone form, lying on his side, the black phone base partially hidden under his body. Blood spattered the collar of his white shirt.

They rolled him over onto his back, pushing the phone console and handset to the side. His skin was gray, warm to the touch, though the room was hot. His eyes were slits. His mouth hung partially open and from the odor Suzanne suspected he may have regurgitated into his lungs.

She bent down, close to Kurt's ear, and yelled, "Kurt, this is Suzanne. Open your eyes." No response.

"Suzanne"—Paul rested back on his heels—"he's—"

"Call 911," she snapped. She placed her ear directly above Kurt's mouth and nose, and listened. Nothing. She turned his head to the side; her hands came away sticky with blood from his hair. She opened his mouth and pulled his tongue forward. She hyperextended his head by tilting it back with one hand, supporting the back of the neck with her other hand. She listened again above his mouth and nose, praying the airway had been opened. Come on, Kurt. *Breathe*. Nothing. The sharp smell of digestive acids made her stomach churn.

Paul held the phone receiver to his ear, punching the plunger on the base. "I'm not getting a dial tone. I'm going to my office to call an ambulance." He took off.

She quickly placed her thumbs over Kurt's eyelids and lifted, examining his pupils. The black circles were large, dilated, and unresponsive to the bright fluorescents overhead. The failure of the pupils to react to light usually indicates that brain damage is about to or already has occurred. Last summer she and Paul had taken the Red

Cross CPR course, the first time for her, a refresher for Paul. You never assume it's too late.

With one hand supporting the back of Kurt's neck, she pinched his nostrils together, took a deep breath, and covered his entire mouth with hers. She blew into his mouth. She moved back and turned her head to see if his chest fell during expiration. It did. She felt air rush from his mouth. No obstructions in his throat. Blood from her fingers smudged his nose. She inflated his lungs three more times, but no spontaneous breathing occurred. She slid her fingers laterally into the groove between the trachea and the muscle at the side of the neck. No carotid pulse.

She shifted to his chest, placing the heel of one hand along the lower half of the sternum. She placed the heel of her other hand over the first and interlaced the fingers of both hands. Her arms were in a rigid line, her shoulders above his sternum. She depressed the sternum a couple inches, one hundred pounds of vertical pressure, then released. She counted each compression out loud, "One-one thousand, two-one thousand, three-one thousand . . ." The rhythm left no space for thoughts, but her eyes caught on the bruise at his inner arm. The injection site. A deep anguish tightened her throat. When she reached fifteen, she quickly shifted to his head and inflated his lungs twice.

After a few minutes, Paul returned. "I propped open the main door downstairs for the paramedics."

He knelt down on the opposite side of Kurt's body and readied his hands to take over the fatiguing job of compression. He counted along with her. " . . . thirteen-one thousand, fourteen-one thousand, fifteen-one thousand." She switched to Kurt's head and they changed to the two-rescuer ratio, one lung ventilation following five chest compressions. They performed in unison, but were unable to communicate. Kurt did not respond.

The paramedics came and she turned away, facing the window, unable to watch. Because she knew. She had known before she slammed open the door to this office. She touched her forehead against the glass. "I'm sorry, Kurt." Her breath fogged the surface.

Paul's hand brushed her shoulder. "It's not your fault." His voice sounded drained, but she had no energy to comfort him. "Suzanne, you couldn't have saved him."

Ah, but I could have. If I hadn't pulled back during the presensory experience of Kurt's death, I would have seen, sensed, much more clearly. I would have recognized the lake, the position of this building. I could have prevented his death. Of all the things she'd done and regretted, that knowledge was one that would—and should—permanently scar her soul. A mourning that would last forever. She gazed down at the lake. The lamplight glinting from the water was overlapped by internal images, the bruise at the crook of Kurt's elbow, his cyanotic bluish lips, the unresponsive pupils. *I will find your murderer*, she promised.

CHAPTER 14

"How was Beverly?" Suzanne slouched against the wall between the upstairs bedrooms, the receiver pinched between her ear and shoulder. Her hair was still damp from the shower. It was early Tuesday morning.

"In a state of shock." Paul had gone with the police to the Pooles' house last night. He was calling from his apartment. The parrot squawked in the background. "Lethargic. Confused. The officer had to ask everything two, three times. Beverly said that Kurt had an appointment yesterday for a blood test. Cholesterol. Apparently he had some symptoms of coronary artery blockage, heart trouble runs in his family. Anyway, that explains the marks on his arms."

Except that she knew differently. The killer had used the existing injection sites to mask a lethal dose. She couldn't tell the police, two guys right off the stage of *Dragnet,* that she'd presensed Kurt Poole's death. They didn't want speculations, much less a vision, from her, they wanted the facts, ma'am, just the facts. Their ears perked up when they found out she was a doctor, then drooped when they found out she was a scientist, not a physician. They had taken her statement, including her concerns about a drug overdose, but it was clear they didn't suspect foul play. A task for today: Convince the medical examiner to check for intravenous drug injection.

Paul continued. "The police think he had a heart attack or stroke, and that caused him to fall. There'll be an autopsy sometime in the next couple of days." He paused. "I keep running it through my mind, that he's dead, and even after last night, I can't believe it. Kurt was only forty-nine."

"What about the person Kurt was supposed to be meeting?"

"Beverly didn't know who it was."

"Last night, when she phoned here, she said she thought he was meeting you."

"She assumed that."

"Because . . . ?"

"I've been seeing Kurt professionally."

"Professionally?"

"For counseling. You see . . . when we argued, I did realize, usually after the fact, that your complaints were valid. Kurt was a sounding board."

Another thing she hadn't known about Paul. He had been seeing Kurt for counseling. "You discussed Carolyn with Kurt?"

"Yes. He knew her from USC—"

Neurons fired unwelcome speculations. What if Paul, drawn out by Kurt's gifted therapeutic manner, revealed his part in Carolyn's death, whatever that was? What if Paul regretted confiding in Kurt and decided to kill him? The chasm of the unknown was deep.

Paul was saying, "It's ironic that your not calling me back did more good than all the sessions with Kurt combined. Look, I know we have a lot more to discuss. This morning I'm driving down to San Diego State to pick up the daughter, Julie—"

"Janey."

"Right. Janey." He paused. "We could talk this morning, if you want to ride down to San Diego with me."

"I have to go into the lab. A new experiment." There's another thing she hadn't told him, her decision to do a heart-rate study on Vitalol. The list of things she was keeping from him was piling up.

She said, "But I was planning on taking off this afternoon, see if there was anything I might do for Beverly or the kids. Why don't you come with me?"

"I can't. I've booked a full afternoon of subjects for the presensory experiment."

Stalemate. "Paul, I need to know some things we didn't get to discuss. I need to know them now."

"Go ahead."

"How did those bees get into Rusty's Jeep?"

"A hornets' nest was under the front seat. We figured some kids, some hikers, dropped it in the back as a prank, and Carolyn's feet knocked it under the seat when she climbed in. But we never found out how the nest got there."

"And Carolyn. Where was she buried?"

"Forest Lawn. The mortuary that always advertises on TV."

"Do you have any pictures of her?"

"Probably. In storage. Suzanne, I'll tell you anything you want to know. I want to come over tonight. I want to be with you."

She hoped her suspicions were wrong. She needed him. "I'll be here."

She hung up. She hadn't asked him what was on the tip of her tongue. She hadn't asked where he was last night before he showed up on her doorstep at nine. Too many questions, too few answers. She dropped her glasses into the pocket of her robe and rubbed her face with her hands, a washing motion that, for some reason, soothed. Her palms covered her eyes and she thought, Whoever killed Kurt knew how to inject intravenously. However, threading a needle into a human-sized vein wouldn't be so hard, particularly if that human was unconscious. Perhaps more telling is that the killer had access to a syringe and some sort of pharmaceutical. No, that's not particularly helpful, either. Even with the security precautions at Bolton's labs, it wouldn't take a genius to steal the keys from Mariette and swipe a syringe and vial. Probably the campus was even looser. She needed clear impressions from presensing, no holding back. She had tried and tried the relaxation sequence last night after Paul dropped her off. She only managed to fall into a troubled sleep, haunted by Kurt's slack dead face and her own miserable guilt.

A touch on her wrist made her jump. She lowered her hands.

Kelly looked at her with concern. "Are you all right?"

She realized she was hunched over. She

straightened. "I'm fine."

"Maybe you shouldn't go into work today. Finding Dr. Poole like that, and you didn't get home till late."

"I have a lot to do"—she slipped on her glasses—"and I'd rather keep busy. Hey, you took off your bandage."

"Allan helped me last night. Do you think it's noticeable?" She turned. A barrette caught hair from both sides and centered the fall over the shaved area.

"You can't tell." Suzanne lifted her hair. A small skin-colored bandage covered the black stitches. "Looks pretty clean, too."

Kelly turned back to her. "Allan dabbed away most of that orange stuff"—she meant the antibacterial scrub—"and I washed sections of my hair. I didn't get the stitches wet."

"Did you use the bactericide?"

She nodded. "Patted it on like the doctor said. I'm surprised that there's so little discomfort. To my fingers, those stitches feel like wires poking out of my scalp." She studied her a moment, a mom-look. "You have circles under your eyes. You should at least eat something. Let me fix you some breakfast."

Kelly wanted to help. Suzanne considered, then said, "How about a yogurt drink?" She thought she could manage to swallow that.

"In the blender, you mean? What's in it besides the yogurt and orange juice?"

"Banana and a dash of vanilla."

Kelly started down the stairs. "Coming right up."

In her bathroom Suzanne followed the PosiBlu instructions. When she had a clean catch of urine, she added a few drops to the shallow depression on the test kit and slid the little drawer into a white rectangle. Life should be like this simple chemical test, you add the right ingredients and the color tells you yes or no. No misinterpretation, no confusion, no wondering. All in a sweet five minutes.

She was buttoning her white blouse when Kelly came in with the drink. "Thanks." Suzanne tasted the shake and pronounced it excellent.

"Last night," Kelly said, "Allan didn't get a chance to tell you some good news."

"I can use some good news."

"He said that Danny—he said you'd know who that was—he said that Danny would probably rent the room."

"Oh, great. Did he say when?"

"I don't know if he knew that yet. He had to leave early this morning, something about an observation he had to make for his research." She looked at Suzanne and her look said something. She opened her mouth, sighed, and angled her chin down, blond hair curtaining her expression.

"What?"

Kelly shook her head. "This isn't the right time." She turned to leave.

"Wait. Wait." Suzanne touched her on the arm, held her back. "What is it?"

Kelly whirled. "You don't tell me anything."

An echo of Suzanne's complaint to Paul. Talk about instant karma. "What do you want to know?"

"I didn't know you were having financial problems. Allan told me. It's not much, but I'm going to pay you half of whatever I earn." Kelly held up her hand before Suzanne could respond. "There's more. On Sunday we did the trial run. After the guy who was the subject gave his impressions of where I would be, the computer selected the Hughes plant on Alton. I walked there and when my watch reached twelve-thirty P.M. on the dot, I took two Polaroids of the building and recorded my sensory impressions on the microcassette recorder. Back at Paul's office I typed the transcript from my tape and put everything in his in-basket." Her voice came in a rush. "There was this manila folder on his desk. Inside was the transcript of the presensory experiment you did on Saturday. It was all there, the walkway, the bird, the dog, the blue car. Suzanne, you saw all that before it happened. You knew about the little girl's *legs*."

"I didn't say anything to you because you were upset enough after the accident. I don't quite understand myself what's going on."

"Can you do this presensing thing?"

"It seems so."

"Have you seen anything else, something else that's going to happen?"

"Nothing as clear as the car accident."

"But what, then?"

"Nothing to do with you."

"You don't trust me. What . . ." Her mouth hung open a moment. She licked her lips. "Did you know about Dr. Poole? Did you presense what happened to him? You acted so upset last night, much more anxious than Paul, after Mrs. Poole called. Like you knew something terrible had happened."

Suzanne didn't want to lie to her. "I can't say anything, Kelly, because . . ." Because Paul might be a murderer, and you're working with him. "There's something going on that I don't understand. I don't . . . I don't think you're safe here, Kelly."

"Safe? I don't understand."

"I think you ought to go back to—"

"No."

"—back to Utah."

"*No*." She gave a hard swipe at her hair. "You're trying to control my life like I'm a kid. I came to California to get away from that. Being the youngest, I've always had other people, *seven* other people, making decisions for me. I thought, I hoped that we would become friends."

"Hon, it's just that—"

"No. It's not fair that you keep things from me, and expect me to blindly do whatever you say." She blinked back tears. "I'm staying here. With you. I'm not going back to Utah."

"I just think that this could be dangerous."

"What could be dangerous? *What?*"

She didn't, couldn't, respond.

"Let me know when you decide I'm trustworthy." Kelly pivoted sharply and stalked out of the bedroom.

Oh, nice going, Reynolds. A class act. She propped her elbows on the counter and steepled her fingers over her eyes. She loved Kelly and wanted to protect her. Right now that meant keeping her in the dark, and causing her pain.

Was she wrong in not confiding in Kelly about the presensory experiences? Was she acting less like a friend and more like a parent? Parent. She spread her fingers wide and looked through them at her reflection. The test.

She rotated, still peeping through her fingers as though seeing something from the safe bars of a cage. The window in the white rectangle was no longer colorless, but a distinct watercolor blue.

Blue for yes.

CHAPTER 15

Suzanne eased her Buick into the Texaco and pulled over by the phone booths. The morning sun burnished a swinging sign announcing oil changes for $14.99. A navy Pontiac with a brilliant red Firebird emblem on the hood was at the pump. A bald man, his stick-thin white legs poking out of baggy shorts, held the nozzle to the Pontiac's tank. Two mechanics in overalls poked around the underbelly of a van in the bay. No sign of Elliot or his Toyota Camry.

She tapped her fingers on the steering wheel. Until Elliot called, the morning at Bolton had gone smoothly. Linda started the Vitalol/heart-rate study, the other technicians were progressing on the antiinflammatory work, she had finished up a New Drug Application report on a compound for dilating pupils. She'd been ready to leave when Elliot phoned and asked her to pick him up. She was certain he had said the Texaco on El Toro Road.

A figure stood behind the station's window, shadowy through the reflective glass with red block letters spelling Texaco. Was that him? She tapped the horn. The mechanics in the bay glanced over, but the person in the station didn't move. She put the car in reverse and guided it to the station door. It was Elliot, all right. He wore mirrored wraparound sunglasses with a brilliant purple-gold lens, blond hair sticking out every which way. His brown suit, white shirt, and paisley tie were rumpled. He had a cigarette in his mouth and was lighting it with the stub of another. He dropped the stub and seemed to be crushing it out on the floor.

She sounded the horn again and he glanced up, recognized her, and made his way to the passenger side. He slid in, along with an odor of tobacco and dried sweat. The smoke sent a nail of pain through her sinuses. Her stomach did a little flip-flop. The baby didn't like tobacco, either. She had crackers, the age-old remedy for nausea, in her purse.

"Would you mind holding off on the cigarettes? I've got a headache."

"Huh? Oh. All right." He tossed the cigarette out the window toward the pumps.

"Elliot."

"Thanks for picking me up."

"Elliot, there's gasoline out there."

"Shoot. Wait a minute." He got out, stomped on the cigarette, got back in.

"How come the lab answered the phone?" He combed his oily hair with his fingers, a middle-aged rock star refugee.

His appearance, topped by those bizarre shades, was definitely odd. She put the car in gear. "Seat belt." While he fumbled the strap over his chest, she said, "Mariette won't be in till later. Her son had surgery this morning."

"Oh, yeah, right, right, right."

She looked at him. He didn't know about Manuel. "Her son's going to be fine. The surgery went well."

"Good. Good."

Elliot was often intense, preoccupied, but never distracted like this. She merged with the traffic on El Toro Road. "Elliot, where's your car?"

"My car?"

"Your car wasn't at the Texaco. And you look like you've spent several hours in a wind tunnel."

"Yeah, it was windy. I walked."

"Walked from where?"

"You know, I was driving to work"—he lived in San Clemente, about ten miles south of El Toro—"and the traffic came to a dead stop. Gridlock. So I'm sitting in the car, thinking in a minute we'll start moving. Five minutes go by, then ten. People are getting out of their cars and standing on the freeway. A woman in front of me, wearing this maroon business suit, her hair braided Grecian style, she gets out and is talking on her car phone. The guy next to me climbs on top of his truck and stares. I get out. Cars are stopped as far as I can see. Nothing's moving. KABC doesn't have a report. We're stuck. I'm stuck, for no reason."

He was talking fast, a substitute for chain-smoking. "I hate to drive in the first place, and the traffic is always a mess. People drive like maniacs because of it. It's insane, when you think of it. Every day we drive on the freeways with a bunch of other people we don't even know, strangers in the control of lethal weapons. A slight misjudgment, and you're dead."

"A cheery thought." She was on the freeway now, heading north for the Irvine exits.

"So I started walking on the shoulder. Ever do that? Take a stroll on the interstate? There's all sorts of junk there, beer and soda cans, shoes, parts of a cappuccino maker, a doll's head without eyes, condoms. Why so many condoms? After about half an hour, I see the source of the problem. Up ahead are the California Highway Patrol, and they're letting cars by in a single lane. All over the road are thousands of shiny red rectangles. The pavement looks wet. There's a funny smell, like a gigantic burp."

"Where's your car, then?"

"You know what those red things were? Squashed cans of Coke. *Coke*. About another half mile there's a huge truck filled with cases of soda. Well, not filled anymore. This Hispanic was pointing into the truck and a CHiP officer was writing on a clipboard."

"Elliot, *where's your car?*"

"I left it." His expression was hidden by those goofy sunglasses.

"Where?"

He thumbed south. "Back there."

"No." She darted a look at him. "No. You don't mean you left your Camry on the interstate?"

"I'm not driving anymore. It's refreshing. I feel like I've taken control of my life."

"I can't believe it. You parked your car in the middle of the freeway. What is this, some orgy of self-destruction?" She changed lanes to reach the

Culver Boulevard off-ramp. "You know it's against
the law to abandon a vehicle. They'll impound your
car, fine you out the wazoo. God only knows what
other laws you've broken. Elliot, you could have
sold the thing and have been done with it."

"What are you doing?"

"We're going back. Maybe . . . I don't know. We
should go see if it's still there."

Fifteen minutes later she said, "You're sure this
is the area?"

He nodded.

A couple of miles ahead flattened Coke cans
littered the shoulder. Still no Toyota Camry. "The
police must have towed it."

"Actually, they could have driven. I left the
keys."

If he weren't his usual hyper self, she would
have thought he was drunk. "Then anyone could
have taken it. I hope the police did. Then you can
plead insanity and at least get the car back."

"It's just as well. Anyway, I thought this would
be easier. Like fate. Outside the office. The tox
guys answered the phone first, and I told Harold
where I was, and he offered to pick me up, but
then I thought, it's kismet."

She felt like her head was in a blender. "You
talked to toxicology? What does that have to do
with anything?"

"This wasn't my idea." He tapped out a cigarette and rolled it between his fingers. Tobacco
flakes cascaded down his shirt to his lap. "Weis
called me at home yesterday. He wants you gone.
Today."

CHAPTER 16

Beverly was almost unrecognizable, as though Kurt's death had changed the underlying bone structure. Pale flesh stretched over sharp planes of cheekbones, shoulders hunched chest into a concave shape, grief a spider that had drained all the juice from her body. Her brown hair hung lank and thin, without the usual curls. Though Beverly's hands trembled and her gray eyes were shot through with scarlet threads, her voice flowed in a diffuse, dreamy way. She seemed to be staring into times gone by. Suzanne wondered if she'd been given a sedative.

They sat on the window seat in the Pooles' study. They rested silently for a few moments, the family pictures and Kurt's diploma on the wall opposite them. This room, this house, exuded pheromones of pain. Suzanne felt helpless, her words inadequate things. It was perverse, expressing sympathy when she should have prevented Kurt's death.

Being passive had cost the life of a friend. She wouldn't commit that error again. Suzanne said, "Did you know Carolyn?"

The corners of her mouth dropped. Her eyes connected with Suzanne's. "Who?"

"Carolyn. Paul was engaged to her when he was in graduate school."

"No, I don't think so."

"She died from an allergic reaction to wasp stings."

"Oh, the girl who died." Her head seemed loose on her neck. "Awful. She was so young. That was years ago. When Kurt was a professor at USC." Her sentences were short tiring efforts. "He advised Paul and Rusty on their doctoral dissertations. But it was Rusty. Rusty was the one." Her eyes clouded. "We haven't seen him for a long time. I wonder if he's happy."

"What about Rusty?"

"Kurt thought Rusty would have been a good therapist for children, but then he wrote a screen-play—"

"I mean when you said that it was Rusty. I asked about Carolyn."

"Oh. Yes. That young girl. A terrible misfor-tune. She was an undergraduate. He'd bring her to our cookouts." Her tone sharpened. "We only had the three children then. Not all these. Kurt always joked that we should have plenty of spares."

Suzanne's scalp prickled. "Who brought Carolyn to the cookouts?"

"Rusty."

Rusty? "What about Paul?"

"The three spent a lot of time together. Carolyn was engaged to Rusty. Rusty loved kids. He and Kurt had that in common."

Beverly was confused, shock had mixed her memories. Had to be. Why would Paul say he was engaged to Carolyn if it wasn't true?

"Any one of them." Beverly nodded at the photographs. "All of them."

Suzanne looked at the pictures.

"The kids. Kurt called them the tribe." Beverly spoke with sudden intensity. "Any one of them."

"What?"

"Any one or all."

Suzanne waited.

"Kurt had a full load as department chairman, then another full-time job seeing clients. Then he got the humanities position. The income. We needed the income for the kids. He wanted a big family. If he hadn't been working so hard . . ." She raised her hands, clenched them, and jammed her fists hard against her cheeks. Her eyelids squeezed shut. Tears ran in rivulets around her knuckles. A wrenching cry escaped from her throat. She gulped for air. Anguish radiated from her. Suzanne scooted closer, reached an arm around the woman's stiff shoulders. Beverly fell into her embrace, wracked by pain. Suzanne rocked, her own eyes stinging. "I'm here," she said, again and again. "I'm here."

Time passed. Janey, the daughter from San Diego State, opened the study door and Suzanne waved her away. After a while Beverly composed herself. When she dried her eyes she seemed to have regained some clarity as well. "You're very nice," she said. "I'm okay."

She took a deep shuddering breath. "It's a terrible thing for a mother to feel, isn't it?"

"What's that?"

"What I said before. Any one or all." She glared at the photographs. Her eyes were fierce and bright. "I would trade any one of the kids or all of them to have Kurt back."

"Mom?" Janey stood at the study entrance.

Inwardly Suzanne winced. Had Janey heard?

"Mom," she said, her thin smooth face unreadable, "the Petersens are here."

"Okay." Beverly stood, brushing down her skirt.

Suzanne rose. The older woman caught Suzanne off-balance in a sudden fierce hug. "Thanks." The release was just as abrupt.

When Beverly reached the door, Janey traced fingers down her arm. She pulled away, a slight motion not lost on her daughter, and left the study.

Janey gave Suzanne a wistful half smile. She was about Kelly's age, wide brown eyes under thick dark eyebrows, crimped shoulder-length hair the color of burnished hickory nuts, and a small vulnerable mouth. She wore lace-edged black leggings under a large forest-green San Diego sweatshirt. "Paul drove me from San Diego this morning. He told me how you . . . how you tried to save my father."

"I'm sorry."

"All the way here, in the car, I kept thinking that I'm half an orphan now." She leaned against the desk and folded her arms. "Dumb." She sighed. "Paul didn't talk too much. He really loved my dad." She dashed a tear away with her fingertips and straightened. "I heard you ask about Rusty."

She must have heard her mother. She tossed back her hair.

"How is Rusty faring in Hollywood?"

"You know him?"

"I'll never forget him. I had a terrible crush on him when I was ten."

Suzanne nodded. Rusty charmed children. "Did you ever meet Carolyn?"

"Oh, yeah. I didn't like her. Competition. I'd planned on marrying Rusty myself when I got older."

It was too much to expect that both Janey and her mother were confused. So the question had to be asked: Why had Paul lied about his relationship with Carolyn?

Janey chewed her lower lip. "You know, I haven't seen Rusty since the fight."

"Fight?"

"When we lived in Long Beach, my bedroom looked out over the side of the house. It was Sunday night and I was asleep when I heard men's voices. I got up and looked out my window and there, in the dark with only a little light from the street, were Rusty and Paul. I couldn't make out what they were saying. I knew they were mad. Paul shoved Rusty, like he was saying something emphatically. Then Rusty threw a punch at him and they got into it. It was frightening. I didn't know what to do. Then Dad . . ." Her voice faded as her mind came back to the present. She coughed. "Dad broke them up."

"Did your father say anything about it?"

She shrugged. "Only that sometimes people do things they regret, and it was best not to talk about the fight. It was a grown-up thing, him trusting me." Her eyes glistened. "I respected my father. He was a good man." She glanced at the door to the hall where her mother had exited. "He was easy to love."

CHAPTER 17

Fuchsia bougainvillea covered the stone walls on either side of Rusty's yard. The back of the lot dropped off steeply, making the pool appear suspended in endless blue sky. Beyond and below his property lay smog-smudged Bel Air, simmering in the afternoon heat. Two white stone lions, paws raised, regurgitated water onto the wet sleek heads of three Hispanic children. The smallest, a girl with yellow water wings on her chubby arms, shrieked in delight as her older brothers ducked underwater and grabbed her feet.

Suzanne sat on a glider under a huge potted tree and balanced iced tea laced with NutraSweet on her thigh. A winged seed pod fluttered down onto her skirt. "There's a service on Thursday afternoon."

"Yeah, I know. Paul told me when he phoned." A woven palm Panama hat hung at the nape of Rusty's neck from a leather cord. Black micro-swim trunks, barely more than a glorified G-string, covered his loins. He was, as Suzanne's grandfather would say, one long drink of water. He propped his elbows on the lawn-chair arms.

"Hey, stay in the shallow end. *The shallow end.*"
He waited until they had done as he said, then
toed his sun-saturated tabby sprawled on the glossy pebbled aggregate. It rolled on its back from
side to side. "I'm not planning on going. I really
haven't had a lot of contact with the Pooles since I
left USC. Paul and Kurt were always much closer."

His voice kept the bogus British lilt. He didn't
sound very upset. "You don't mind talking out
here, do you? Just until Benita returns from the
grocer's." Benita, the mother of the children, was
his housekeeper.

She shook her head in the negative, sipped her
tea. Was he being deliberately offhand? He hadn't
asked why she drove a blessed hour and a half to
see him in the middle of a workday.

"I would like to come down to Orange County
and visit your lab. Maybe Friday. Then dinner,
you and Paul, my treat. Have your sister—Kelly,
isn't it?—have your sister join us."

"I've been fired, Rusty."

He gave her his full attention for the first
time. His astonished look was genuine. "No.
How? Aren't you under contract?"

"Not any more."

"What happens to the payback?"

"I don't know." She'd expected alarm to explode
like a grenade in her stomach, yet her financial
problems paled in significance compared to Kurt's
death. "I hope the lawyers will allow a revision of
the contract for a reasonable payment plan. Also,
I think they'll find they need me to wrap up a
few studies." How far would Linda get with the
heart-rate study before Elliot noticed?

"Why fire you then?"

"I'm against human testing of a flawed drug. The animals are having a side effect. Bolton's chief scientist doesn't want to hear it."

"This drug will be used on people?"

"I won't let it happen. I'm still submitting a report to the New Drug Application people. The whole point of animal screens is to discover exactly this sort of problem before a chemical is used on humans."

"Certainly it must be illegal to force you out under the circumstances."

"Unethical, at the least." After the weird drive back to Bolton, after Elliot canned her, he had sequestered himself in his office. Benson and Hedges smoke diffused from under his door. She hadn't been able to reach Weis before she left Bolton. She had, however, mailed her Vitalol heart-rate study and conclusions to the monitor at the Food and Drug Administration. More than enough evidence to postpone human testing until further qualifying studies were done. When Weis found out about that, it would push his loathing of her to new heights.

"You can still go by the lab. Call and ask for a tour by Linda, she's one of my—correction— used to be one of my technicians. She's sharp. She'll give you enough to make your screenplay credible." Right now she had other things on her mind. Her pulse quickened. "Rusty, I talked to Paul about Carolyn."

He nodded. Up came the index finger to stroke above his lip. What did that mean, that unconscious gesture? Hush? Quiet? Don't tell?

She watched him carefully. "You were engaged to Carolyn."

His expression didn't change, but his chin lifted. He slouched, squashing the Panama hat against the chair back, and laced his fingers over his stomach. "She was . . . yes. I knew her first, you see. She was my student when I was a grad assistant. We had a thing going for a while, a short while. And, you know, it fell apart. I rather suspected she'd been drawn to Paul all along." He squinted into the sun as though something odd had appeared in the sky.

"Is that why you and Paul had a fight?"

His face jerked to one side very slightly, slapped by an invisible palm. "A fight?"

"Janey, one of Kurt's children, saw you and Paul fighting outside late one night."

Hesitation. "She said we were fighting about Carolyn?"

"No," Suzanne admitted, "Janey couldn't hear."

"It's likely she saw us arguing, but not over Carolyn. Paul and I had many heated discussions. We were young psychology graduate students, passionate about our slightest opinions. Is toilet-training traumatizing? I said no, Paul said yes. Are slips of the tongue indicative of the unbridled id expressing itself? Paul said yes, I said no. He was, at that time, very neo-Freudian and a royal pain in the ass."

He paused for her reactions. After a moment he filled the void. "After we broke up, Paul and Carolyn dated, became engaged. They had a lot of problems, though. Mainly Paul wanting her to take care the way he wanted her to, and her being defiant."

"And you and Paul remained friends."

The slightest hesitation. "Yes."

"Why would Beverly and Janey only remember you and Carolyn?"

"I don't know. Maybe Carolyn and Paul hadn't been over to the Pooles' place as a couple."

"But surely Paul would have told Kurt."

"What does Paul say?"

Suzanne smiled. "Nice therapeutic technique." A therapist avoids intimidating "why" questions—Why haven't you asked Paul?—and uses less-threatening open-ended "what" questions. A subtle hint that Paul is the person to ask. She set her glass on the ground. "Paul told me about the day she died. I'd like you to tell me what happened."

"I feel responsible for opening Pandora's box. Mucking around in the past like this, you're sure this is right? Helpful, I mean, for you and Paul?"

"Please. It's . . . important. Something about this still bothers Paul." Something bothers me.

"He can't still be blaming himself."

"For what?"

His ersatz British accent faded. "We both blamed ourselves. It was awful. I'll never forget. Carolyn . . . she couldn't breathe. Finally she was unconscious, so I don't think . . . I hope she wasn't feeling anything."

"Wasn't she carrying a kit with injectable epinephrine?"

"God . . ." Rusty watched the kids for a moment. "Yes." He rubbed his face. "In the Jeep, in the

back with the cooler and other stuff, was her
knapsack. There was a yellow case, this small
plastic case, with the syringe with the stuff in
it."

Suzanne nodded. Epinephrine. "Go on."

"The syringe was cracked. Most of the fluid had
run out. He fitted the needle onto the syringe
anyway, hoping some might—"

"How did that syringe break?"

"God only knows. We threw everything into the
back of the Jeep. She must have tossed her knapsack in there, then we loaded the cooler—it was
heavy, we had lots of beer, cola, water, ice."

"How . . ." She stopped. "Who got the antivenom
kit?"

"Paul. I was with Carolyn. She was choking,
clawing at her throat. Her panic was terrible."

"Paul brought the kit, this plastic case, to you
and when you opened it, the syringe was broken."

"Not . . . no. He told me it was broken, then
showed me the damaged syringe."

She didn't like the direction of her thoughts,
but they went there anyway. What if Paul planted
the nest, broke the syringe? But why, why, why
would he want to kill a woman he loved? "How
many times was she stung?"

"I don't know. Not that many. Maybe six, ten
times. A dozen. It happened so damn fast."

"Who injected Suzanne?"

"Paul."

She was silent a moment.

He said, "What is it?"

"What is it that Paul's not telling me?" A rhe-
torical question. She thought of something else.

"How would a hornets' nest get into your car?"

"There were a few other hikers at the park. Not many. Someone might have tossed it in the back seat as a joke. Or it could have been a kid from my neighborhood, pitching in the nest before I left Venice Beach. I had a tiny bachelor's flat at the time, parked my Jeep on the main drag. Didn't always lock it."

"You would have been stung as soon as you got in the car. How could a hornets' nest be undetected all the way from Venice Beach to Joshua Tree?"

"When Paul and I were kids, we took wasps' nests and chilled them in the fridge, then planted them in a classroom or somebody's locker. They'd go into a dormant state for quite some time." He shrugged. "Might have been something like that."

Paul could have placed the chilled nest in the Jeep.

"You drove from Joshua Tree to the hospital in Palm Springs."

"No. Paul drove. I knew CPR. At that time he didn't."

Last night flashbacked, her hand cupping Kurt's chin, Paul's hands on Kurt's sternum. "He knows it now."

Rusty nodded. "It grieved him that he didn't know what to do. He started Red Cross classes after that.

"So I stayed in the back with her. I should have been driving, but I couldn't do both. We got lost."

"In Joshua Tree?"

"It was a mess, I had driven in too far. Paul couldn't find the main roads. I'm not sure I would have remembered. In any case, the emergency-room doctor said she'd never seen such a severe reaction. She said even if we'd been able to dose her with the serum and reach the ER within thirty minutes, an impossibility, it would have been too late."

Anaphylaxis through insect-sting challenge could be a brutal though quick way to die.

"Did you . . . did . . . was there an open casket?"

"No." He shook his head. "The swelling was horrific. Her family knew she wouldn't have wanted to be seen that way."

"How do you know her body was interred?"

"How . . . ? Suzanne." His forehead crinkled. "I don't understand where you're going with these questions."

It seemed unlikely that Paul had returned to Joshua Tree and buried Carolyn. Besides, the visions were clairvoyant, of the future, right? Why would she suddenly be seeing the past?

A child's shrill brief scream ripped through her thoughts. The little girl, her lavender swimsuit hiked up over one small tanned haunch, splashed under the lions. When she noticed them watching, she shrieked again for their benefit. Her brothers were already out of the pool, blotting their legs and arms with large white beach towels with the Paramount logo.

Rusty stood. "Sylvia, I think that's enough swimming for today." The child obliged, climbing carefully up the pool steps. She came to Rusty, who pulled off the water wings and wrapped a towel around her.

My instincts brought me here. Why? "What is it about Carolyn—"

"How about a rousing game of hide-and-seek?" Rusty's voice interrupted.

The kids loved the idea. They jumped on spring-loaded legs and cried, "I'm it! I'm it!"

Suzanne thought he'd send them off to hide, but Rusty said, "I'll be it this time. You count to twenty. Slow." He waggled his finger at the children. "No cheating, all right? Suzanne's going to make sure you don't cheat." A shallow smile.

He turned and walked into the house. She stared after his minuscule butt under the stretch of black fabric. What the devil is going on? They were in the middle of a conversation.

The boys counted to twenty, the girl chiming in with "One . . . one . . . one . . ."They rushed through the French doors into the kitchen, their bare feet slapping the marble tiles.

Suzanne reviewed the pieces, seeking a pattern. What I have is a woman's body in the desert and a man coming to bury her, Carolyn at the national park dying of anaphylactic shock, Kurt Poole killed by injection. Had the irritable clerk answering at the medical examiner's actually checked that her suspicions were in Kurt's file? And why had she experienced the auto accident of the little girl? That didn't connect with the others at all.

The kids returned. The tallest boy, about ten or eleven, said, "We can't find Mr. Ames."

"We looked everywhere," the other boy added.

"You help us."

Three pairs of large dark eyes stared at her with earnest concentration. Sylvia wiggled her fingers, the nails with chipped pink polish, into Suzanne's hand. She allowed herself to be led into the kitchen. Rusty's house was a small, though expensive, piece of real estate. How many hiding places could there be for a grown man in a three-bedroom rambler?

The decor in the kitchen, like the rest of the house, was ultramodern, stiff and precise as Rusty's hairstyle. He believed in rampant consumerism, provided the items were white. No place to hide in the whitewashed oak cabinets of the kitchen. The white tiled counters held a juicer, a computerized food scale with readouts for weight and calories, an espresso machine, a pasta maker, a gelato churner, a bread baker. Elongated brown pods filled a tall glass jar, exuding the fresh sweet scent of vanilla. A huge inset refrigerator with clear glass doors was next to a closed pantry. No Rusty among the caviar tins and artichoke hearts. The kids followed, their chocolate-brown eyes wide in anticipation.

She peered behind the big screen television in the bedroom converted to a media center, under the mirrored platform bed in the master, even in the wheeled trash cans in the garage.

Where the heck was he?

She returned with her silent crew to the vaulted living room and plopped onto the butter-smooth white leather sofa. On the glass coffee table was a photo of a young brunette laughing over her shoulder, eyelids at half-mast over crystalline blue eyes that seemed to follow you, full glossy lips showing just above the rise of her shoulder, a yellow silk blouse slipping down her back. A publicity photo, one of Rusty's starlets. The only photograph, she realized, in the whole house.

Next to the photo was a manuscript with a pale yellow cover, the drilled sheets held together by brass fasteners. A screenplay. "Nightblood by Rusty Rydalch-Ames" was typed on the cover.

The three kids watched her soberly. "Where is he?" the oldest boy asked.

"A very good question. Let's listen."

An unhealthy silence.

"Okay," she called out loudly. "You win, Rusty. We give up."

The kids echoed, "We give up, we give up."

The little girl added, "Come out, come out, wherever you are."

Even when the children's mother hauled in groceries, Rusty didn't emerge from his hiding place. He had vanished into thin air.

CHAPTER 18

Suzanne turned onto Harbor Boulevard, pointing the Buick in the direction of the freeway. Night had fallen while she and Kelly talked in the Japanese restaurant, but this part of Costa Mesa didn't succumb easily to the dark. Spotlights scythed the night, swooped from automobile dealerships on both sides of the street, clowns danced with big pointing hands, strings of balloons floated, stuffed animals perched on the hoods of cars, salespersons lurked like hungry vampires.

This frantic commerce was unsettling, as though motivated by fear, as though time were running out. She braked at the red light near Fedco. Her sister stared straight ahead, twirling a strand of taffy-colored hair around her finger. Thinking.

Kelly bent a leg under her, rotated to the left, her knee nudging the thin brown purse between them. She pulled the seat-belt harness away from her shoulder. "I agree with you that those desert presensory experiences, Dr. Poole's and Carolyn's death and the way Paul and Rusty behave is suspicious, but . . . I just can't see Paul as a murderer. I mean, I've worked with him and he's . . . kind. He's, you know, *nice*. And now he's willing to discuss everything with you. Right?"

"I hope so. I'll know better after he and I talk tonight." Suzanne hadn't told Kelly about the pregnancy. She wanted to tell Paul first.

"Plus," Kelly said, "these presensory experiences are clairvoyant, not . . . I don't know what you'd call it . . . not of the past, anyway. They're predictive."

Suzanne smiled. Her sister was picking up some vocabulary from Paul's research.

"Carolyn died years ago," Kelly continued. "Maybe there's some other reason Paul and Rusty acted so weird. You know, like wild sex orgies, drugs."

"If so, then we're still left with the man in the desert coming to bury the body of a woman. If that's yet to come, who is the man? Who is the woman?"

"You've tried the presensory exercise, but it didn't work?"

"Last night, after we found Kurt, I didn't have any luck. I was too upset and exhausted." The light switched to green. Suzanne eased the Buick forward. "It doesn't seem to be an ability that I control. I can't make it happen when I want. Not yet, at any rate."

"Hmm." She pulled on a lock of her hair. "You do the relaxation sequence?"

"Right. Last night I fell asleep."

"How do you focus? What do you ask yourself?"

"What do you mean?"

"You have to give your mind a command, something to link to. I've been typing my own transcripts after I go to the site the computer chooses.

After I'm done with that, Paul allows me to read the transcripts of his session with the subject. He always asks leading questions, where is so-and-so going to be at three o'clock, keeping the subject oriented on the future."

Suzanne was thunderstruck. "That's it. *That's it*. I haven't been trying to guide myself to a specific person or incident. Not like Paul did on Saturday. He guided me to that time and place."

Kelly nodded, obviously pleased. "You need to focus. I could help. I could ask the questions and then, if you seem like you're getting scared, like with Dr. Poole's death, I could stop the session."

"That has to be the difference."

"What difference?"

"I kept turning the presensory experiences over and over in my mind. A little girl killed by a car, a killer coming to bury a woman in the desert, Kurt Poole's death. There must be a connection other than death itself. People are dying everywhere all the time. Why was I zapped by these three specific instances? There had to be a connection, but the little girl didn't seem to . . . fit, somehow."

She thumped the steering wheel. "Now I see the difference. I was guided specifically to that accident. It isn't connected to the others. But Kurt's death and the woman in the desert . . . I feel something about those. A resonance. And those are the two that came to me without focusing."

"The synchronicity Paul talks about. How events that appear unrelated actually have a connection."

Suzanne nodded. "I think the killer of the woman in the desert is the same man who killed Kurt

Poole." Suzanne drove the car onto the freeway entrance ramp. "If the murderer is someone I know, then the list of suspects is somewhat limited. Paul, Rusty, the men I work with at Bolton, Allan—"

"You know Allan was in reform school?"

Suzanne darted a look at her sister. "What?"

"A stabbing. He stabbed some kid at his high school with a kitchen knife."

"Great. Wonderful." She merged into the freeway traffic, keeping to the right lane. "Since when is Allan baring his soul to you?"

"We talk when Arsenio's on. But I don't see Allan as the murdering type, either. He was a kid when that happened."

He wasn't a kid when he shook Danny like a sack of potatoes. "How much a kid?"

"I don't know. A senior in high school."

"Seventeen, eighteen. Maybe a year younger than you." Allan and his bats and his fierce unexpected temper.

"Don't forget the neighbors. How about that strange guy who walks his dog on the bridle path at midnight? Or who's the man about four doors away who clips his lawn with scissors—"

Kelly stopped, clapped her hand to her mouth.

Suzanne saw the movement out of the corner of her eye. "What?"

She dropped her hand and faced Suzanne. "I didn't know."

"Know what?"

"That it was a secret. Oh, Suzanne," she wailed, "I told him."

"Told who what?"

"I told Paul that I thought you'd had a presensory experience of Dr. Poole's death. I didn't know you wanted it kept a secret. What if Paul's the one?"

Suzanne turned her head and said, "It's all right—" when a crack resounded through the cab. A rush of air, small and inconsequential, blew by Suzanne's forehead. The driver's side window was completely crazed, framing a small round hole. The spidery fractures obliterated the view. Her mind momentarily refused to compute. The tiny hole, the fractured safety glass, the hole, the glass. *A bullet.*

"Kelly," she yelled, "put your head down! Put your head *down*!"

"What was that? What happened?"

Suzanne reached over to shove her sister's shoulder, yanking the wheel, and the Buick fishtailed. She let up on the gas, corrected the steering, desperate to duck down herself, yet she couldn't risk careening into other lanes. A second bullet twanged through the metal of the fender, pinging against the engine block.

Damn damn damn damn damn damn damn damn *damn*.

The San Diego Freeway was always a zoo and Tuesday nights were no exception. Cars and trucks sped by. The driver behind sounded his horn, flashed his brights, annoyed at the Buick's deceleration. Suzanne jerked the wheel, bouncing the car onto a downsloping shoulder. She stomped the brake and the car slammed to a stop, throwing their torsos against locked seat belts. Kelly's purse lay on top of her feet. Her heart tried to climb up her throat. She unlatched her seat belt and grabbed Kelly's face with both hands. "Are you all right?"

"Yes," her voice came in gasps, "but what—"

"Bullets. Someone was shooting at us." Suzanne flipped on the dome light. Her hand, seeking evidence of a wound, trembled down Kelly's arm. The tan sweatshirt was unmarred. "People often don't know when they've been shot. Remember President Reagan? A ricochet hit him?"

"I'm okay." Her eyes were nightmare-wide. "I don't . . . I'm sure I'm not hit."

"Where did that bullet go? It must have hit something in here."

Kelly thumbed toward the door on her side. The window was rolled down. "I think I felt it go out that way. You know"—she laughed, a ragged sound—"in one window and out the other."

Cars zipped by. For the few seconds they'd been stopped, a hundred cars had sped along, unseeing and uncaring. No glowing red taillights of a vehicle stopped up ahead, the shooter coming to finish the job. Whoever it was, at sixty-plus miles per hour, was long gone.

Warm odors of steak teriyaki wafted from the tipped container at Kelly's feet. Suzanne righted the small box. A coil of liquid, dark and viscous, stained the floor mat. Her sister's sandals moved away from the fluid.

Suzanne's heart beat in quick tempo. A big rig fled by them, the car shuddered in its wake. Forces as immutable as the rotation of the planet were shifting, settling into place, and she, Suzanne, was at the core.

She cupped her sister's chin in her palm. "It would kill me if I let something happen to you." She picked up Kelly's purse from the floor, dropped it on the seat, then slid out from the driver's side, legs shaking. Her eyes studied the crumbled glass as though some answer might be deciphered there like the random patterning of tea leaves. She ran her hand along the fender and found the other hole, neat and round and perfect. The traffic ten feet away sent jittery waves of air laden with fumes.

"A drive-by shooting?" Kelly stood on the downhill side. "Is that . . . ?"

Kelly and Suzanne exchanged looks.

Knowing looks. This wasn't a random act of violence.

Suzanne banged her fist on the hood. A creature deep in her howled. She was getting close, too close, and the killer was putting a stop to it. His intent was as intimate to her as the lion's breath upon the deer. She had moved around in his mind just as she moved through Bolton's laboratory, past equipment, to the animal rooms, and a shocking question occurred to her. Did the killer feel her presence in his thoughts? Was she a haunting, leaving a trace of disturbance like gossamer, like the beat of a moth's wing, like prickles of heat before the onset of fever?

What if he was circling around even now, coming back to level a gun at them while they stood here, easy targets?

"Suzanne, shouldn't we report to the police? I mean, tell somebody—"

"Get back in the car."

Kelly obeyed.

Once behind the wheel Suzanne keyed the ignition and it growled, already on. She pushed down the turn signal lever and spun wheels getting into the traffic. If she couldn't outrun her demons, by God, she'd turn and fight them. First, she'd arrange for Kelly to be as far from this as possible. Then she'd find out the truth about Carolyn, whatever that took. And then—

"Suzanne, where are we going?"

To the right glide slope indicators and green threshold lights illuminated the John Wayne Airport runway. A jumbo jet skimmed over the freeway, coming in for a landing. The next exit was for MacArthur Boulevard and for the airport. She guided the car onto the off ramp.

"Suzanne?"

The blacktop coiled to the right. She rolled the car to a stop at the MacArthur Boulevard traffic light. "I can't risk your safety."

"What do you mean?"

She pressed her lips together. She would not allow anything to happen to Kelly. Let the killer come to her, Suzanne, but not to this young woman who, in spite of her eighteen years, was still a little sister. Still her baby sister.

"Suzanne, what do you mean?"

The light changed and Suzanne turned the Buick left onto MacArthur Boulevard.

"Are we going to the police?" The peaked skylights of the John Wayne terminal were ahead and to the right. "The airport? Hey, wait a minute—"

"Kelly, listen—"

"No."

"Someone shot at us. Someone just tried to kill me, and he wouldn't have cared if he killed you, too."

"Making me leave doesn't solve anything. I can help—"

"It solves something. You'll be out of danger."

Kelly crossed her arms and turned away.

Her sister's anger and frustration didn't matter. What mattered was getting her on a flight home to Utah.

When the Buick reached the entrance to the parking structure, Suzanne pulled up to the ticket dispenser at the crossarm, swung open the door to punch the red button and grab the stub. The crossarm angled upward. She drove through. She found a spot near the terminal entrance and parked the car.

Kelly said, "I'm not going."

Suzanne pocketed the keys, then withdrew her wallet from her jacket pocket. She peered inside. American Express, don't leave home without it. "Okay." She tucked the wallet back into her pocket.

"Kelly?"

Her sister shifted position more toward the right door.

"Kelly, I can't protect you if you're here."

No response.

Suzanne slipped from the car and walked to the passenger side. She pulled open the door. Kelly rotated away. Suzanne reached over her and unlatched the seat belt.

"Don't you see, Kelly, I can't stop this. It's going

to happen, the killer, the desert, the woman—"

"I'm not going. You need me."

"I need you to be safe."

"You're not giving me a chance. You're deciding for me."

"This is not a game." She picked up Kelly's purse from the seat and held it out to her. "Come on."

"No."

Suzanne grasped Kelly's arms and pulled her from the seat. Her sister resisted, but her smaller size was a disadvantage. Once Suzanne had her out of the car, Kelly clutched Suzanne's lapels and said, "You can't make me." She became a dead weight, pulled Suzanne off-balance and down with her to the grease-covered concrete. Suzanne's knee rasped against the ground, the loosening sensation of nylon tearing. Kelly lay completely prone, her hair fanned out over the ground. Suzanne struggled to sit up, but her sister held firm. Grit rasped against the smooth fabric of her jacket.

She tried to pry Kelly's fingers loose. "I can't believe you're doing this. Of all the—"

Kelly yelled, her voice outraged, "I can't believe *you're* doing this!"

"Let *go.*"

"No!"

"You have to leave, Kelly. It's not safe here."

"No."

"Hey. *Hey.* What's going on here?" a man's voice said.

Their heads swiveled at the sound.

A tall, thin man with a lopsided smile stood near

the trunk of the Buick, looking down at them. He uncertainly slung a black garment bag over his shoulder. "What do you ladies—"

Kelly let go of Suzanne, sat up, and hollered, *"Beat it, this is none of your damn business."*

His chin moved back as though struck. He cocked his head, raised his hand in a brief mock salute, and walked away.

Kelly blinked. "I'm not leaving. You were the oldest, you had an easy escape. You don't know what it's been like for me." Her lip trembled.

"An easy escape?"

"From home. From them. From Mom and Dad, from Mark, Matt, Doug, and Jim. From me. You were the oldest. No one told you what to do. Everyone told me what to do. It's like by hanging on to me, they were hanging on to something else. They suffocated me."

She rubbed a fist into her eye, smearing black on her cheek. "I'm not going back."

Suzanne thumbed at the spot, succeeded in spreading it. "I guess you're not."

CHAPTER 19

The white stucco California-style house, its beveled glass windows sparkling, glittered against the velvet night sky. It was, Suzanne thought, a place for women in long gowns, men in tuxedos, good fairies, and magic wands. Nellie Gale Ranch, this bedroom community of equestrian estates on multi-acre lots, was only ten minutes from Suzanne's house, but eons away in terms of prestige and value.

"Look at that." Kelly pointed to the north side of the house where a large turret reached for the sky. "What's that make you think of?"

" 'Rapunzel, Rapunzel, let down your golden hair.' "

Kelly grinned. The glow from the driveway lamps reflected in her green eyes. After the tense drive from the airport, on the lookout for drivers brandishing weapons, it was good to see her smile. Suzanne stopped the Buick inside the wrought-iron gate, to give them both a little time to gawk and adjust.

Bricks in patterns of intersecting ovals paved the circular drive. The putting-green lawn was bull's-eyed with a spotlighted fountain, the waters rippling in sheaths over glittering stones. A fine mist swirled and cocooned the Malibu lights. Suzanne killed the engine. Over the splash of the fountain came the cricker and ghee of insects. The effect was one of a tropical sultry world, an oasis in the desert climate of California. A haven.

"Is this friend of yours, Olivia, rich or something?"

"Apparently so. Or maybe her husband came from money."

"He's running for the Senate?"

"The House." A fresh scent, wistful as a memory, swirled in with the breeze. Honeysuckle. Her childhood playmate, George, had shown her how to peel away the white petals and to touch her tongue to the honey-sweet nectar.

A strange sensation flooded over the memory. She felt the hot winds of something racing toward her at terrific speed, a chasm yawning at her feet, the winds pushing, pushing. It was close. Very close.

She keyed the ignition and steered around the driveway. Two immensely wrinkled and worried-looking brown dogs rowfed from the tiled steps. As her car rolled under the arched portico, they ducked behind a huge white planter of a tall broad-leafed palm. She removed the keys as Olivia stepped out of the house. The dogs, grinning up at her, skittered on the tiles to rub against her black slacks. Their rears whipped from side to side.

Olivia hurried down the stairs. When Suzanne stepped out of the car, the older woman embraced her. "Your call," she said in her raspy voice, "had me worried as hell."

The frizzy coil of the braid around Olivia's head brushed Suzanne's cheek. Chlorine tang. "I know this is an imposition. Not only did I forget about meeting you at the pool this afternoon—"

"Not a problem. No one is thinking straight today, not after Kurt's death." She released Suzanne.

Suzanne felt the appraisal of those quick hazel eyes, their taking in of her rumpled clothes, then the fractured window. "We have a lot to talk about. Olivia, let me introduce my sister, Kelly."

Olivia turned to Kelly, whose smile was uncertain and strained. Kelly held out her hand, but Olivia hooked an arm around her shoulders and squeezed. "You have no idea what a relief it will be to have some company. My husband seems to live in Sacramento more and more, and I loathe being alone in this house." She guided her to the steps. "It's too damn big for one person."

It was just the right thing to say. The tense edges to Kelly's expression softened. When the three of them climbed the tiled steps, the two dogs wiggled furiously and made sounds that were a combination bark and cough. "Ufff. Ufff."

Kelly asked, "Are they friendly?"

"Friendly? Hell, yes. Too friendly. The only way they'd overcome a burglar is by drowning him in drool."

Kelly reached out a hand. One dog positioned his head under her palm and she patted him, his eyes rolling in ecstasy. She stopped and he nudged her hand, his wrinkled face pleading. She laughed. "I think they're cute."

Olivia shook her head, though her gaze on the animals was tender. "You're being kind. Butt ugly is more like it." She grasped the brass handle and pulled open the door for Kelly.

"I can't stay too long," Suzanne said. Paul, after working up the transcripts from this afternoon's sessions, had planned on visiting the Poole family, then going to Suzanne's house. He was probably already there. And this thing, this whirling vortex, hissed in her ear.

"A few minutes"—Olivia gestured for her to enter—"you need to relax for a few minutes."

The dogs squeezed through at the same time as Suzanne and stomped on her feet with amazing weight. The two pooches took off to the left, their toenails scrabbling on the whitewashed oak floors. "We'll have to go to the kitchen," Olivia said wryly, "and give them their biscuits."

Suzanne and Kelly followed her to a massive great room with an elevated round fireplace. Its mirrored chimney reached to the top of the vaulted ceiling where stained-glass skylights alternated with exposed oak beams. The back wall consisted almost entirely of tall arched windows that, in daylight, must offer a view of the ocean ten miles away. Glass and light and reflections, punctuated here and there by modern sculpture on pedestals.

After the dogs wolfed down large biscuits, Suzanne and the two women settled in cream-colored leather chairs. A vibrant Oriental rug in blues, greens, and beige covered the oak floor.

The coffee table was an oak trunk, its white surfaces carved with intricate marsh scenes of waterfowl. Hand-blown glasses, irregular and rimmed in pale blue, sat next to a matching pitcher of iced orange-banana juice. The dogs sprawled like road kills at their feet.

Olivia poured juice into a glass and handed it to Suzanne. "Okay. Why do you two look like you've been rolling on the ground? What happened to the car window?"

"First of all, I don't want anyone to know Kelly's here. That includes Paul, Rusty, the Pooles, Allan, everyone."

"What about classes tomorrow?" Kelly asked. "Wednesdays are my full days. And I don't have any of my stuff, clothes and things."

Olivia filled another glass and gave it to Kelly. "My stepdaughter, who's at Yale getting her doctorate and falling in love, has a wardrobe, a veritable store of things in the tower. We'll have no trouble finding clothes for you. And we've got one of those cute Daihatsus, a Rocky? Like a little Jeep, an automatic. Jade and gray, cute. It sits idle too often, needs to be driven. You can use that."

Kelly's cheeks pinked. She swirled the ice cubes in her glass. "I feel like I'll be too much of a burden."

"No," Suzanne said sharply, "this is not an option. You have to stay here. There's no other choice."

Olivia sat on the edge of the chair, legs apart, elbows on her knees. "Tell me what's going on."

Suzanne cleared her throat, swallowed some juice. "I told you yesterday about the little girl and the car accident, and the desert premonition." She described Paul's and Rusty's reactions to questions about Carolyn, her presensations of Kurt's death, finding his body, Kelly's input about focusing, and the gunshots on the freeway.

"You have to notify the authorities," Olivia said immediately.

"And tell them what? That I'm psychic? That I have visions of a dead woman somewhere in a desert?"

Kelly nodded. "Report the shooting, at least."

"It won't do any good. And I don't have time." Suzanne stood. "I have to go." She bent over Kelly and kissed the top of her head.

Her sister reached for her hand. "What if it's Paul?"

"Then . . . then it's Paul. It's coming. All I can hope to do is head things off."

Olivia and Kelly spoke at the same time. "What's coming?"

"A feeling . . ." She bit her lip. "A pressure is building up. All the things I've sensed, they fit a pattern and that pattern is nearly complete. I'll talk to Paul. Try focusing on the man, the desert location." She made a cutting gesture with her hand. "I have to go." She crossed the great room, the mirrored chimney shot back her reflection. Olivia followed.

At the door Olivia said quietly, "I'll take care of her. You don't need to worry." She leaned closer. "Did you take the pregnancy test?"

Suzanne nodded. "Positive. On top of every-thing else. I know, I know." Her mouth quirked, failed to smile. "It could be worse. I could be in Belize."

"Yeah. Right. Could be worse." But Olivia's words didn't match her worried expression.

CHAPTER 20

Suzanne parked her car on the street in front of her house. No sign of Paul's car. Allan's truck was positioned nose-first in the driveway. The garage door was open. Fluorescent lights revealed Allan working under the hood. The open bed faced the sidewalk, its gate showing the white block letters TOY against the brown finish. Allan had told her, when he first rented the room, that the previous owner had painted over the last three letters of Toyota. She had smiled at the time. He had wanted to make sure she understood that he wouldn't have done something so . . . what? Frivolous? Childish?

Destructive?

Her thoughts glided off into images, Allan wielding a knife, Allan hauling a man completely off the floor and holding him there. Paul handling a cracked syringe, injecting subcutaneously into the flesh of a dying young woman. Fingers holding another syringe, guiding the needle through an existing puncture wound at the crook of Kurt's arm.

The hurricane whirl of the thing approaching her.

Closer now.

She left the car, took a few steps on the sidewalk, and walked alongside the truck. She circled around the grille. The green hose, coiled and turgid, hissed at her feet. An orange extension cord snaked up to the underside of the hood, ending in a caged lit bulb. The crown of Allan's head gleamed under the light. Black smears across his white undershirt. He dipped a toothbrush into a plasticfoam cup and scrubbed a white paste onto a battery terminal. A blue-green froth bubbled. Grease smudged his fingers. A scent of hot motor oil.

"Allan."

His head came up. "Hi. Didn't hear you." His gaze flickered away from her to the battery. He dropped the toothbrush in the cup. "You just missed Paul."

A surge of adrenaline. "Did he say if he was coming back?"

"He didn't say anything to me when he left." He gestured toward the hose. "Would you spray the terminals? My hands are gunky."

She lifted the hose, aimed the pistol nozzle, and squeezed the control lever, rinsing off the blue-green foam. A puddle formed near her feet under the chassis.

"That's good."

She released the trigger. "Was Paul here for a while?"

"I don't know. I didn't get in till, what? Nine, I guess. He was already here."

Over an hour ago.

The engine ticked like a bomb as it cooled. "Wish I knew why these terminals corrode so much." He set the cup on the air filter cover, and pulled a smudged rag from the back pocket of his jeans. He blotted the top of the battery, then wiped his hands on the rag. "I tried calling you at work today, but whoever answered said you weren't available." He pressed one palm against the fender and lifted his gaze. "Suzanne, I'm sorry about your friend. Professor Poole. It must have been terrible to find him like that." His words were simple, sincere.

"Thanks, Allan."

He set the rag on the windshield-fluid reservoir.

"There's something I wanted to ask you—"

"I know. It's taken care of." He pinched open the red cable clamp and fitted it over the positive terminal. "Danny's coming over this weekend to look at the room. If he likes it, he'll want to move in the first of the month."

She had been going to ask him about the stabbing, but this news surprised her. "How did you manage that?"

"Took him out to eat, apologized. Promised it would never happen again." He wiggled the clamp.

"Is that true?"

He looked up at her.

"What's this about you stabbing someone?"

"Oh, yeah. I told Kelly . . ." He wiped his palm across his stomach. "There's a bit of a story attached."

"I'd like to hear."

His thin eyebrows tented. "You don't need to worry about . . . about my flying off the handle, Suzanne."

"Tell me."

"I was a boy. High school. Fifteen years old. Then I was a little guy, short, puny. Puberty seemed to be passing me by. Everybody picked on me. Especially Manfred. Manfred. That was his name."

He worked the black cable onto the negative terminal. "Fit him, too. He was solid, biceps out to here, not tall, but built like a throwback to Cro-Magnon. Tiny deep-set eyes. Knuckles nearly dragging on the ground. Manfred and his gang, they made it their goal to not let one day go by without bumping books from my hands, knocking me around between classes. Sometimes they'd apologize profusely. You know, look all around above my head and then startle, 'Oh, sorry, I didn't *see* you.' "

She winced at the misery he must have felt.

He continued. "Not the sort of stuff teachers would readily notice. I guess this sort of thing doesn't tend to happen to girls."

"Not like that. Not enough testosterone."

"Yeah, well, Manfred had plenty."

He took the cup from the air filter and set it on the concrete. "And I didn't complain. To complain would have been a big mistake, it would have *offended* Manfred and his psychopath buddies. I was furious, but I wasn't stupid. I didn't want to make things worse. The last thing I wanted was for Manfred to feel the need to go beyond a few rough shoves, beyond minor humiliations."

When he dropped the hood, a gust of air puffed out. "At least, I wasn't willing to risk that until this new girl started at school." He wiped his brow with his forearm. "Donna. I thought she was beautiful. Brown curly hair. She always wore a black velvet headband. She was quiet, liked to read. Most important of all, of course, was that she seemed to like me. So when she responded to me, sat with me during lunch, that sort of thing, I lived in dread of Manfred knocking me around in front of her. And it was going to happen.

"Just a minute." He picked up the hose, directed the nozzle under the truck, and rinsed the concrete. He carried the hose around the side of the garage. When he returned, from another pocket he pulled out a plastic Ralphs grocery bag. He put the cup, toothbrush, and rag in the plastic bag. "I managed initially to avoid her during the dangerous times. Manfred and I had different schedules, different lunch periods, so the few minutes between classes were when he and his buddies would strike."

They walked into the garage. He tucked the bag on a shelf near the door. The shelves were lopsided, loaded with storage boxes. She and Paul had built those shelves that first summer. Already the particle board had bowed, cracked.

He held his grimy hands up like a surgeon. "Could you . . . ?"

"Here." Suzanne opened the door for him, and followed him through the narrow laundry room to the family room. "You never told your parents about this bully?"

He cocked his head, smiled. "It's clear that you've never been a boy. First, my father would have been ashamed that I was a sissy, not fighting back. Probably would have knocked me around himself. Second, even if I'd managed to convince him to complain to the principal or, God forbid, if my mother complained, every kid would see me as more wimpy than I already was." He went into the powder room and turned on the faucet.

"So you decided—"

"One morning I came to school with a small paring knife, the one my mother used to peel potatoes." He pumped the soap dispenser, soaped up. "Longer knives were too conspicuous, hard to hide. This one fit on the inside cover of my three-ring binder, held by tape. I sweated all day long. Donna noticed I was distracted, upset. But that day nothing happened. I didn't even get pushed once, kind of unusual. Relief made me so weak I could barely walk home.

"The next day I came to school sick with anticipation. But for the next few days, nothing happened other than the normal shoving, and never when Donna was in view. But the next week . . ." He rinsed, dried his hands on the finger towel. "The next week it happened."

In the family room he flopped on the sofa, she took the BarcaLounger.

"Donna and I had the same English class in the afternoon. From there I went upstairs to a different class, she stayed on the same floor. So the critical time was from when we left English until we reached the stairs. Less than a minute. Manfred should have been upstairs. He had a

study hall, then history, both on the second floor.
I know. I checked."

Suzanne nodded. It paid for the prey to know
the movements of the predator.

"This particular day Donna and I parted at the
stairs. I took one step up, had just turned away
from her, when I found myself staring at these
pearl snaps on Manfred's shirt. He had stopped
on the step just above me, a couple of his buddies
loomed behind him."

"Had Donna gone on?"

"I wasn't sure. I didn't dare look around to see.
Manfred must have positioned himself there on
purpose when he saw me. Our principal was insist-
ent that if you're going up the stairs, you stayed to
the right. Down the stairs, stay to the left. Kids
pretty much did that anyway. But there I was,
on the right side of the stairs, Manfred looking
down at me with this big shit-eating grin. It felt
like my heart was going to explode."

"Weren't there teachers around?"

"Not right there, but sure. Yeah. But though
this seemed like it took forever, when it started
happening, it happened fast. The whole incident,
start to finish, lasted maybe a minute. Manfred
says, 'Out of my way, douche bag.' And I'm ready
to oblige. I figure Donna hasn't heard that. It's
pretty noisy, feet shuffling, people talking. There's
kids pressing around us, climbing the stairs.

"So I shift to the left and, of course, Manfred
moves to block me. Grinning. He had a space
between his front teeth you could fly a plane
through. He mimics John Wayne, 'Thought I told
you to move your ass, pilgrim.' The guys behind

him giggle. I'm holding the binder, *the* binder, and some books under my arm. My palms sweat like mad. I shuffle to the right, so does he. To the left, so does he. He says, 'Jesus, what a fuckwit you are,' and he shoves me.

"I fly backward, knock into some other kids, and hit the linoleum. My books scatter, but I have a death grip on the binder. I'm on my butt. I don't see her, thank God. Kids stop, curious. I don't think many saw him actually push me. But she's not here. She'll hear about it, of course, but I can handle that, I'll come up with something.

"And then Donna squeezes through and she stops, her mouth this big O. I want to die. Manfred steps down from the stairs and says, 'Hey, douche bag, you dropped something.' With the pointed toe of his cowboy boot—he always wore these leather boots with a built-up heel—he kicks one of my books into the crowd.

"Then the absolute worst happens. Donna *defends* me. The girl I'm trying to impress defends me from the school bully. She says to him, 'You stop that right this minute.' Manfred gets a kick out of this, he laughs and turns to say something to his two buddies. A final humiliation, that he turns his back to me, like I wasn't more worrisome than a fly.

"My brain . . . catches fire. I slip my hand under the cover of the binder—I practiced at home—and rip loose the knife. I'm up and slashing before anyone even sees what's in my hand. It's like an Alfred Hitchcock movie. You know when the camera is positioned so the viewer sees the actor's arms and hands like his own? Like a camera is where the actor's head is? It felt like that, like I was watching someone else hold a knife. You know what I mean?"

"Yes. Like a disassociative reaction. Separating yourself from the behavior."

"So just as Manfred says in this falsetto voice, 'Oh, I'm so scared,' I slice his back, cut this big diagonal in his shirt. He screams, turns, reaches for his shoulders with both hands, he doesn't know what the hell is going on, and I cut his arm here"—Allan touched the skin below his elbow—"and I stab him in the chest. He falls, screaming.

"It's noisy, everybody shouting, yelling, scattering away from me, even his two buddies. For a split second, there's something neat about that. Everyone's reacting to me, they're afraid of me. I'm a force to be reckoned with. There's this bloody knife in my hand. Then I see Donna. Her mouth is open like she's about to cry. She's . . . repulsed. Afraid. All of a sudden what I had done hit me. There's a kid, crying and moaning on the floor, maybe dying, because of me."

"What happened to Manfred?"

"The blade was short and wide, so the chest injury was minor. The blade glanced off a rib. He needed over a hundred stitches to his back, though. And surgery to repair the severed tendon in his arm. I wanted to go see him in the hospital, to apologize. The juvenile court judge was in favor, but Manfred's parents weren't."

Allan twisted his mouth, exhaled an abbreviated laugh.

"What?"

"My father. He drove an eighteen-wheeler, would be gone for a week, maybe two. Come home, cruise around on his Harley with his drinking buddies. He had a temper. Unpredictable. My father, when he learned what happened, was proud of me. He thought it was great. My mother was horrified. They argued. He said I had been defending myself, that the apple doesn't fall far from the tree. He had never taken crap off anybody, why should his son? That horrified *me*. From an early age I'd promised myself I wouldn't be like him, and there I was.

"When I had been at school, standing there with the knife, seeing Donna's reaction, everyone's fear . . . their expressions were just like the ones my father's friends wore. Uneasy. Afraid of offending him. Afraid of not laughing loud enough at his jokes. It sickened me."

"Given that, how could you have treated Danny the way you did?"

"There's a certain amount of conditioning that I've worked to overcome. Danny's . . . well, you'll get to know him. Danny's Danny. He can be irritating, innocently thoughtless. The fourth time he screwed up the timer for the animals, I blew my cool. It won't happen again. I swear. Off and on I see a therapist at the U who's helping to recondition my—"

"A therapist?" Her antennae quivered. "Who?"

"A guy at the Student Health Center. Robinson."

The name didn't ring a bell. "Did you know Kurt Poole?"

"Never met him."

She wanted to believe him. Yet antagonism had cranked up to murderous fury in Allan once. Once that he would admit. Had it happened another time?

Suppose it had. Suppose he had told someone about another scenario of rage and violence, ending with a woman's body in the desert.

Suppose he had confided in Kurt Poole.

His narrow face, his clear and unwavering gaze, gave her no answers. If only she could read his mind.

CHAPTER 21

In her bedroom Suzanne peeled out of her dirt-smudged skirt and jacket, rolled off her torn nylons. She stood in the walk-in closet, staring blankly at her clothes. Her mind wanted to glide off into a large empty space and rest, isolated from chaos and confusion.

But chaos and confusion approached fast.

She selected a pair of no-name stretch jeans, a blue-and-white-striped polo shirt with three-quarter-length sleeves, anklets, and a comfortable though ancient pair of Reeboks.

There had been no answer at Paul's apartment. The next step, then, was to try to presense using a focusing command. She washed her face, felt marginally better, clearer. She used Ivory soap on the lenses of her glasses, rinsed, then dried them off with a tissue. She settled them on her nose and walked to the bed.

Thunder in her head.

The revolver. Her gun.

What if her gun, the Colt, was the one he used? Paul.

What if it was gone?

She raced around the bed to the opposite side,

dropped to her knees, yanked open the drawer.

The case was there. When she lifted it, the weight told her the gun was still inside. She unzipped the case, picked out the Colt, brought it to her nose, sniffed. Scent of oil from the last cleaning. Unfired since the time, months ago, when she had practiced at the police range in Huntington Beach.

It hadn't been used.

She released the cylinder. The six chambers were empty. Though heavy, the gun looked like a toy. Short black barrel, an oak crosshatch grip with a silver medallion of a colt rearing on its hind legs.

The Colt elicited memories. Summer mornings, mist floating in depressions in the field, the call of birds, cows in distant fields with foggy plumes of condensation at their nostrils. The smell of hay, sod, manure. Her father, Levi's stuffed into mud-encrusted knee-high boots, set up empty cans on the stake-and-post fence. He wore a droopy Wyatt Earp mustache. She was eleven. The oldest. The boys were back at the house with her mother. Kelly wasn't born yet. He stood behind her, arms around hers, his big rough hands over her small ones clutching the Colt. She used both thumbs to cock the stiff hammer. He corrected her aim. They held their breath as she squeezed the trigger. The loud crack, the thrill as it jumped in her hand, the dry burnt scent of gunpowder. "A gun is always loaded," he said. "You never ever point a gun at a human being unless you intend to use it."

Did she intend to use it?

Could she if she had to?

She picked up a small yellow Winchester box and slid out the cardboard drawer. Tiny missiles of brass with silver tips. She dropped five rounds into the cylinder. The Colt didn't have a safety. Even though firing the gun without cocking the trigger took a fair amount of pull, she left the first chamber empty as a precaution.

"Suzanne?"

She nearly dropped the gun, expelled a strangulated gasp. Paul stood at the bedroom door. His hair was windblown, a dark brown forelock curving over his brow. His beard and mustache looked recently trimmed. A strong, burly man who'd make the perfect Santa in thirty years. He wore a short-sleeved gray plaid Oxford shirt, unbuttoned at the throat, gray chino slacks, and a hesitant tired expression. In his hand was a tan canvas satchel.

He had brought his overnight things.

She came to her feet, leaving the handgun on the carpet. She wanted to go to him, to fit herself into the curve of his arms, to listen to the drumroll of his heart, to forget about everything else.

She didn't move.

The space between them congealed.

She stepped around to the foot of the bed. "We need to talk."

"Here? Or do you want to go downstairs?"

The Colt was on the floor. Did she really need to consider the possibility of protecting herself from this man? But she said, "In here's fine."

He left the satchel by the door and walked to her.

She sat on the frame of the bed. A signal.

He read her. He sat, too, but a couple feet away. The vertical lines between his eyebrows had deepened. He was weary, yet he radiated heat. "I spent the evening at the Pooles'. The oldest, the married daughter? She and her family had arrived."

"Any news about the autopsy?"

"It's scheduled tomorrow."

His hand lifted, then dropped to his thigh. "Kelly said something about you presensing Kurt's death. Is that why you told the police—"

"Let's talk about that later, all right?"

"But it's true? You had another presensory—"

"Paul, I have to understand about Carolyn before we discuss anything else."

He nodded. "I'll tell you everything."

"Everything?"

His gaze skittered from her to the floor. "Everything that—"

"Wait. That's what I want to know."

His eyes found hers again. "What?"

"Whatever it was that just made you look away."

He caught his lip with his teeth. "My reaction to Carolyn's death, the way time eroded my feelings for her, those are the things that have affected my relationship with you. Kurt helped me see that. That by avoiding intimacy, I invested in superstitious ritual. Avoiding a deeper commitment because I feared I'd eventually lose you. Being too boneheaded to notice that I was alienating you. That's it. I swear."

"No. Listen. The one thing that you're keeping from me, that thing I sense, that's what's causing me to distrust you *now*. I have to know what that is."

He shook his head.

"Why? Why can't you tell me?"

He reached toward her. "I'm sorry—"

"No." She shifted away. " 'Sorry' doesn't cut it. Don't tell me it happened in the past, that it has nothing to do with me. It has everything to do with me." Her throat constricted.

Paul scooted over, his arms wrapped around her. "I don't know how I can make you see—"

She shoved him away, stood.

"Did you kill Kurt?"

His mouth opened, closed. A wounded look. "How can you ask that?"

"Did you?"

"I did not."

Their eyes locked.

And she didn't believe him.

He understood her expression. "For God's sake, Suzanne. It's the truth."

"Tell me the truth about Carolyn."

His eyes were pained.

"Can you at least say if this secret has something to do with her death?"

No reaction.

"Does Rusty know?"

An uncontrolled blink.

Rusty knew.

Rusty's disappearing act.

"Everything's over, we're finished, unless you tell me."

"Suzanne . . . I've been an idiot in the past. Stupid. But I wouldn't do anything to hurt you. Can't you just trust me? Just trust me?"

"How . . . ?" She blew out a breath, exasperated. "How can you be so hypocritical? Why can't you trust me? Tell me?"

He clamped his mouth shut.

She felt its presence, the thing he refused to reveal, so close, a throbbing pulse just beneath the skin.

"I think you'd better go."

She didn't think it was possible for her world to shatter much more, but the sound of his car pulling away from the house splintered her heart.

She hadn't told him about the baby.

CHAPTER 22

"Suzanne." Rusty blinked at her, surprised. A narrow sliver of his body showed from the door barely ajar. His hair looked like he'd been yanking on it. Stubble smudged his chin. Sparse chest hairs showed in the V of his pale blue silk kimono. Bare feet. "It's . . . what time is it, anyway? Past midnight?" Rusty's voice was subdued and had whispers at its edge.

"It's time to talk. Let me in, Rusty." Over her shoulder hung a limp denim daypack. Miscellany from a camping trip, her wallet, and the loaded Colt were inside.

"Uh . . ." He glanced behind him, then tugged the kimono over his chest, a curiously protective gesture.

"We have to talk. Now."

"Well, sure. Come in."

He widened the opening and shuffled aside. "Are you driving that truck?"

"It's my roommate's. My car has a broken window." She hoped, unless the shooter was Allan, that the rusty truck might provide anonymity.

Unless the shooter was Rusty.

Inside his house it was dark. No lights except for one glowing from the recessed water dispenser in the kitchen.

"Something to drink?"

"Coffee?"

"Sure thing." He led her through the dining area to the breakfast counter. His silk robe billowed.

She pulled out one of the white stools, a modern design with S-shaped legs and white leather covering the round cushion. "Can you make that decaf?"

"I can."

He didn't ask why, for the second time today, she'd driven so far to see him. She swung the daypack onto the counter's white tile. There was the yellow-bound manuscript she had noticed earlier.

He twisted the dimmer dial and brought up a faint illumination from the ceiling. He opened drawers and pulled out a paper filter, a snap-ring glass jar filled with ground coffee, a tablespoon measure. He set about making coffee in the white Krups. When coffee dripped down into the carafe, a noise came from the corridor.

He looked edgy, glanced toward the hall. "I'll be back in a sec." Weak smile.

"Not on your life." She slid off the stool. "Where you go, I go."

His smile eroded.

"I'm not letting you out of my sight. Not after what you pulled this afternoon."

Muscles flexed along his jawline. He tightened the sash around his waist.

"Paul and I had . . . a talk, of sorts."

His eyes narrowed. "Did you." Combative.

"Why did you hide from me this afternoon?"

He snorted, crossed his arms over his chest. Light rippled from the fabric. "What is it you want me to say, Suzanne?"

She pressed her palms flat on the tile. Cold. Hard. "What secret is Paul keeping about Carolyn?"

"What . . . ? I thought . . ." Caught off-guard. Up came the hand, the finger stroking above the lip. "Did Paul say you should ask me?"

"No. He wouldn't answer any questions."

He rested his chin in his hand.

"I've had some other presensory experiences. Like the one with the little girl and the car accident. I have to know about Carolyn. What it is about her death that Paul refuses to—"

"Her death?" He walked toward her and stopped, the counter between them. He stared at her a moment. "Paul really hasn't told you then, has he?"

"He hasn't told me anything."

His eyes stayed on her, but his thoughts took him elsewhere. When he came back, the harsh planes of his face softened. He said, "Cream and sugar, right?"

She nodded. Settled herself back on the stool.

"Did you know"—he retrieved a carton of creamer from the refrigerator—"that I had started to specialize in child psychology? When I was in graduate school?"

"No."

"Childhood was a magical time for me. When

Paul and I were boys, the sand, the sky, everything had this special crystalline glow." He set the creamer in front of her and moved a white porcelain sugar bowl closer. He leaned his elbows on the counter. "I wanted to work with phobic kids. Kids who feared the dark or wide-open spaces or snakes, monsters, the bogeyman. Help them overcome those fears and replace them with . . ." He straightened.

"With what?"

He shrugged. "Happiness. The pure unsullied kind you can only have in childhood, before you start reality testing every belief."

He padded to a cupboard and took out china cups and saucers. He poured coffee, brought the filled cups and spoons to the counter.

"But you didn't complete your doctorate." She stirred in cream and sugar. "You sold the screenplay."

"That was later. Much later."

He was easing into something the way you step into freezing water. Acclimating himself.

"I'm the archetypal screenwriter. I exude just the right amount of bashful, self-deprecating wit and wild, barely controllable enthusiasm. What the producers, directors, actors want, I give." His voice constricted. "You want bad dialogue? You got it. You want brain-damaged plot? No problem. You think the thirty-two-year-old undercover DEA agent ought to be an anorexic eighteen-year-old cello player? Sure thing. If a screenplay ever becomes a 'go,' gets the okay from the studio executives and somehow, miraculously, makes it to the theaters, it's the actors, the director, the producers who get the credit. Every screenwriter knows what the horse feels like when the jockey accepts the trophy."

He sipped his coffee. "Ultimately your soul rots. But, as I said, selling that first screenplay came much later." He came around the counter and pulled out the other stool. He adjusted the kimono, sat down. His hand rifled the pages of the manuscript.

"I loved Carolyn. Make no mistake about that. If she would have had me, I would have married her. I would have made it work. I still believe that."

Made it work? "What do you mean?"

"Paul told her. That was what the fight was about." He punched a fist into the palm of his other hand. "And Paul told Kurt."

Her scalp prickled. She waited.

"He broke his word. Paul had promised never to tell."

His face turned toward the hallway as though he had heard something. A thin young man peered into the kitchen. Long curly blond hair cascaded over his bare chest, two diamond studs twinkled from the lobe of his left ear. Almost invisible blond eyebrows. He smiled, then grimaced. "Am I interrupting? I wanted to get some orange juice." He had remarkably huge hands and tried to tuck one into the front pocket of his tight jeans. Bare feet, long narrow toes.

Rusty gestured for him to come over. "Suzanne, this is Dana."

He walked to the counter and thrust out a big hand. A firm handshake. His eyelashes were thick and pale, the same color as his hair, covering startlingly green eyes. Smooth poreless complexion. "Nice to meet you."

"Help yourself to coffee," Rusty said.

"Ah, no. No, thanks." Hair shimmered. "I'll get some juice and go back to bed. Early cattle call in the morning."

He took a plastic container of juice from the refrigerator.

"Cattle call?" she said.

"A soap has an opening," Dana explained. "God and everybody shows up. Cattle call."

"Dana's an actor," Rusty said.

"Last year's Dr Pepper commercial, that was me jumping around like a fool in the background." He poured juice into a glass and returned the container to the fridge. "I think my mom was the only one who noticed. She taped it and sent it to all our relatives." He grinned. "Good night."

After Dana left, they were silent a moment. Rusty said, "I was engaged to Carolyn. She didn't know I was gay. Paul insisted I tell her."

"But you didn't."

"No. I wanted . . . I thought a relationship with Carolyn would work. That I might force myself to be straight. At least fake being straight. Maybe I sensed how doomed I was."

"Doomed?"

"This was before AIDS, but still. Think of it. A child psychologist. What parent would send their child to a homosexual for therapy? The hours of playtime. If I was married, had kids myself . . . Well, marriage, psychology became the road—the roads—not taken." His cheek muscles tightened.

"Thanks to Paul. It was a trap, that night at Kurt's house. Paul had told Carolyn, then arranged this meeting at Kurt's house to confess his deceit. Paul couldn't tell me himself, he needed the reinforcement of Kurt. A double blow. Not only had Paul told Carolyn, but Kurt, too. His adviser at USC. My adviser. Of course, a few days later Kurt *advised* me about the pitfalls being a homosexual and a child therapist. Paul and Kurt. My friends. I hated both of them. Then."

"You made an adjustment, though. You spent time with Paul and Carolyn afterward."

"Yeah. Sure. I'm great at making adjustments. My life today is one big adjustment. This business I'm in now, Hollyweird, not many last long under the best of circumstances. It's an industry that promotes paranoia in all things. In spite of publicity to the contrary, Hollywood has a bad case of homophobia. I've seen it happen again and again. Word gets around, true or not, that a certain up-and-coming actor is HIV positive. No director wants to work with him. Hell, nobody wants to come within breathing distance of the guy."

She thought of Angela and the dozen or so women before her. "So all those dates—"

"Yeah. Exactly. So all those dates."

Paul's pained expression. Determined not to make the same mistake twice, determined not to betray Rusty again. Willing to pay the price of losing her, Suzanne.

Not a secret about the circumstances of Carolyn's death.

A secret about Rusty.

How bitter had Rusty been? Betrayed by the

friend he trusted, rejected by the woman he loved.
A hornets' nest worth of anger?

"The funny thing," Rusty interrupted her
thoughts, "is that Carolyn didn't want him,
either."

"What?"

"They'd fought over her avoidance of medication. She came from an overprotective family, and
getting the same treatment from Paul drove her
crazy. She was working up courage to tell him
that it was all off."

"Did she?"

"Apparently not."

"You're sure she didn't tell him."

"I don't think she did. Paul never mentioned
that she'd broken off the engagement. And I never
told him that she had intended to. After she died,
I couldn't see the point."

Her spirits sank. If Carolyn broke off with Paul,
then Paul had a motive. She switched channels.
What if Rusty's lying? What if Carolyn didn't
intend to cancel the engagement to Paul? Or
even if what Rusty said was true, that didn't
erase his hurt, his hate.

Her thoughts entangled in barbed wire. It was
time to stop struggling with logic. Another way,
another path, led to the answers. She hoped she
had the courage to find them.

BOOK THREE

DESERT

CHAPTER 1

Suzanne stood on a grassy knoll, part of Ocean Park in Santa Monica. A three-quarter crescent hung in the sky. Beyond the sand the ocean pulsed, constant as the moon in its rhythms. She inhaled. A wet salt tang. Waves, their froth a luminescent white, lapped against the shore. The water swelled, receded, swallowed into inky and secretive depths.

She had wanted to feel the infinity of the ocean, of the moonlit sky, before she descended into a tiny dark corner of another mind. She tilted her head up at the heavens. The periphery of her vision filled with stars.

The presensory technique recalled the way you perceive faint stars. Look directly at their pallid glow, and their photons strike the cells of the retina called cones. Cones interpret color, not low levels of light. The stars are invisible. But look askance at the stars, and the angle of their rays strikes the rods, cells sensitive to the intensity of light. To perceive the dim universe of another mind, she needed to look to the side. To relax, to drift, yet focus. A meditation.

She turned, plodded over sod spongy with moisture, the damp seeping through her sneakers. A blooming jacaranda sheltered Allan's truck from the street lamps. Once in the cab, she considered a hotel. Considered the print bedspread, the stale odor of tobacco smoke, the white paper stripe across the commode, the minuscule blocks of soap, some sad stain on the carpet, the attempts at homey comforts that only emphasized alien surroundings. Considered and rejected. She preferred staying here, within earshot of crashing waves, where sea breezes tantalized the skin. Close to the world she hoped to return to.

She straightened in the driver's seat, placed her feet flat on the floor, rested her hands palm-down on her thighs. Closed her eyes. How to focus? Where to direct the travels of her soul?

A specific time—tomorrow at three P.M.—wouldn't help. She didn't know the actual location in time of any meaningful event.

To the man in the desert? To the killer?

To his victim? But what if the victim was herself?

To the time when the killing occurred?

The questions circled, closing in on just the right one. She sensed its nearness the way a homing pigeon must recognize the end of its flight.

It came to her.

Not a question, but a command. Simple and elegant, like all truths.

A few deep breaths. The relaxation technique, muscles complying, easing. Finally the silence.

She cast out into the still spaces of her mind:

Take me to the desert.

CHAPTER 2

The nightmare. The nightmare has him again.

Thermal waves rise like steam from the asphalt, only there is no humidity. Chalky high desert. A place where the dead finally become cremated. The pavement of the highway shimmers with a startling heat. The car speeds by Harper Lake, a dry bed. Once a body of swirling blue waters, eons ago, before life was sucked from this place, before moisture evaporated.

Before the ghosts.

The anger of the land, like its heat, rises in palpable waves. He violated this place. He committed a transgression, and it wants him, it *lusts* for him. It wants not his life, no, nothing so simple as that. It wants his anguish, his wet, wet tears. This is the heat of hell. The poetry he'd felt here, before the killing, the magic of its arid dust, has fled. Now there are always hot winds, robbing succulence from flesh. The chinook, it was said, drove men insane. One town, in particular, had dwindled to a dozen inhabitants who, the rumor went, hacked each other to bits after a month of the howling juiceless wind.

This area is dotted with ghost towns.

So it demands him, this inhospitable wilderness. The immortal rocks want nothing so fleeting, so unsatisfying, as his death. This desolation wants his soul. Forever. He wondered if it didn't already have him. If it hadn't already clutched him to its shriveled bosom, filled his skull with dust. Cut his veins, scorched red sand would trickle out.

The road sign whips by as though on roller blades. Gone. There is dread. Up ahead a ghost town sign, black letters parched gray by the sun of too many summers. The ghost town sign thrusts forward—Blackwater—then speeds away, eager to avoid the journey of the damned.

You can believe in ghosts, when the dead come back to you with their torn faces, with their wide gaping tongueless mouths, their shrieks. There must be penance. There must be punishment. Lurching up and over an old dirt-dry path. This is several miles past the ghost town sign. The road throws the car around, the steering wheel twists as a rut grabs the tires to wrench them off, to keep him here forever, to wilt and desiccate his fragile flesh in the desert air.

This land thirsts for him.

He has the shovel. He has brought the shovel, a talisman against fate. An irony. A shovel to cup his own grave in the mummified hard earth. The ground beats at the belly of the car, a terrific scrape as though something has torn off the oil pan, and still he presses the accelerator, turns and rolls to a stop. He doesn't want to go. But this wasteland, this nightmare, owns him. This desert has a right to him. Everything else in his life is temporary. This is infinity.

He gets out with a panicky heart, a scream building deep in his chest. This is the fine-tuning of the nightmare, the suspense of the horror to come. His legs carry him, though he doesn't want to go. The shovel is in his hand, the shaft hard yet with a secret pliancy, thick as a serpent.

He has added a ghost to this place and it is now evil. The ground is evil. What waits for him is worse than his own death. Terror mounts. Perspiration pops out on his brow, the desert sucking moisture from his body, osmotically draining him. He looks up. There. And there. And there. Always the airborne wheeling shapes. The birds. The scavengers. Circling and waiting. Their needs so simple, their beaks so sharp, their patience so long, their life without concerns except for instinct that glides them down, down, down to the dry dirt, to the wet that is blood, before the desert consumes that, too.

He walks. He tries many times to turn back, but he walks. Gravity, an enemy, pulls him down the steep slope. A snarl of creosote, branches as brittle as ancient bones. A mausoleum for the murdered. She waits for him, as the dead do. The harsh cry of the ravens, the two turkey vultures, great hopping shadows like deformed old men; they wait. He holds the shovel. Why can't he untangle his thoughts from this endless horror? Why can't he rise up from this nightmare?

The handle of the shovel is in his fists. The stench. Her stench. The putrid scent of meat left to rot in the sun. The birds rise, connected together in a fathomless pattern. Up and up, silent. The silence worse than sound. No, there is a sound, from behind the brush. Someone chokes, moans. His legs tremble. He holds the shovel. He rounds the creosote. Sweat stings his eyes.

She is there, lying quietly. The birds are gone, circling overhead. He will bury her without looking. He must not look. He knows what he'd see. He's done this so many times, this penance. He will bury her again. But she won't stay under the dirt, she always draws him back.

Sounds from her. Coughing, gagging, obstruction in the throat. Oh, God, please, she is dead, she is dead. His traitor legs carry him to her. She lies on her side, her naked back, narrow and small as a child's, toward him.

He bends down to her, she rotates and lunges, an ungodly screech from her throat, empty eye sockets, her tongue bloody ribbons, because this is what the desert does to you, what its creatures must have, this parched wasteland needs the choicest parts first. Her bloody tongueless mouth, teeth sharpened to piranha points, rushes toward him, to devour him, the torn face sightless but drawn to his odor of guilt as she has been drawn to him all these years, draining the life juices from him in order to have back her flesh.

She comes at him, comes at him teeth first, a thing of hell, and he stumbles back, sand in his loafers like tumors, he stumbles back and back, at the last second grasps the shovel in both fists like an ax and swings hard, the shovel blade slices through the air with a whoosh, its edge dead-on for her neck, striking, decapitating like her spine was butter, a whirling spray of red, the nightmare head falling, falling, thudding to the ground, bouncing, and now the face is whole, uninjured, and laughing, smirking at him, inexplicably the wrong face, completely wrong, the face of Suzanne Reynolds . . .

CHAPTER 3

The face, her face, head at an angle, defocused, blurry, mouth opening, mouth closing, a tapping, teeth clicking, lips pressed together, then separating. Transforming. A square jaw, full lips, squashed nose, heavy-lidded eyes. Not her reflection. A man. A man at the windshield, knuckles rapping the glass. His voice muffled. "Miss?"

Suzanne blinked.

A uniform.

A cop.

She rolled down the window. An explosion of minutia. The weak rays of the rising sun. The soft rasp of fabric against metal as he moved from the windshield, the subtle displacement of the cab, the soles of his shoes grinding against pavement, a drifting cloud of molecules bringing the scents of soap, lime cologne, strong coffee. The radiant warmth of his skin.

He peered at her. A small cut on his dimpled chin. "Are you all right?"

"Yes." The power of speech returned with an effort. "I fell asleep."

His irises mingled radial lines of green, brown, and gold. "Your driver's license and vehicle registration, please." Good teeth, though the incisors were trying to go catty-corner to the rest.

She turned to the right, unsnapped the denim daypack, slipped her hand inside. The oily metallic odor of the gun. A shiver of alarm. Just what I need, to end up in jail for carrying a concealed weapon. Her fingers clutched the slippery leather of her wallet. She pulled it out, flipped open to the plastic sleeves, plucked out her license. She handed the card to the officer.

While he studied that, she ripped loose the Velcro tab holding the glove compartment closed. An extension cord, squashed white napkins, a folded brown paper bag, pencils without points, a heavy black tape measure, a gray envelope. Inside the envelope she found the current registration.

After the cop looked at that, he handed the items back to her. "At six A.M., you'll have to move your vehicle."

"What time is it now?"

He didn't check his watch. "Almost five-thirty." He thumped the roof, walked away.

Her senses expanded. The same thing had happened Saturday, after presensing the death of the little girl.

She gazed out over the flat line of the horizon, spellbound, possessed by a preternatural clarity, aware of another time, a different reality, existing simultaneously with the moment in which her own heart pulsed. Double vision.

The external world was still the same. She saw every detail with microscopic precision, the rays of morning sun glinting off floating seaweed, every blade of dewy grass, the individual feathers of swooping gulls.

But it was the other world that captivated her mind. And here there was heat, an everlasting suffocation, punctuated by the screams of birds slicing through air, the agonies of horrific expectations. The reign of the desert, its intelligence without mercy, no kinder to the dead than to the living.

She didn't know the identity of the killer.

But the killer knew her.

She didn't know the identity of the woman.

But she knew the location of the grave, whether it already existed or whether it was soon to be. She knew where to find the grave. And once she found the grave, she would find all the answers.

CHAPTER 4

Suzanne stopped at a gas station, fed quarters to the public telephone, and dialed Olivia's number. Olivia barked into the phone after the first ring. "Suzanne?"

"Olivia, let me talk to Kelly."

"Are you all right? Where are you?"

"I'm all right. I'm somewhere on Wilshire Boulevard, near the beach." Horns blared. Exhaust fumes. Not yet six and already the thick of the rush hour. "I have to talk to Kelly."

Clicks. She thought she'd been disconnected, but Kelly's voice said her name.

"It worked, Kelly. Focusing."

"Do you know who—"

"I know *where*. Where the desert grave is. I'm driving out there this morning."

"Then let the police handle it."

"I don't know if the murder has taken place. I need to go to the site, to see for myself. Then—"

"Then what?"

"I'll know. Everything. I sense it, events unfolding. Waiting. I . . . I can't explain any better."

"Come get me. Take me with you."

"No. I know you're safe . . . that's the most

important thing."

"Then call me as soon as you can. I'm staying here at Olivia's house. I'm not going to class unless you call."

"I'll call you."

After she hung up, she filled the gas tank, then went through the accordion grated storefront to pay. She hunted the aisles of the minimart, picking up packets of trail mix, a map of southern California, several liters of spring water and Gatorade. She lugged everything to the checkout counter. The attendant, steroidally bulked, hair slicked back in a ponytail, rang up the charges. When she paid, he caught Suzanne's eye, tapped his cranium, wiggled his eyebrows.

Suzanne followed the arrow of his gaze. A short, dumpy woman stood by the newspaper rack near the door. She grinned, showing wide-spaced tobacco-stained teeth. A curdled, sallow complexion under scraggly reddish-brown hair. Eyeglasses, the left lens cracked, tilted cockeyed on her nose. A thick wrapping of filthy tape held the frames together at the bridge.

"Harmless," the attendant said. "Will talk your ear off."

Suzanne gathered up the paper sack, headed for the door. The woman, pushing along a wave of body odor, followed her out.

The woman scuffed along in too large men's shoes. "I been waiting for more of you. Didn't think I'd recognize you, what with this, that, and the other. The plumbing's been a problem. Always been a problem." She jabbered about the economy, the coming wars, and pointed.

Suzanne looked at the rusted tan Ford, a pickup truck with a wood and tar-paper makeshift camper shell, parked at the back of the lot. The fender, the roof of the shell, everything at crazy angles as though dropped there from a great height.

". . . . so I says we don't know the magnitude of the problem, the way you can leave something right there, right there in plain sight—" Something was getting the woman steamed.

Suzanne put her groceries in Allan's Toyota and paused before getting in. The symphony of the mind was badly out of tune for this ragged woman. Suzanne took some bills out of her wallet and held them out.

The woman stopped her litany, squinted, plucked at her multiple layers of clothes, a ragged leather-look jacket, untucked flannel shirt, men's work pants rolled at the cuff. Averted her eyes. Breathed hard, bosom heaving. Shuffled. Scrunched her face.

She said, "I dream the dreams of another. The FBI insisted on it."

"I know." Suzanne shook the bills. "This is your salary."

The woman's face puckered, relaxed. She snatched the money and turned, mumbling, lumbered in her too large shoes toward the ramshackle Ford.

Suzanne looked up. High above, closer to the clouds, flapped a distant V-formation of white birds. A northward trajectory.

North toward the high desert.

CHAPTER 5

Suzanne veered the Toyota off the asphalt, downshifted onto a dirt trail, a vehicle-wide swath cut through clawing brush. A lonely unused road. The tires kicked up plumes of dust. Here even the prickly pear cacti, with their flat jointed pads, were scarce. Wind pummeled the truck, pelting bits of gravel against the windshield. A tangle of tumbleweed leapt up, bounced on the hood, slid away. Another rolling mass of the stuff, otherworldly spoor of a long-dead animal, caught on the grille. The path looped sharply, widened. At a certain point, she had trouble getting sufficient traction and decided to stop. She was close enough.

Her footfalls were soundless on the chalky dirt. The daypack's contents pounded her shoulder blades, the bottle of spring water sloshed, the gun thumped with its own mean weight. Sweat trickled between her breasts. Gusts of heat whipped her hair, threw invisible grains of sand against her glasses, her cheeks, sucked away her breath. A magnetic attraction tugged and pulled.

The land sloped up, endless and deceivingly steep. A few clouds blotted out the merciless sun.

She walked on.

Her thigh muscles burned. She pressed into the wind, past tinder-dry mesquite, feeling a profound emptiness. Life had stopped clinging to this place.

A quarter mile farther she reached the summit. Suzanne hunched over, panting. Air currents ripped at her clothes. The soles of her feet burned as though an inferno roared beneath the surface. She pulled off her glasses, wiped a gritty film from her face with a shirtsleeve. With uncorrected vision, the landscape softened to a tapestry of blurred, depthless tans.

Formless shapes, without meaning.

Easy to turn away from.

A small voice in her head. *Go back. Leave. You'll be safe if you go. Now.*

Seductive, that small voice.

Deceitful.

She slipped on her eyeglasses and walked to the edge. The forty-five-degree hillside bottomed out into a broad tangle of mesquite.

The sight of the brush set off explosions of recognition.

And dread.

Behind the bramble of twisted bushes was a malignancy. Timeless. Waiting for evil. She felt its pulse, like a huge malformed heart.

The source of terrible answers. But answers, all the same.

She sidestepped down, knees bent, hands grasping the brittle stumps of weeds, planting one foot firmly before shifting the other. No bushes on the steep angle of the slope, no cacti, only broken

stalks, as though scythed by the embodiment of
hot anger. Thick stems protruded, stems that
would become jagged stakes if she fell. So don't fall.
As she thought this, a rock dislodged under her
sneaker and her foot flew out from under her.

Her body slid over crumbling dirt, ruins of flora
snapping in her fists like straw, dull knives of
stubble punching her jeans. A piercing scrape
to her right forearm. An outcropping of rock
slammed against her hip. The force rolled her
to her stomach, rubble abraded her chin, and she
jerked to a shuddering halt. Gravel and stones
thudded past her. A firm pull at the left strap of
the daypack. Her right cheek against the slope,
dirt in her mouth, the thunder of rushing blood in
her ears. Her glasses against her lips. She gulped
air, trying to minimize movement at the same
time. Two inches below and pointing at her left
eye was the splintered tip of a thick stalk. The
strap of her daypack was hooked around it.

Two inches closer and . . .

She shut her eyes, shaken. Stupid stupid stupid
to attempt to walk down the hill. Her stomach,
with its tiny new life, pressed against the rough
surface. The fragile biology of flesh was no competition for the earth's crust, for the evil of this
place. She opened her eyes. She eased up her left
hand and wrapped her fingers around the base of
the stalk. Pulled. Firmly rooted.

Her feet found toeholds. Keeping a firm grip
on the stalk, she raised her torso, slipped the
daypack strap over the splintered tip with her
right hand. Blood dotted a long superficial abra-
sion on the white skin of her inner arm. Her hip

throbbed with the promise of a nasty bruise. The prices of passage. Her glasses were coated with dust but miraculously unbroken.

Chastened and no longer naive, she scrabbled crablike the rest of the way. At the base, her feet stumbled over scree, rocks, and stones from landslides, testimony to the land's fundamental instability. Though she faced away from the cancerous sprawl of mesquite, she sensed a profound difference. Stillness. At the top of the hill a sandspout, a miniature tornado, drilled into the dirt. Where Suzanne stood, not even a ghost of a zephyr stirred the air.

But there was a presence. The hush of something lying in wait, somnolent in the heat.

The pull was unmistakable. She shrugged off the daypack, unzipped the main compartment, pulled out the tall plastic Evian bottle. Rinsed out her mouth, took a generous drink of the warm water, then patted her cheeks with a handful. An anointing of sorts.

She was ready. She swung one strap of the daypack over her shoulder, turned, and staggered back under a spasm of impressions. Being handled, being undressed, the elastic waistband of slacks pulled off hips, muscles lax, unresponsive, a sleeveless sweater yanked over the head, naked skin against a velour blanket, darkness, suffocation. The sensations stopped.

Suzanne hung her head, recovering. Grieving. The woman was here. Dead. Not a death in the future, but a death in the past. Suzanne's role was not to prevent a murder, but to reveal one. She stepped around the mesquite to the grave.

The clouds drifted and the sun shone full of horror on the dry featureless sand. She had a sudden sense of tectonic activity kilometers below, a reverberation. Stronger as she approached an area of barren soil in the sheltering curve of the brush. Terror, old and dry as dust, snarled through the dirt. She dropped the daypack, responding to a compelling urge. Kneeling down, she held her hands above the ground. Petrified fear radiated a heat all its own. She pressed her palms flat on the dirt. Hot. Rough pebbles and small sharp twigs thrust up against her skin.

Vibration. Tingling up through her fingers to her arms, to her shoulders to arc in her mind, a bright white light—

A woman's moans.

The birds. Wild. Violent. Carrion eaters with bright cunning eyes.

The woman's skeletal muscles are paralyzed, but not her voice. Loud garbled cries.

Vultures, sly and obscene, jump back three, four times before their shrewd eyes realize this quarry makes only harmless noise. Skinny devilish creatures. They step forward on scaly feet and legs, one scrabbles onto her chest.

Terror fuels a tremendous effort. She manages to turn her face, but it's the last move she makes. She can't use jaw muscles to close her mouth, helpless to protect her eyes and tongue from the jabbing beaks. Carrion eaters have no mercy, they have only hunger. Insatiable hunger.

The hooked beaks dart—

Suzanne jerked away her hands, jerked away her mind from bloody memories that were not her own. The suffering. Her lungs struggled as though shriveled by the furnace air. An abomination, a perversion, for the dead to give up their secrets. Yet those moans were reluctant to let go of her, bonded by violence. The heat had brought a fierce, almost painful tightness to her cheeks. Her arms ached in their sockets as though she had been dragged to this desolate spot.

This psychometry, this receiving impressions from being close to the remains, would give her the answers. Don't give me your pain, she pleaded to the dead woman beneath the soil. Show me your murderer. She lowered her hands to the dirt.

Cloth covering her face. Limp arms, legs. Swinging hammocklike in soft fabric. The hands carrying her are silent, knees thumping against her flanks, her buttocks. Grunting with the effort of her lax weight.

Being lifted higher, up over something. Head thuds against a hard surface. The smell of exhaust. Hands shoving her legs, pushing her shoulders. The cloth slips. From slitted eyelids she sees two faces looking down, one in shadow, hard to make out. The other—

Her mind screams a single word.

Suzanne recoiled, a protective reflex. Fear, anguish, surprise, terror, her emotions and the emotions of the dead woman spun in a vortex, as intertwined as strands of DNA. The dizzying whirl blotted out the heat, the sun, the desert. The face. Years younger, but a face that Suzanne knew well.

The face of a murderer.

She stood just as a voice called her name.

CHAPTER 6

His words had the wheezy sound of very old age, the ancient voice of depression. He took a step, jerky and mechanical, arms limp at his sides. Crescents of perspiration under the arms of his white shirt. His chest heaved. Temple veins swollen, sweat glossed his brow. The look of a man who had failed to outpace his demons.

Dr. Franklin Weis.

He stayed near the bramble, over fifteen feet from the grave. His white hair glinted in the sun. His fleshy face was pink. Gray gaberdine trousers, black laced wing-tip brogues. Ready for a day at the office, not a climb down a desert slope. A wonder that he hadn't taken a dangerous fall.

Suzanne eased over to the daypack. "How did you know I was here?"

He ignored her question, seemed dazed. "Ironic. You look so like her. So like Tracy. My daughter. And now you're here. You're both here." His cheeks belled out with each pant. He eyed the barren soil. "Ironic."

The terrified mental scream of the woman replayed in Suzanne's mind: *Daddy.*

He rubbed his hand across his chest. "Fifteen years it's been. In all that time, you'd think she could have . . . forgiven. Could have stayed buried."

He had the look of a man whose sanity was rapidly escaping like air from a leaky balloon.

"Why did you kill your daughter?"

A spasm of pain. "It was meant to be a mercy. A release from suffering. She was no longer the person she was meant to be. One day she's a junior in high school, already accepted at Harvard and MIT, the next day she's lying in intensive care. Closed-head injury. Ski accident. I prayed for her to come out of the coma. And when she did, after it was clear that she was changed forever . . . I prayed that she would die."

Suzanne lifted the daypack. The center compartment was still unzipped. Weis made no move toward her, was intent on confessing, his eyes locked on the ground covering his daughter.

"My wife insisted, though Tracy needed constant watching, that we keep her at home. Over the next two years my daughter deteriorated. Suffered rages, terrors that we had no way of understanding. She became crafty, would hide, sometimes run away. When my wife became ill, too sick to watch over our daughter, she arranged to place Tracy in a nursing care facility in Santa Barbara. Even there she'd disappear, find a way of slipping by security. She'd end up with . . . scum. Homeless men who'd . . ." He placed a shaking hand to his forehead. "You can see that there was no choice, can't you? That death can be the only alternative?"

She reached into the daypack, slipped her hand around the gun. "You injected her with a skeletal relaxant."

"Succinylcholine. A massive dose. I thought . . . I was sure she had died. But . . . she was on so much other medication, there must have been some sort of delayed paradoxical effect."

She nodded. "When you left her here, she was alive."

"Yes. I returned to bury her and . . . her face. From the birds. Too much blood. Gouges in her skin. Her empty eye sockets, her mouth. The dead don't bleed, not like that. But the living . . ." He squeezed his eyes shut, raised his hands, clenched them into fists. "She won't let me forget. Nightmares. Haunting me for years." He focused on Suzanne. "Then you. The image of what my daughter should have been. She worked through you." His right fist unfolded, fingers splayed, arm extended. He stepped forward.

She pulled out the gun.

Weis blinked. "This land, it's a relentless force. Vengeful. It wants slaughter. I was wrong to reverse the order of death, to take you before your time."

Talking like she were his dead daughter. "There was someone else. Who helped you kill . . . me?"

She saw that he didn't want to come closer, as if he feared a skeletal hand might burst from the grave, grab and pull him under the parched dirt. Or that she herself might do so. His hands were raised, not in attack, but in supplication.

He didn't answer her question, but said, "My sin. My sin. Do what you will."

Weis's complexion had deepened to an unhealthy raspberry, streaked with lines of moisture. His jowls loosened, pouches of despair tugged his mouth. His eyelids fluttered. He swayed. He looked like he was going to faint.

She relaxed. He hadn't intended to attack her. He sought relief from a guilt that was driving him mad.

Suzanne hunkered down, put the gun on the dirt, took the bottle of water out of the daypack. She stepped toward him, wondering what had triggered his impulse to come here, whether he had, on some level, been in tune with her.

Weis blinked at the proffered water. The whites were completely visible around the blue iris, too many years of looking at the terror within. He squinted, slightly past her, as though seeing into the past. His lips blanched, his chin lifted, perceiving some answer. He came back to Suzanne. He said, "The desert must have its blood," in a disembodied voice.

That made no sense. His personality had continued its insidious meltdown.

"Drink the water." She lifted the bottle. "Then we'll head back."

A click, followed by a gunshot that pierced the stillness. Weis staggered, shoved by an invisible force, his arms flailed out, knocking the bottle from her hand, he crumpled to the ground. When he fell, Suzanne's confusion lifted, spheres of insight rising to the surface and exploding. The realization was instantaneous. Victims. She'd been in the minds of victims, *never* the killing mind. The little girl crushed by the car, Kurt Poole . . . and Weis.

Weis as victim.

A fusillade of questions.

Who knew Weis all those years ago?

Whose face was in shadow when Tracy was loaded into the car trunk?

Who had medical experience, the knowledge to kill Kurt Poole?

The final question, the real kicker, the one that held the answer to all: Who knew Suzanne was coming here?

She held her hands carefully out by her sides. She did a slow about-face. Standing by the daypack, holding the Colt with a firm grip, hands in brown leather gloves, was Olivia. Titan-red hair pulled severely away from her face, caught in a chignon. Tan gauze blouse tucked into brown slacks, oil-tanned leather hiking boots. Prepared for the climate. Standing strong, unruffled, her mouth a thin firm line. Cool, as though bred for the desert elements.

Suzanne stepped back, to check on Weis and keep Olivia in view.

"*No.*" The hammer cocked with a distinct click. "Leave him be, the damn fool." She rasped out a laugh. "Failure to perform."

Her voice scared the hell out of Suzanne. The tone was calm, regretful, conversational.

"What do you mean?"

Olivia sighed, used the gun to motion at Weis's prone form. "Failure to perform. An epitaph for Frank's tombstone. He was going to offer himself up like some goddamn sacrificial lamb. Offer me up. The weak bastard. All these years, it was fucking ages ago, all this time and we were safe.

Safe. No one knew. His daughter had wandered off so many times, no one questioned when she vanished again."

She curled her lips in scorn. "And his fucking *conscience* was bothering him. Worse than ever. Because of you. You triggered the memories. He talked like you were some sort of avenging angel, what his daughter could have been if she had been whole and well and alive. How she had come back in your body to torture him. Why he thought she looked like you I'll never know. Same color hair, but Tracy was a tiny girl, wiry. But he was convinced she had come back. Crazy talk. No stamina. I saw it back then, when he was too puny to actually inject her himself, to put her out of her misery. Spineless. Lost his nerve at the last second. Thank God for what I learned helping that doctor in Belize."

"My sister—"

"She's all right. She's at my house, gawking at the horses. A sweet kid. I wouldn't hurt her, Suzanne." She sounded offended. "I'm not some nut offing people for the hell of it. She's not in my way. You and Weis are obstructions to my goals. Your sister is, and will be, fine. You and Frank are another matter. I'll return home today and at some point the police will discover your bodies, obviously the result of a struggle."

She waggled the Colt and smiled. "Almost threw me off when this damn thing didn't fire the first time. But thanks for bringing the revolver. Is this frigging destiny or what? Frank is killed by this little Colt, your gun. And you"— she put the Colt in her left hand, pulled a sleek black semiautomatic from the back of her waistband—"you are killed by Frank's gun. The ballistics will match up with the bullet, if the authorities find it, that struck your fender."

"It was you."

"Thought I had nailed your ass on the 405. He always kept this gun in his nightstand. When Blake and I visited him and his current wife, I slipped into their bedroom. Thought he'd have the guts to eat it one day, do us all a big favor. But things have a way of working out for the best, don't you think? And I don't care if they unearth her"—she pointed the pistol to the unmarked grave,—"because there'll be no one alive to say I had anything to do with her death."

Sweat, like teardrops, trickled from Suzanne's temples. "Why did you help him kill his daughter?"

She expelled a short burst of air. "At the time, Frank and I were lovers. An embarrassing lack of judgment on my part. Me and Franklin Weis. But Frank was going places, had made big discoveries in pharmacology. Anyway, his wife was dying. Ovarian cancer. We'd planned to marry after a decent interval. His wife had the money, money that her last will would piddle away keeping Tracy locked up in this resort-style home. So I helped him see how cruel it was to keep Tracy in agony. But then, afterwards, he was so damn . . . haunted. Unstable about his daughter. Tortured about the grief he'd caused his wife before cancer took her. The backbone of a jellyfish. Marrying him would have been a big mistake. In any case, I had met Blake."

A thought struck Suzanne. The presensory experiences always dealt with the future of the victim. The future. "Blake doesn't know."

"Of course not." She grimaced. "It's a shame you won't get to know my husband. An intelligent man. He and I have worked hard for years to get to where we are today. Blake will win the seat in the House, then the Senate in a few years, while I'm UCLF's university president, and you and Weis will be dead.

"Suzanne, I'm so sorry. I really liked you. I promise you, I'll be grief-stricken when I hear the news." Her voice was apologetic, as though she were canceling a dinner party.

Olivia stepped forward. "It'll be bad for Frank's current wife and little boy. But Frank was disintegrating, right before my eyes. He was talking to Kurt Poole, did you know that? Frank insisted he hadn't told Kurt—yet—about his daughter. He promised not to implicate me, but it would have come out, my part in Tracy's death. Then there was you and your visions."

Suzanne gauged the distance between them. Her mouth was dry. Her heart lurched against her rib cage.

Olivia hunched down, put Suzanne's Colt on the ground, stood up. "I damn near choked when you described the desert premonition. For a while I suspected Frank must have confided in you, that maybe you were testing me, working up to blackmail. But you seemed innocent as the day is long. This . . . thing you do, this presensing, it's for real, isn't it? You knew about Kurt's death." She cocked her head, talking as though they shared some camaraderie.

"How did you kill Kurt?"

"Now this is damn scary. Just the way you described in your presensing experience. I called Kurt, said I had something I wanted to discuss in confidence. You know him. Secrets were second nature. Kurt had some god-awful jazz singer on the cassette player, he didn't hear me come in. I hit him with an obsidian bookend. That would leave a wound, I figured, like his skull hitting the edge of the desk. Then I injected the same drug we used on Tracy."

"Succinylcholine."

"Right. According to Frank, a large dosage should kill quickly."

Suzanne knew that the drug metabolized quickly. An autopsy assay wouldn't pick up a trace. Death from acute respiratory depression, cardiovascular collapse.

Olivia widened her stance, lifted Weis's pistol with both hands. "You deserved to have your question answered, but I can't waste any more time. I am sorry, Suzanne, truly, about the baby. The only innocent in all of this."

Suzanne directed her gaze behind Olivia, letting an expression of relief mingled with concern wash over her face.

"Paul!" she cried. When Olivia spun around, Suzanne pelted toward her and sprang headfirst into the void.

CHAPTER 7

Olivia twisted, caught sight of Suzanne just as she was completely airborne, the nanosecond before Suzanne's body, outstretched arms first, slammed into her. The impact shoved Olivia against the dried mesquite, Suzanne pressed full length against her, the pistol discharged. The element of surprise was Suzanne's advantage. She grasped the automatic with her left, swept up the heel of her right, and chopped hard against Olivia's windpipe. Olivia released her grip on the pistol, brought both hands up to her throat, her mouth contorted with pain, with the horror of being unable to breathe.

Suzanne staggered back, off-balance, the pistol in her grasp, a sympathetic pain in her own lungs. Olivia dropped to her knees, twigs of mesquite snagging in her hair, snapping, her eyes wild, fingers clawing at her neck. She tumbled to her side. She wheezed and choked, a sibilant hiss squeezing out with each labored breath.

Suzanne stumbled to the daypack, keeping the automatic leveled at the other woman. Weis groaned. She glanced at him; his legs shifted. Not dead. She had to hurry. She tugged at the zipper to the outside pocket of the denim daypack, her fingers thick, stiff. Inside she found a jumble of small items from her last hike, compass, empty film canister, Swiss Army knife, a mini-flashlight. Where was the twine? An unrestrained Olivia was a deadly Olivia. Before she tended to Weis, she had to render the woman immobile. Then her gaze lit on Olivia's hiking boots, ankle-high, tough leather laces threaded through the many eyelets in the flaps.

She walked to Olivia, whose constricted gasps were lessening in intensity, whose eyes squinted into the sun and sparked with venomous hate. Suzanne's foot nudged Olivia's leg. "Take off your boots," she ordered.

Olivia kicked, caught Suzanne square on the shin. A lightning bolt shot up Suzanne's leg, up her hip, detonating a painful stitch in her side.

"Don't be stupid, Olivia. Listen to me. Those presensory experiences I had of the desert. The woman and the birds. That woman . . ." Suzanne paused to catch her breath. The air thickened into hot syrup, viscous in her lungs. "That woman wasn't Tracy. You said Tracy was tiny, petite. I thought, when I had those desert experiences, I thought I might be in my own body. The proprioceptive cues, the sense of skeletal dimensions, were very similar to my own. But I wasn't in my body, sensing my own fate, the attack of the vultures. I was experiencing the sensations of a woman built like me. My height. My proportions."

She crouched out of range of Olivia's legs, the pistol aimed at the woman's heaving chest. "Take off your boots. If you make me shoot, you won't be lucky enough to die from the bullet wound." She glanced up. Orbiting silhouettes, wide-spread wings. The flesh eaters. Had the scent of Weis's blood drawn them?

Olivia's eyes, following Suzanne's gaze, widened in comprehension.

"Take off your boots." Suzanne gestured with the pistol. "Now."

Olivia eased to a sitting position, gagging with the effort, reached down to her boots, and loosened the leather cords. She pulled off the boots, exposing thin oatmeal-colored socks with pale tan toes and heels.

"Remove the laces. Then throw everything to me."

Olivia did as directed. Each strip was sixty-inches long. Suzanne had the woman roll over onto her stomach, ignoring a choked protest. She bound Olivia's wrists together behind her back, then lashed the second lace around her ankles. Suzanne had her kneel, bending her knees, bringing her feet toward her wrists. She tied the ends of the thin cords together so that Olivia's wrists and ankles were connected.

She picked up the Colt and daypack, hurried to Weis, her stomach twisting, the stitch in her side a dull pulsing ache. She dropped the daypack, knelt. A crimson wetness colored his left chest and shoulder, trickled down his armpit to pool on the dirt. The round had pierced his skin under the collarbone and above the heart. Lucky the bullet had missed his heart. His eyes were open, his breathing shallow, complexion white, glossy with sweat. Lucky if shock doesn't kill him. A mnemonic from first-aid classes popped to consciousness: Face red, raise head. Face pale, raise tail. But there was no way to treat him for shock.

"Dr. Weis?"

He blinked, focused on her. Eyes narrowed against the light.

"Unless you can walk, I'm leaving now to get help."

To her surprise, he heaved himself up on his elbows, grunting, then pushed to a sitting position. "No." He huffed. "You . . . go." He rocked with each exhalation. Olivia's coughing pulled his attention. He stared like he had never seen her before. "It has . . . what it wants. You . . . go."

The bottle of Evian lay on its side, mouth propped upward on the uneven dirt, some water still inside. She righted the bottle, set it next to the daypack, ignoring her own thirst. "Here's water." She glanced at Olivia, who was kneeling, hands behind, swallowing with obvious discomfort.

Would those leather strips hold?

Suzanne held the automatic and Colt in front of his face. "I'm leaving these with you." Weis kept his eyes on Olivia, the two guns invisible. Suzanne set them next to the bottle. When she stood, a rushing blackness spotted the landscape, then dissipated. Sunstroke. Her feet seemed to weigh tons. The stitch in her side was worse.

Olivia sat awkwardly, leaning forward from the tied wrists at her back. Her voice croaked something unintelligible. Pause. Another try. "Bleeding." Olivia pointed at Suzanne with her chin.

Suzanne looked at her shirt. A roan-colored stain, a traitor wetness, had turned the white stripes to red, the blue to purple, below her right breast. A sparkler of adrenaline burst in her stomach. Reflexively she pressed her left palm against the wound and a red-hot knife stabbed her ribs. During the struggle with Olivia, the pistol had fired. She marveled that until now, until seeing the red evidence of injury, the pain had been negligible. A worse injury than Weis's. The hinges of her knees threatened to give. She staggered.

"You won't"—a raw cough—"make it. Untie me."

"No." Her right lung was filled with boiling lava. "I can't trust you."

"Hell," Olivia's voice rusty, but stronger, "you can't *not* trust me. You'll pass out before you reach the car."

She forced her feet to move. Looked up at the black shapes circling overhead. "You better pray I make it."

Now the woman yelled in her raspy androgynous voice: *"For God's sake, don't leave me here."*

Suzanne paused by the edge of the mesquite. "Relax, Olivia. It could be worse. You could be in Belize."

CHAPTER 8

An eternity up the steep slope. Sweat trickled from her brow. A pulsing red-hot coal lodged in her lower right torso. Suzanne clutched fragile stalks endlessly, a hellish Twilight Zone existence, continually climbing, feet slipping over gravel, never reaching the summit. With every stretch of her right arm, the grating of a shattered rib. When she regained the peak, she took a few paces and her legs gave out. The ground rose up to slam against her. Fire erupted in her chest, a smoky gray obscuring her vision. She lay there, oxygen condensing into molecules of burning grit, abrading her lungs. A copper taste deep in her throat. The gray compressed, darkened, into several black triangles wheeling in a sun-bleached sky. An interior image fluttered, the desert, lying helpless, sharp hooked beaks.

Did the desert demand her corpse? And that of the tiny life floating within her? A bargain. Two for the price of one.

Damn it, no.

Rolled to her side. Drew knees up. A surge of pain, but not so bad. Another roll, centered her weight over her legs. Then palms against the dirt,

straightened her arms. Mostly vertical now. Then
she was upright, swaying. A force pressed against
her back, a massive soft hand.

The wind urged her away from this place.

One foot scuffled, dislodged pebbles.

Then the next.

A thought, discrete as an electron, for each dragging step:

First Kelly. Make sure Kelly's all right.

Then Paul.

He had told her the truth about Carolyn.

He had feared losing intimacy, so he avoided
it.

She had accused him of murder.

Apologize.

Had she been mean to Allan?

Apologize.

Had she told everyone how much she loved
them?

Tell everybody.

Gusts of air shoved this leg, then that one.

The desert pushed her away, back to the cars.

Weis's sedate black Mercedes was in front of
her, its gleaming grille like an insincere smile.
Allan's Toyota wore a tumbleweed above the fender, a bushy brown mustache. She shuffled to the
truck. Her fingers grasped the handle and pulled.
The door was stuck. She pulled harder, her ribs
pounding, and managed to open it. She leaned
across the seat, reached past the stick shift, and
picked up the Gatorade. Twisted off the cap, the
yellow plastic smeared with sticky red. Drank.
Warm citrus flavor. Alligator piss. That's what
Paul said it was.

Her thoughts cleared. The stick shift. Could she manage the stick shift? The steering column. What was it about the steering column? The ignition. *The car keys.* Her daypack was with Weis. Her trembling legs could not repeat that distance, descend that slope. Tears trickled down her cheeks, into her mouth. Salty.

Better to walk to the highway. How far was it? Two miles?

Two miles downhill.

She'd have to try.

She took the other liter bottle of water, stepped away from the Toyota. Turned and looked through the tinted windows of the Mercedes.

Keys in the ignition.

CHAPTER 9

Weis grunted. Sweat slicked the grip of the semiautomatic. He heaved himself up, the effort an electric shock to his shoulder. But she wanted something from him, and if his life had any meaning now, it was to do her bidding. His daughter stood over her grave. Naked. Bulbous distended stomach. Her flesh was iridescent, nearly translucent, casting no shadow. Torn mouth, the corners streaked with gore. Empty eye sockets, the extruded strings of the optic nerve. But she could see him. Her hand beckoned him forward with large slow-motion sweeps.

He said, "What do you want me to do?"

Olivia squirmed to an upright position. She had been scuttling on her knees like a mendicant over the distance between them, tumbling to her side on the uneven dirt. Retching. Rocking up to her knees. The way her wrists and ankles were tethered behind her back made her balance precarious. "Untie me, Frank." Her voice rough, hoarse. "You won't survive out here. Untie me. I'll get you to the car, to the hospital. It's all over now. I won't add to our mistake of long ago. I swear." Words tight with panic.

His daughter pivoted, her feet unmoving, not touching the earth. Her movements were mechanical yet languid, her body floating in a medium more viscous than air. Her head swiveled around, chin pointed down. Toward Olivia.

His temples throbbed with the ebb and flow of blood. "Tell me what to do."

Olivia shifted her weight to one cheek of her buttocks. "Come over here. Untie my hands. I can do the rest."

A shadow rippled over the ground past Weis, an inky stain that raced toward Olivia, slithered over her. She recoiled, cried out, and fell to her side. She struggled up to her knees again, her gaze focused up, then shifting frantically, tracking. *"Frank!"*

Tracy's head rotated back to him. Her hand drifted, closed into a fist, forefinger extended, up came the thumb. The forefinger pointed at Olivia's back. Down came the thumb.

He nodded. His daughter had become a thing of this arid wasteland. A wraith in service of the land. She hunted souls of the guilty. Hunted for the bounty of suffering.

He moved his legs woodenly like a man in a dream.

"Turn over," he said to Olivia. He knelt down heavily.

She rolled onto her side.

Perspiration stung his eyes. He looked up at his daughter, her pointing forefinger. The thumb moving down. Up. Down. He nodded. He understood. He placed the pistol above Olivia's bound wrists.

"What are you doing?"

The position of the weapon was critical. He didn't want to hit her heart, spleen, something that would kill. Lower intestines, okay. Flapping sounds. A huge turkey vulture scrabbled atop the mesquite. The bravest. Or the hungriest.

Weis angled the barrel down, aiming for a trajectory that would destroy a portion of the spinal column. Render Olivia paralyzed, not unlike his daughter had been.

"Frank? What are you doing? You have to hur—"

He squeezed the trigger.

CHAPTER 10

A crack echoed, a sharp report like a tree limb snapping in the wind. Suzanne paused before sliding behind the wheel of the Mercedes. She lifted her head, listened. The same sound again.

From the direction of the grave.

CHAPTER 11

Except for the road, you would not suppose that anyone had been this way before. An inhuman landscape. It wasn't the real world. No. Not the complete bona fide kit and caboodle. Suzanne marveled that this wasn't everything. She felt giddy, light-headed, intoxicated by the splinters of silver glinting from the chrome hood ornament, from specks of silver on the road, imbedded in the blacktop itself. A universe of hidden treasures. The road dipped and bounced. She was stationary; things whizzed by her. The pain receded, a small river flowing through a distant body.

Nice car, Frank. Okay if I call you Frank? By the way, do I get my job back?

She made a wide turn onto the highway, narrowly missing a green and gray Rocky Daihatsu. Must be what Olivia drove. Clever of her to leave it out on the highway. No tire tracks for her.

The Mercedes's left tires rumbled over the gravely shoulder, not a good place for the tires to be. Why did the car insist on staying in the wrong lane? Frank ought to get this looked into. Guiding the car back to the right side was an immense effort. The steering wheel had become a thing of dreams, irascible and contrary, leadened in her hands.

The desert landscape gleamed with a snowlike intensity. She was no longer certain of the identity of the ground. What was this place? Jupiter? Pluto?

The inescapable beat of her heart had migrated to the lower right side of her chest, where it ached, throbbed to leave. There her heart fluttered, fighting, a bright dove thrashing under the magician's red scarf.

A black-and-white, a police car, say it southern, po-leece, a po-leece car was up ahead, on the shoulder, its hard shine had materialized out of sunlight, shimmering like a mirage, the officer stooping to talk into the driver's side of a funny-looking car, an old sports car with too much orange. Still, orange is safe. Orange is the best. She twisted the rebellious wheel to the left, pointed the Mercedes at the po-leece car, and couldn't seem to lift her foot to the brake. Her foot was glued to the floor, that can happen in dreams. She swerved across the median. Getting dark. Night was falling fast. No, it was an eclipse, a massive shadow, a spongy comforting blackness. Her foot came up, such an effort of will! To the left, to the left, her quadriceps straining, pressing down, muscles tightening in her chest, squeezing out the bright dove, it pulsed, a shining, a soaring, a great hope taking wing in the darkness.

CHAPTER 12

Suzanne was skimming prone and parallel to the floor, a wonderful weightlessness, a magic carpet ride. Someone yelled in her ear. "Stay with us. *Stay with us*. Good. That's good. Are you allergic to anything?"

Why wouldn't the voice leave her alone, let her descend into blissful dreamland?

"Are you allergic to anything?"

"Penicillin."

A babble of murmurs. Collapsed lung, hemorrhage, bleeding into the peritoneum. Ghosts swarmed around her, hot-blooded anxious ghosts. She felt their heat.

"Are you pregnant?"

"Yes."

Cacophony.

"What's the BP?"

"Single bullet, entry and exit."

"Start another IV."

A shout. "Shit. *Shit*."

"Bag her."

"The officer wants to ask about the shooter."

"Tell him to go fuck himself. Where the hell is Fielding?"

"I'm getting rales."

"Page Respiratory, stat!"

"We're giving you—"

The bullet had drilled her a second mouth. The hole in her side, where her wandering heart had taken flight, suddenly formed a mouth that began to scream.

Fragments of light. Paul. Kelly. Their faces multiplied. Many Pauls and Kellys. Enough spares to last forever. Reassuring. They floated. She floated.

CHAPTER 13

Suzanne was awake. For the first time, fully awake. Snippets of conversations came to her, dreamlike memories. Kelly's ashen complexion, eyes glistening, her little sister saying over and over, "I'm all right. Don't worry about me. You just rest. I love you, too."

A voice had been babbling. Her own voice, she realized now. Paul's wrinkled brow, his warm hand stroking her cheek, responded to her, "I'm not going anywhere. I'm staying right here."

Now she was fully awake. The room was blurry. A starched white sheet stretched from her toes to armpits. Her chest was bound tight, preventing a good deep inhalation. But since it felt like a two-by-four was imbedded to the lower right of her rib cage, she wasn't complaining. IV tubing ran from the crook of her left arm to a clear plastic bag hanging from a metal stand.

Were those her eyeglasses on the nightstand? She slowly wormed her right arm through the side rail bars, retrieved her glasses.

Paul was slumped in an ugly green chair with dark wooden arms. Hospital issue. His hand cupped his bearded chin, his long dark lashes touched his cheeks. Dark bruised crescents under his eyes. Looking at him, she felt her heart swell against her rib cage.

"Hey," she croaked.

His eyes flew open and he leapt up. He leaned over, brushed her bangs from her forehead. "Hey, yourself. How do you feel?"

She swallowed, the desert in her throat. "Thirsty."

He reached to the tray and aimed a cup with a bent straw at her mouth. Apple juice. It was the most wonderful thing she had ever tasted.

She smiled at him. "Ever vigilant."

"I told you I wouldn't leave. Your sister and Allan went to the cafeteria. Oh, and Elliot came by briefly. He said, and I quote, 'Suzanne is un-fired.' What's that all about?"

"A long story that can wait. What time is it?"

"About eleven. In the morning."

She nodded, trying to orient. She'd been in the hospital for almost twenty-four hours. "What happened to Weis?"

"They dug the bullet out of his shoulder, treated him for dehydration. He was released from the hospital. He's been talking up a storm. He and Olivia will be tried for the murder of his daughter. I saved the newspapers for you."

"Newspapers? Plural? How long have I been in here?"

"Three days. You were in ICU for almost two days, talkative but disoriented. A medical marvel."

His smile trembled. She saw now how upset he was.

"The doctors don't know how you drove so far with a punctured lung and internal hemorrhaging."

"How far?"

"Over fifty miles. Almost an hour, they figured. They wondered how you stood the pain."

She didn't remember pain while she had been driving. And today, now, she felt pummeled but renewed, a creature who had shed its old skin. "The last thing I recall clearly is hearing two gunshots right before I got into Weis's car. I assumed he had shot Olivia, then himself."

"Weis shot her twice, the second round severing her spinal column. Paralysis. He said, he claimed, that his dead daughter told him to do it. After he shot Olivia, he sat back and waited for the vultures."

"It was Olivia, then. I kept tapping into Weis's nightmares, his future nightmares, where he relived over and over the burial of his daughter. Then there was the clairvoyant sensing of vultures attacking a woman. Olivia. Two separate experiences: Weis's nightmares and Olivia under attack by the birds." She blinked. "I guess this doesn't make much sense to you."

"Kelly told me about the other presensory experiences."

"How is Olivia?"

"The police got there before the birds had done much damage. She had been able to move her head from side to side. Kept them at bay for the most part. Weis sat there and watched."

She remembered presensing the attack. "Olivia must have been terrified."

"Damn straight she was. She deserves everything that's happened. She killed Kurt. She tried to kill you. She's still in ICU. The paralysis looks permanent. They had to perform a colostomy. She bloody well deserves it all."

He looked embarrassed at his vehemence. He squeezed her hand. "I'm sorry I screwed up. That I wasn't there for you."

"No, this time it's my turn. I'm sorry. When you told me that night in my bedroom about Carolyn—"

"I know. You've apologized."

"I have?"

"Many times. And I told you it was my fault."

"Rusty told me why you didn't want to say—"

"I know." He grinned.

"Told you that, too, did I?"

"More than once. And Rusty and I have talked."

"Is there anything I didn't tell you?"

As soon as the words came out of her mouth, she remembered what she hadn't yet told him. He didn't say anything. From the look on his face, he knew.

A sudden panic flared. "Did I lose the baby?"

He shook his head, a smile lifting the corners of his mouth. "He's still firmly attached."

"He?"

"Or she. Seems too impersonal to say 'it.'"

"So . . . what do you think?"

He kissed the back of her hand. "Can I lie down next to you?"

"Sure. Probably against hospital policy, though."

"Sounds like a personal problem."

He lowered the side rail and carefully maneuvered his body next to hers. He eased an arm across her hips, avoiding the IV. His breath was sweet on her cheek.

"Did you stop to think," he said, "that your presensing the future never happened before you were pregnant?"

"It did occur to me. I know you said that this presensing technique worked for people who'd never shown any psychic ability before, but that just didn't feel . . . right, true, in my case. Before last week I never even had a glimmer of the future. So I wonder about the baby. What would the mother feel if the fetus was psychic? I mean, what if the unborn baby reached a certain stage of cerebral development and then at that point— but no sooner—there's a placental-utero transfer of clairvoyant ability? What if that's why I could see into the future? And how would a psychic newborn behave?"

"Time will tell."

"Yeah. In about seven months." She thought for a moment, recalling her discussion with Allan in his bat laboratory. "It's like the next step."

"What is?"

"The next evolutionary step for the human race. Our brains have remained unchanged for millennia, right?"

"Right."

"So a baby, a fetus even, with sixth sense might be the dawn of a new age for human development. The next step in evolution."

"I'll be happy if he, or she, is healthy. You asked what I thought about us, baby included."

She waited.

"I think I'm damn lucky that you didn't dump me. And if you're willing, when you're released from the hospital, I'd like to move in with you."

"No." She heard his faint intake of breath.

A pause. "No?"

"I want you to move in *before* I'm out of here. Today. Everything, including that awful parrot."

A whistle of air escaped from his mouth. "Consider it done. And listen, Suzanne, I'm sorry about . . ."

"Later." She kissed him. "Apologize later when I can take full advantage of the situation."

They rested, entwined. After a while Suzanne dozed, and an image fluttered. A tiny bundle in her arms, a swaddle of cloth, the scent of baby powder, a tiny face beaming up at her, the mouth opening into a wide yawn. Blue eyes blinked, regarded her with calm assurance. A warm radiance, like early morning sunlight, flowed from the baby, glowing, straight into Suzanne's heart.